Angels
IN THE
ARCHITECTURE

STEPHEN J. COOK

First published in January 2024 by Westcourt Publishing
This revised edition published in February 2024
Email: westcourtpublishing@gmail.com

Angels In The Architecture
Copyright © Stephen J. Cook, 2024
ISBN 978-1-7385076-2-7

Stephen J. Cook asserts his moral right under the Copyright, Designs and Patents Act of 1988 to be identified as the author of this work.
All rights reserved. No part of this publication may be reproduced, stored in a retrieval system, or transmitted at any time or by any means, electronic, mechanical, photocopying, recording or otherwise without the prior permission of the copyright holder.

This is a work of fiction and although it contains historical facts and real places all characters, their situations and actions are imagined. Any resemblance to actual persons, living or dead, is purely coincidental.

Typeset by Kevin Moore

For my mother -
Lillian May Cook

Halo

The dim yellow glow of the streetlight illuminated the top of her head creating a halo effect.

The night-air was still warm. With the light behind her the oversized white shirt she was wearing, gathered at the waist with a black leather belt, looked like a shroud. Leaning against the wall she stood with her head tipped back, revealing her slender neck. Her right leg was crossed over the left leg at the ankle. With her eyes closed she took another long drag on the cigarette. Letting her arm fall back to her side she extended her bottom lip, breathed out and directed the smoke up above her head.

Suddenly she felt her legs give way. She hadn't seen it coming - the kick that lifted both her feet off the ground and sent her crashing to the floor with her head banging against the wall. Before the sense of surprise could turn to pain or fear she was aware of somebody kneeling over her and felt the hands around her neck, the thumbs pushing harder and harder.

For a few seconds she could see the shape of the person above her but then everything went black. For a few seconds she could hear their heavy breathing; she could hear the distant sound of traffic; she could hear the sound of water lapping against stone.

And then nothing.

Toast

The early morning sunlight shining through the kitchen window illuminated the quickening spiral of smoke as it rose to the ceiling. The unmistakable smell of burnt toast reached him just seconds before the urgent, shrill alarm of the smoke detector sounded.

"Bollocks." He jumped up, pushing the chair from out behind him, but in his haste to reach the toaster he knocked the table with his knee and this minor collision was enough to send a splash of coffee from his mug across the floor.

"Bollocks," he shouted again, slightly angrier than before, as he stabbed at the cancel button on the side of the electric toaster as if his life depended upon it. Reaching into the empty washing up bowl he grabbed the dishcloth and threw it onto the floor where the small, dark pool of coffee was slowly spreading. Without bending down he stamped on the cloth with his right foot and moved his leg from side to side in a strenuous but ineffective mopping action. When finished he shook the dishcloth from his foot with a sharp flick that sent it flying into the kick board of the corner unit. And there it stayed.

Picking up what was left of his mug of coffee he walked from the kitchen into the lounge, his favourite room. This was where he listened to his music. In the alcove to the left of the fireplace, around eye level, were two shelves supporting nothing other than a CD player and an amplifier. Either side of the grey stone hearth was a large speaker balanced on a black metal stand: a pair of old but trusty KEFs. The whole back wall opposite the front room window had been fitted out with bespoke wooden CD storage units that went from floor to ceiling. Housed here was an A to Z of twentieth century rock music, from AC/DC to Frank Zappa with almost everything in between.

Putting the coffee mug down he instinctively reached for his mobile phone on the arm of the chair and saw straight away that he had a missed call. He recognised the number so he hit call-back and walked to the bay window. The signal was no better here than anywhere else in the room but this was where phone conversations always started. Waiting for the call to connect he walked from one side of the bay to the other, stopping to part the blinds and look outside, checking up and down the street.

"Good morning - can I help?" the voice asked just before he had completed his second return journey.

"Who's that?" he barked angrily.

"PC Sharma."

"DI Page here," he confirmed, slightly less angrily but still well-short of polite.

"Hello Gov. I was asked to give you a call before you came in this morning. Have you had a good holiday?"

"It wasn't a holiday. It was ten days I was made to take off or I would lose my leave entitlement. Big difference."

"Yes, of course," Sharma said, clearly wishing it wasn't him having to pass on the news. "Anyway first things first, DS Stevens is still off sick so they've put you with…"

"Don't tell me Sharma. Let me guess." Page was staring out of the window and watching the couple from next door get into their car. They seemed to be arguing. Somebody else's day off to a bad start too he thought to himself and felt a little better.

"Gov - you still there?"

"Yes Sharma. Go on - make my day."

Sharma hesitated before saying: "For at least the next three weeks you will be working with DC Connor."

"Bollocks," was all Page could say. "Not Loopy Lou!"

"Afraid so Gov, and yet she speaks so highly of you," Sharma added with a certain lack of reserve and respect.

Luckily for him this attempt at humour wasn't noticed by Page who was still observing the comings and goings in the street outside. Taking Sharma's comment at face value he growled: "I don't really care what she thinks of me. Is she in yet?"

"Yes, she's waiting for you in the office. Wants to know what she should do about the shout."

"What shout?" Page asked, now watching the couple from next door finally pull away, their disagreement seemingly resolved.

"That's the other thing I've got to tell you. A woman's body has been found on Castle Park."

"Brilliant," Page sighed sarcastically. "Tell Connor to go on ahead. Send a car for me and I'll meet her there."

"OK Gov, I'll..." but before Sharma could finish Page had already hung up and was walking away from the window. The conversation was over.

Jim Page was in his late fifties and had been a copper all his adult life. He lived alone but that wasn't because he was 'married to the job' as was often said of single, career minded people. If that were the case it might better be described as a marriage on the rocks. He'd had some good times but now he felt like he'd had enough. He sometimes wanted out completely but wasn't sure he really wanted to leave; after all, this was all he'd ever known. Or perhaps it was more a marriage of convenience where the possibility of a happier existence was outweighed by the cold comfort of certainty. Better the devil you know and all that.

Back in the kitchen Page put the empty mug into the washing up bowl, bent down, picked up the dishcloth and flung it into the bowl as well. The washing up would have to wait, as would sorting out the burnt toast that was still standing to attention, half out of the toaster as a reminder of how badly Page's first day back at work had started.

On the way upstairs to clean his teeth and put his tie on Page let out a long sigh. He didn't always get on with DS Stevens but over the last couple of years he had got used to working with him. And now that was going to change. It might only be a temporary thing but it was one more thing he could do without. DC Connor was a strange one, in his eyes at least. With every step on the stair the thought of working with her worsened in his mind until he reached the landing and lamented to himself: "Bollocks. What have I done to deserve Loopy bloody Lou?"

Chalk And Cheese

The morning sun was bright but not yet that warm. DC Louise Connor was leaning against a blackened stone wall of the derelict church. She'd arrived at the scene half an hour earlier, been met by a uniformed officer and introduced to Dr Charlotte James the pathologist.

"Anything I should know?" Connor had asked.

"Too early to say. Give me another ten minutes," the pathologist had said without looking up or moving away from the body. Connor had walked back to the church building where she was now waiting for Page to arrive.

Her morning had got off to a good start. A half hour on-line pilates session in her garage (which now served as a home made exercise area) and then a light breakfast and a quick shower. Before leaving for work she had put a bowl, spoon and cereals out for her teenage son, along with a note reminding him of the things he needed to do before she got back from work that evening.

Louise Connor was in her late thirties. She had joined the police at twenty-five and spent most of her time in uniform. She enjoyed the job but had never expected to have a career. For a start she never saw herself as being that capable, just dependable. And then of course there was the fact that she also had a family. Juggling the demands of shift work, a young child and a needy husband wasn't easy. In the end it was her marriage that came crashing down. She had been a single, working mum for over ten years now but it wasn't getting any easier. She just found herself having to work harder. And then out of the blue, about three years ago, she had been offered the chance to join the Major Crime Investigation Team as a Detective Constable. Up until now she had been tasked with a lot of the administrative work that nobody else wanted to do or else sent out door knocking when the public needed a visible sign of police activity for whatever reason. It was only when she had reached the Bridewell office that morning that PC Sharma had told her about the discovery of the woman's body and the fact that for the next few weeks she had been assigned to work with DI Page.

And here she was waiting for him to arrive. She looked across the paved area to the wooden coffee kiosk, and beyond to the pedestrian crossing at the junction of Wine Street and Union Street, the direction from which she presumed Page would come. But she couldn't see him.

She moved her head back until it rested against the wall and she let out a long sigh and thought to herself: "DI bloody Page. What have I done to deserve this?"

She didn't really know him, but she knew of him. Just the thought of working with him made her anxious. 'We're as different as chalk and cheese,' she thought to herself, and then remembered the comments she had heard about him when she first arrived at Bridewell:

"He doesn't suffer fools gladly."

"He isn't mean, just moody."

"He's a man's man. Doesn't get on with women."

She sighed again and took her mobile phone from her pocket. Unlocking it she opened her diary and smiled when she was reminded that it was Monday and that evening she had her yoga class to look forward to. A flexible body leads to a flexible mind she had always been told, and then for some reason she wondered how flexible or open DI Page's mind might be. Staring at her phone screen she started thinking whether or not it would be best to remove the dream-catcher hanging from her car's rearview mirror. She wasn't sure that mysticism or alternative thinking would be Page's thing. She was so deep in thought that she didn't see or hear him approaching.

"So, what have we got?"

She was startled and felt a little annoyed with herself that she was already on the back foot.

"So, what have we got?" Page asked again.

"Sir… Sorry Sir." She immediately regretted apologising. Not the way to show somebody that you were confident and fully in control of the situation at all.

"Anything to report?" Page asked.

"Too early to say apparently."

"How long do they need for God's sake?" Before Connor could regain her composure or answer the question Page was striding impatiently towards the pathologist who was now standing up removing her protective gloves.

"Bollocks," Connor said angrily under her breath. She knew full well that there were no second chances to make a first impression.

Mystery Tramp

"Charlotte. Good to see you," Page said smiling broadly, before adding: "So, what have we got?"

The pathologist tossed her used gloves into the large opened holdall bag acting as the forensic waste bin. She smiled back at Page, happy to play the old game: "This is where I say - *I'll know more once we get her back to the lab and do the PM.*"

"But first impressions Doctor?"

"I'll know more once we get her back to the lab and do the PM, but I don't think there is much here to concern you. Woman, late fifties, rough sleeper in poor health, no signs at all of foul play. Been dead between six and ten hours before you ask."

"ID?" Page asked.

"Nothing," the pathologist confirmed, closing her briefcase before handing Page a clear plastic bag. "This was all she had on her. A few scraps of paper, receipts, and an empty packet of cigarettes in her coat pockets."

"Not much to go on," Page muttered despondently.

"What did you expect?" Dr James asked, picking up her case and turning to go: "A passport? Driving licence?"

"Not really," Page answered shrugging his shoulders, not knowing what he had expected. "When will you have the PM results?"

"Later this afternoon. I'll give you a ring." With that Dr Charlotte James walked back to the car that she had parked on the pavement next to the cafe kiosk.

Page walked towards Connor who was standing ten yards or so away from him, her back turned. "Hey," he said, and as she turned round he handed her the plastic bag: "Look after this."

"What is it?"

"The only personal belongings she had on her. Not much help, but it's all we've got."

"Do we have a name?" Connor asked.

"No. Just a mystery tramp with no alibis."

"I'm not with you." Connor was looking confused.

"Like a Rolling Stone," he prompted.

"Who is?"

He was about to say Bob Dylan but decided to save his breath. He simply smiled and said: "Don't worry Connor. Go over and get me a coffee will you."

Page didn't want to watch the woman's body being manhandled onto the trolley and then wheeled across the uneven flagstones to the waiting private ambulance. It was so undignified. Instead he walked through the formal garden alongside the church and down the slope to a grassed area overlooking the river. He sat down on one of the benches and his eyes were drawn to the new foot bridge snaking across the river, joining Castle Park to the old brewery site that was now being 'regenerated' into apartments, bars and cafes. He could remember coming into Bristol as a child and the warm, damp smell of fermentation from the Courage brewery would cover the whole of the Broadmead shopping centre if the wind was blowing in the right direction. Or the wrong direction. It was not a particularly nice smell if his memory served him well.

He was brought back to the present by Connor's voice, sounding slightly frustrated: "There you are. I didn't know where you had gone."

"But you found me. We'll make a detective out of you yet." Page hoped he hadn't sounded too sarcastic. He had meant it as a joke. Connor handed him a large take-away cup of black coffee, three individual portions of long-life milk and two paper tubes of sugar.

"I don't know how you have your coffee," she said defensively.

"That's fine," he replied. "A couple of milks and no sugar." And that was as close to a thank-you as she was going to get.

Connor sat down next to him as he balanced the cup on one of the bench slats so that he could open the pots of milk and pour them into the steaming black coffee. "So do we know the cause of death?" she asked.

"Not yet, but it looks unlikely that it was murder."

"Natural causes then."

Almost before she had finished uttering these words Page stopped stirring his drink, sat forward and turned towards her. "There is nothing natural about dying in your fifties, homeless and on the streets. We are supposed to be living in a civilised country and yet somebody can die and nobody else knows or cares." He paused, and his voice became less angry, more contemplative: "I live alone and don't mind that at all, but the thought of dying alone? It's not right. And dying on the street! It's ironic isn't it that Castle Park here and the church are kept as a reminder of all the civilians that died in Bristol during the second world war and here we are more than seventy-five years later and people are still lying dead on the streets. Who needs bombs?"

They sat in silence until Page started to feel too self conscious. "Where do we start with this case?" he asked.

"St Mungo's," Connor answered almost immediately. "It's a homeless charity."

"I know that Connor, but what on earth made you think of St Mungo's?"

"The Physic Garden."

"The what garden?"

"The Physic Garden Sir, alongside the church up there. As I was walking through it with the coffee just now I saw the notice board that explained how homeless people from St Mungo's had worked to restore and plant the area a few years ago."

"Well it's as good a place to start as any I suppose. And if I'm not mistaken St Mungo's have got a place right next door to the Volunteer Tavern in St Judes. You never know, by the time we've spoken to them we could well be ready for a spot of lunch."

They both stood up and Connor walked over to the waste bin to throw their coffee cups away. Page was wondering where Connor might have parked her car when his mobile rang. Reaching into his inside jacket pocket and finally retrieving his phone he answered the call with his usual gruff, single-word greeting: "Page." He walked up and down a few paces before standing still, listening to what he was being told, silently shaking his head. Putting his phone back into his jacket pocket he said: "Come on Connor, St Mungo's will have to wait. We've got another body."

Seven Stars

"There," Page shouted, pointing to a parking space that had just become free at the end of the street.

Connor, evidently flustered, indicated and turned off the main road. Page had no idea whether or not the space would be big enough for Connor to park in. He didn't drive, never had, but that didn't stop him offering advice to others. He was not a good front-seat passenger, but of course he was an excellent back-seat driver. He didn't particularly like walking much either but he was frustrated that the short drive from Castle Park had taken nearly fifteen minutes by the time they had got back to where Connor had parked her car.

"I could have walked here in five minutes," he muttered to himself as Connor managed to guide the car into the parking bay with only one forward and backward manoeuvre. Before she could turn the engine off he had opened the door and was getting out of the car. "Come on," he barked impatiently. "We've wasted enough time already."

As he slammed the car door shut Connor whispered: "The dead can always wait!"

Page reached the narrow alleyway, its entrance barred by blue and white tape. He looked back to see Connor hurrying to catch up with him. The uniformed police officer recognised Page immediately and with a nod and a "Sir" he lifted the tape so that Page and Connor could pass with only the slightest of stoops. Further down the alley, just in front of a row of wooden pub-garden tables, Dr James was crouched over a body. She heard the footsteps and looked up at Page with an expression that even he understood to mean 'no silly comments'.

"It's not good Jim."

"What have we got?"

The pathologist stood up and moved to one side: "Have a look for yourself."

Page looked down and saw the body of a young woman. She had been stripped naked and in each hand was a large glass jug used for serving beer. "Have you finished here?" Page asked Dr James. She nodded. He turned and called to the group of people assembled behind him: "Will one of you cover her up for Christ's sake." He walked away from the body and sat down at one of the wooden tables. The pathologist followed him. "Do we know who she is?" he asked.

"Yes. She worked in the pub."

"And how did she die, or is it too early to say?"

"I'll know for certain once I've had a better look, but the petechial haemorrhages around the carotid arteries are consistent with asphyxiation."

"So she was strangled."

"Probably."

"But why strip her naked and arrange her body like that?"

Dr James smiled: "That Jim, is for you to find out."

As the pathologist tidied her things away DC Connor joined Page on the bench. "Now this is what you call a suspicious death Connor."

"But why was she naked? And why was she carrying those glass jugs?"

"Well, as Dr James has just so eloquently put it: that is for us to find out. However, I suspect she wasn't carrying the jugs."

"You mean..." Connor started to say.

"I mean, she would either have let go of them when she was attacked, or if she was holding onto them then they would surely have broken in the struggle. And whichever scenario you choose, I doubt very much that she was walking around outside serving beer stark naked." That much at least was clear to him. Looking at his watch he sighed: "Come on - let's go and talk to the landlord."

The Seven Stars was one of Page's favourite pubs in Bristol but he hadn't been in there for years. The beer was always good but the interior was very basic and hadn't seemed to have changed very much since the early 1600s. And that was part of its charm: the fact that at over 400 years old it had not only survived the Luftwaffe's best endeavours but had also managed to stay out of reach of the avaricious town-planners and architects of the 1960s. And then of course there was the peculiar twist that unlike the rest of the city the pub was linked to the movement to abolish slavery in the late 1780s.

Walking towards the bar Page was reflecting on the historical and cultural significance of the building when Connor, in the worst stage-whisper possible, commented: "It's a bit dark and shabby in here isn't it."

Page ignored her hoping the landlord, who was stood at the far end of the bar smoking a cigarette, hadn't heard her.

"We're closed."

"Yes, I know," Page confirmed, sounding irritated. "I'm DI Page, this is DC Connor. We need to ask you a few questions. You are the landlord I presume."

"No, I'm the bar manager, but I might as well be the landlord."

The man looked irritated that he had been disturbed, despite the seriousness of the situation. It was hard to put a precise age to him but Page guessed 'in his late twenties'. It looked like he was reading some paperwork, a bill maybe, but he didn't give the impression that he was going to stop reading it any time soon. "I said, we need to ask you a few questions." Page wasn't warming to him.

"Yes, I heard," the bar manager confirmed without looking up.

"Then leave what you are doing and come and talk to us." Once eye contact had been made Page walked away from the bar. "Let's sit down here." The three of them sat down at a small, circular cast-iron table. From bitter experience Page made sure he didn't bang his knee on the protruding lion's head at the top of the table leg. "So, who are you?" Page asked.

"I'm the bar manager. I've already told you that."

"I know. I want to know your name." Page was becoming annoyed.

"Sean Wilson. My name is Sean Wilson."

"And the..."

Before Page could finish asking the question Wilson glanced instinctively at the window behind the two detectives and said: "Clare Harding. She's worked here about three years."

"Any family?" Connor asked.

"I don't know. Nobody local that I know of."

"Boyfriend?" Page asked.

"No."

There was something about the way Wilson answered the question. A slight hesitation before dwelling on the word a little too long. "Go on," Page prompted.

"Look - it's not really my place to say. Anyway I don't know for sure..."

"But you think she preferred girls."

"I don't know," Wilson said, shrugging his shoulders. "It's just an impression I've always had. I've got no problem with it."

"Nor have I," confirmed Page, "but it's worth knowing." He glanced at Connor as much as to say 'make a note of that'. A difficult silence threatened to grow so Page continued with his next line of enquiry: "Where were you last night?"

"Here, until about 8 o'clock. I usually have Sunday evenings off. Go out with some friends for a drink."

"Bit of a busman's holiday." Page couldn't help himself.

"Yeah," Wilson laughed. "I suppose it is. But it's different when you are on the other side of the bar. When you aren't having to make small talk with the merry Brexiteers and laugh at the racist jokes they've read in the Daily Mail."

"And last night?" Page asked, trying to get Wilson back to the point.

"Last night I met some friends on the Grain Barge, had a few drinks and stayed over at Jeremy's flat."

"And who would Jeremy be and where does he live?" Page asked.

"Jeremy Green, an old friend of mine. He lives in a flat up by Brandon Hill."

"Well you can give the address to DC Connor in a minute," Page suggested, with just a hint of impatience. "So you didn't return here until this morning."

"No, yes - I mean I got back here sometime between ten o'clock and half-eleven this morning to find the alley swarming with police."

"That's very vague," Connor said. "Sometime between ten and half-eleven."

Page shot a glance at Connor to let her know her interruption wasn't welcome, but Wilson didn't notice.

"Well I don't wear a watch," he said beginning to sound irritated again. "So I don't know what time I got here. Does it make a difference?"

"It might do," said Connor looking down at her notebook.

'Good girl,' Page thought to himself, now pleased that she had interrupted. He waited a few seconds for Connor's point to fully hit the mark. "Now, before you went out drinking, anything unusual happen? Any strangers hanging around?"

Wilson seemed to be growing ever more agitated. "Look mate, this is a pub in the middle of a very big city and most nights it is full of strangers."

"Firstly, I am not your mate," Page barked, "and secondly don't try and be clever."

Before Wilson could respond Connor smiled at him and said: "What DI Page wants to know is whether or not everything was OK when you left the pub last night."

Wilson sighed as he rather sarcastically confirmed: "Nothing untoward to report, honest," but as soon as he had said it his face said otherwise. Connor raised an eyebrow at him. "Well apart from having to ask Dick to leave."

"Dick who?" Page asked instinctively.

"I don't know his real name. We all call him Dick because he is such a dick."

"And what in particular was Dick doing last night?" Page asked.

"Being a dick as usual," Wilson replied before explaining: "He was mouthing off about Clare. Making comments about what she was wearing and how it was a shame that it was so baggy you couldn't see how big her tits were. And then he said..."

Page interrupted him angrily: "And you didn't think to tell us this at the start?" Wilson looked taken aback as Page leaned forward towards him and in a very loud whisper said: "Enough of this crap. Tell me where Clare lived and where I can find this Dick fellow."

"I'll get you Clare's details now," Wilson said standing up from the table, wiping the palms of his hands down the front of his jeans, "but I don't know where Dick lives. He won't be in here for a while because we had words last night, but he will be in one of the other local pubs that's for sure."

"And what does this Dick look like?" Page asked.

"Tall, scruffy with long hair."

To Page's mind Wilson was being deliberately vague but he chose to let it go for now. "You were about to find us Clare's details," he reminded him, before adding: "And while you're at it you can write down this Jeremy Green's address as well."

Wilson went behind the bar, opened a large desk diary and flicked through a few pages. He returned to the table having scribbled down the addresses he had been asked for on a small food order pad with red numbers on the bottom of each page, the type that all pubs had used before the advent of iPads and digital ordering systems. He handed the slip to Page who without looking at it, folded it in half and made a show of passing it straight on to DC Connor. "Thank you for your help Mr Wilson," he said sarcastically. "Don't go too far, I suspect we will want to speak to you again."

Outside in the alley way things were already calmer. Clare's body had been removed and scenes-of-crime officers dressed in their white paper suits were silently poring over the area like worker ants.

Page could contain his feelings no longer. "Sean Wilson is not giving us the full story and I don't like him."

"That was very obvious," Connor commented.

"Yes, sorry about that. Not very good at hiding my feelings." He laughed. "And how about you? Are you happy with what he's told us?"

Connor shook her head. "No. I don't believe a word he said."

They walked the rest of the way back to the car in silence and as Connor pressed the remote to unlock it and the indicators flashed Page said: "You go on. I'm going to get some lunch, clear my head and call in at St Mungo's to see if there is anything more we can find out about our mystery woman. You go and speak to this Jeremy Green bloke and check out Wilson's alibi; and then get round to Clare's place and see if there is anything of interest there for us or not."

Connor climbed into the car but before she could close the door Page stooped and leaned his head in towards her: "I'll see you back at the station around four o'clock."

And with that he pushed the car door shut and walked away towards Bristol Bridge.

Just Good Friends

The traffic seemed worse than usual and sat waiting at the traffic lights Connor was becoming more and more convinced that she could have taken a quicker and more direct route. She had parked the car outside St George's, formerly a church but now a concert venue, and then walked to Jeremy Green's flat on the edge of Brandon Hill. Upon leaving she had instinctively turned right, taking her down Park Street. Now she was stuck in traffic and what made it worse was that her car was stationary less than a minute's walk from her Bridewell Police Station office. She would be back here again later to update Page on her findings.

The visit to Jeremy Green had been short but no less interesting for that. He had spoken to her on the doorstep 'as he was getting ready to go out', but he had confirmed that the previous evening he was socialising with Sean Wilson, and that they had returned to his flat after having had a few drinks where they stayed until that morning. What was interesting however, was his response when Connor had asked him at what time, approximately, Wilson had left the flat that morning. Green knew precisely what time it was because he had given his friend a lift, dropping him off outside the Old Fish Market pub at half past eight. Wilson had told him he needed to be at the Seven Stars early that morning because there was a lot to do before he could open at noon. Mr Wilson was clearly not very good at telling the time. Or perhaps at telling the truth.

Slowly approaching the roundabout Connor glanced up at St James's Park and as usual the benches were occupied with homeless groups drinking cans of extra strong lager or cider, all of them numbing their senses and waiting for the volunteer soup-run to arrive around dusk. Not for the first time that day Connor wondered why Page had given her this job to do, and why it was that he had been so keen to make enquiries of the homeless woman. She had fully expected to be packed off on that particular wild goose chase whilst Page kept the murder enquiry to himself. Of course she was as pleased as she was surprised, but she was also a little apprehensive. Given the opportunity she didn't want to let herself or Page down.

Arriving at Clare's address she managed to find a parking space relatively easily but then had the job of finding the main entrance way into the correct block of flats. Armada House was one of the tower blocks on the Dove Street estate, but from the external area in the middle of the development it was difficult to identify one particular block from another. Built by the council in the 1960s to replace the Georgian houses above Stokes Croft the tower blocks still divided opinions. For some the sheer scale of the flats, the drab concrete structures, external walkways and rows of ground floor garage blocks summed up all that was bad about council housing. For others the Right to Buy had brought town-centre home-ownership within their reach and these 'apartments' represented a very real stake in a vibrant part of the city.

Having found the correct entrance door Connor pressed the intercom and listened for the electronic ringing sound.

"Hello," a voice said.

"Hello. It's DC Connor here from…" but before she could finish her sentence the loud buzzing sound indicated that the door was now unlocked and that introductions weren't required for the moment.

The flat door was already open as she got out of the lift but she still knocked and waited.

"Come on in," the same voice as before called out.

Connor walked into the hallway and could see the lounge at the far end. There was nothing unusual about the room: a small settee, an armchair, a coffee table and a bean-bag. A television was balanced in the corner of the room on what looked like a modern interpretation of an old-fashioned, upturned wooden tea-chest. Spread across the coffee table and on the floor were various sections from a Sunday broadsheet. "Hello. I'm DC Connor, but call me Louise."

"Hi. I'm Nicola. Nicola Jarvis. Take a seat," the young woman standing in the middle of the room said, stretching out her hand towards the settee.

Connor sat down. "Thank you," she said and the other woman climbed into the armchair, tucking her feet and legs up beneath her.

"This is about Clare isn't it."

"Yes," Connor said, trying to look and sound sympathetic. "There are a few things I need to ask you. Sensitive things maybe."

"Don't mind me. Fire away."

"What is your relationship to Clare?" Connor asked tentatively.

"That's complicated. Let me see: landlord, flatmate, ex-colleague, former uni-pals, bestie. Will that do?"

"Yes, fine," Connor answered, but she had waited just a little too long for her response.

"You seem disappointed. What were you expecting me to say: lesbian lovers?"

Connor felt flustered. That was exactly what she had been expecting her to say. Or at least a form of words that confirmed the two women were actually partners.

"Sorry, there was no need for that," Nicola apologised. "I guess you just need to know who Clare's next of kin is."

Taking the lifeline handed to her Connor gratefully answered: "Yes. We don't know much about Clare's background at all. Do you have anything that might help us get a better picture?"

"Well, I met her when we both started university here in Bristol. She's from Dorset originally. Her mum came up to see her a couple of times but she died during our first year. Her dad had died years before that, and as far as I know she has just the one brother. I think his name might be Rob."

"And where does Rob live, do you know?"

"I presume he's still living in Dorchester, but he never came to visit Clare. She just got cards from him for birthdays and Christmas, but no other contact. No phone calls or anything."

"Sad," Connor said, but she was really thinking aloud. And then she returned to her original line of questioning: "Did Clare have any 'significant others' that you know of?"

"Not really. She was always too disorganised to keep a relationship going. There have been a few different blokes over the years, but nothing serious."

"And nobody on the go right now that you know of?"

"No. I mean I know there is nobody at the moment. Nobody that Clare wants to get involved with in any case."

Connor picked up on Nicola's last statement. Her instincts told her it wasn't a throw away line. "What do you mean by that?"

"This bloke at work has been hassling her for months. Asking her out and getting really annoyed when she declines. But he still keeps on trying. It's started to get her down a bit lately."

"And this bloke, one of the punters, he wouldn't go by the name of Dick by any chance?"

Nicola looked at Connor in puzzlement and clarified: "He's not one of the punters. He's the manager."

Connor sat back in the settee and looked up at the ceiling in an effort to conceal the small smile she could feel creeping across her face. "Sean Wilson," she said under her breath but still out-loud.

"Yes, the little shit. Thinks he's God's gift to young women, but really he's a slimy creep."

"You don't like him then?" Connor asked, rather superfluously.

"I don't really know him, but I know Clare didn't like him, and that's good enough for me. She was trying to leave the pub but Wilson had started holding back some of her wages on the pretext that there were problems with her National

Insurance contributions. She couldn't afford just to lose the money."

"So what was she going to do?" Connor asked, now sitting forward and trying to reassure Nicola who was clearly becoming upset.

"She'd told him last week that she was going to get legal advice about her wages and…" Nicola's voice trailed off.

"And?" Connor asked softly and encouragingly.

"…and about his sexual harassment."

Why was she not surprised to hear that? "And had she spoken to anybody?" she asked.

"I don't think so. I don't think she was really ever going to do it. She just wanted to frighten him off. To see his reaction." Nicola sniffed and wiped away the tear that was running down her cheek.

"I think that's enough for now," Connor said, glancing at her mobile phone. She had turned it to silent when she first sat down in the lounge and she could now see that she had a missed call and a voicemail from Page.

"You don't think that he killed her, do you?" Nicola asked, almost as if she had only just thought of this possibility.

"It's too early to jump to any conclusions," Connor said, conscious that she was quoting the text book. "We'll be back in touch if we need anything else. In the meantime, give me a call if you think of something I should know." She stood up and handed Nicola one of her business cards. "You stay there, I'll see myself out."

Back in the car she listened to Page's voicemail message: 'Connor, it's getting late and not much to report this end so let's skip this afternoon's meeting and call it a day. There will be a briefing tomorrow at nine so see you then.' She deleted the message and tossed the phone onto the passenger seat. No hello, no thank you, no goodbye; and not even a thought that she might have something interesting or important to report. How long would it take to get used to working with this man she wondered to herself?

Diamond Star Halo

That evening he sat in his room remembering the previous night. It had all been much easier than he had thought. He had worried that when the chance finally presented itself he wouldn't be able to find the inner or physical strength to see it through. But when he saw her standing there bathed in light and crowned with a diamond star halo, he knew it was a sign. A sign that the time was right and that the right time had arrived.

She hadn't heard him approaching, and with one kick she was on the ground. The bang to her head must have really stunned her because she put up no fight when his hands went around her throat. He had squeezed and pressed with all his might until her shoulders went limp and her head rolled to one side. Undressing her had been the hardest part even though she had only been wearing two items of clothing. He had undone the belt and unbuttoned the large white shirt, and to his surprise found that she was wearing no bra. Her small breasts had hardly moved as he pulled the shirt fully open. To get the shirt off he had had to roll her from side to side and in reaching underneath her he had scraged his knuckle on the cobbled street. Removing her knickers had been a little easier: just a case of raising her legs in the air, lifting her bottom slightly and giving the white cotton and lace a hard tug to render her fully naked. Retrieving the two glass jugs from where he had hidden them a few weeks beforehand in a gap in the broken stone wall had been the easiest part.

But that was last night. Tonight he was safely at home and was able to start enjoying the fruits of his labour. He looked at the picture on his desk: the naked woman kneeling at a pool with a jug in each hand, and above her head a large yellow star. He picked the picture up, slowly brought it to his mouth and kissed it, very carefully and very lightly as if not wanting to leave any trace at all. Then, standing up, he reached over the desk and fixed it onto the large cork pinboard hanging on the wall.

Only A Pawn
In Their Game

Page had been in since seven o'clock, unable to sleep all night and disappointed that his enquires into the homeless woman had so far been fruitless. He'd got himself a coffee from the machine in the kitchen area and had taken it back to his office where he had gone through all the reports of yesterday to prepare himself for the imminent team briefing.

Through his open door he saw Connor come in and sit herself down at one of the hot-desks. It was just gone eight. "I got the notes you sent through last night. Nothing better to do?" he shouted.

She came towards his office and leant into the doorway. "I thought you might need them so finished and mailed them before I went to my yoga class."

"Yoga. Never seen the point myself."

"Have you ever tried it?"

"No. Far too eastern and mystical for my liking. Anyway, if you are going to get a coffee, bring me back one too would you?"

"Of course, as you've asked so nicely." She gave him a broad grin. "Unlike you though not to have had one already."

"But I have," he said holding his empty mug out to her. He was going to make a reference to the Dylan song One More

Cup of Coffee but he thought better of it. She took the mug from him and turned away towards the kitchen.

The briefing started at nine o'clock prompt. "Good morning ladies and gentlemen," Page called out in a loud voice as he walked to stand in front of the portable whiteboard. "This won't take long, so listen up." The conversation in the room stopped and all eyes were on Page. "As far as our homeless woman goes, her death is not being treated as suspicious but she remains unidentified. I want to know her name by the close of play today. She deserves that at least. Sharma, get a couple of uniforms to go round all the homeless haunts with the photo we have and see if it jogs any memories."

"OK Gov," Sharma said automatically, but Page could tell from the quick glance that Sharma had made to his colleagues in the room that he clearly didn't think this to be a good use of uniformed resources.

Page continued. "Clare Harding died of asphyxiation at the hands of a person still unknown. Her clothes were found a few hundred yards from her body, stuffed into a hole in the old stone wall. DNA not belonging to the victim was also recovered from her clothing, and this was a match to a small amount of blood found underneath her body. Unfortunately this DNA profile is not on our database, but what we can conclude with certainty is that we are looking for a male in connection with this crime." Page looked around the room before saying: "Perhaps DC Connor will update us on her findings."

"Yes Sir. Thank you," she said, clearly unprepared for the invitation. "I have spoken to Clare's best friend and flatmate and apart from a brother somewhere Clare has no other close family. It appears that Clare was having some bother with her boss at work, the manager of the Seven Stars, who DI Page interviewed yesterday, but neither his alibi nor his general account of things seem to add up."

"That's because he's a lying little scrote," Page interjected. "DC Connor and I will go back and speak to Mr Wilson this morning. Yesterday Wilson mentioned a pub regular he called Dick, although that's not his real name. Seems to drink a lot. Is a big fellow with long hair. DC Mills, you visit some of the local pubs and see if you can track down this Dick fella that Wilson claims was around on Sunday night." DC Mills nodded and for obvious reasons looked pleased with the task he'd been allocated. "Sharma, get your team to make a few phone calls and try and trace this brother of Clare's, Rob or Robert Harding." Page waited for Sharma's acknowledgement and then clapped his hands together loudly. "One final thing, and it should go without saying, but the details of our scene of crime stay in-house. The last thing we need is the press getting a sniff that we are dealing with a naked girl and a large pair of jugs." Before the smiles in the room could turn to laughter Page clapped his hands again: "Chop, chop. Let's get going." And with that the briefing was over, and it wasn't yet a quarter past nine.

Back at his desk Page had a pen in his hand and he was clicking it on-and-off as he stared out of the office window. He knew what he should be doing next, but was trying to assess the risk of doing what he needed to do first. How long did he have before he was summoned, again, by his Chief Superintendent?

"Are we good to go?" Connor asked, who had managed to walk unnoticed up to his door.

"Change of plan. Let's get Sean Wilson in here for questioning. Voluntarily of course, but we need to up the ante. Take a uniform with you and bring him in. I need to pop out but I'll be back to interview him with you before midday. I promise." Connor looked as if she were about to say something but before she could Page, in a jovial but persuasive voice, said: "Off you go then."

He was going to ask Connor for a lift but having checked the route on his phone he'd found he could walk it in about half an hour. The route planner had suggested twenty minutes but he knew he wasn't that fit. He had taken the precaution of calling ahead so as not to waste any more of his time than necessary. The meeting had been arranged for half past ten.

Rather than walk all the way along the road he had cut through the Cabot Circus shopping mall and was emerging back into the outside world between the Phoenix pub and the Quaker Meeting Place in Champion Square. How long would it be he thought, until someone found some dirt on poor old John Cabot that stained his reputation to such an extent that the shopping area would have to be renamed? And Cabot Tower of course! How long before he suffered the same fate as Edward Colston?

Arriving at his destination he tried the door, but it was locked. He held the button on the grey box next to the door and put his ear to the speaker. Almost immediately, and to his surprise, he was greeted personally.

"Good morning. DI Page I presume?" And before he could respond the woman's voice continued: "Don't worry, I can see you. I'll be straight down." Page stood up straight and started looking around for the CCTV camera he had clearly failed to spot. "Hi. I'm Abbie," the young woman introduced herself as she opened the door.

Page looked at her in her jeans and T-shirt and hoped that his thoughts on her attire and apparent young age had not been communicated through the half-smile, half-frown that had flickered across his face. "DI Page," he confirmed, determined not to allow his old-fashioned prejudices to show themselves again and possibly mar the meeting.

"Come on through," Abbie said, showing him into a small room with a low table and two soft chairs. A couple of colourful pictures hung on the wall and in the corner was a small shelf unit containing magazines. "How can I help?"

Page sat down and pulled a copy of a photograph from his jacket pocket, placing it on the table between them. "I don't suppose you know this woman?"

Abbie straightened it slightly as she looked, before saying: "Should I?"

"No. It's just a long shot."

"Are you looking for her?"

"No. I know where she is. I just don't know who she is," Page said wearily, picking up the picture and putting it back into his pocket. "I know you run a hostel for homeless women here and I just thought she might be known to your organisation."

"So she's homeless?"

"No. She's dead," and as soon as he had said it Page regretted his matter of factness. "She died a couple of days ago. Nothing suspicious, but I need to know who she is, or rather who she was. What I do know is that she was somebody's daughter and possibly somebody's mother." He stopped abruptly, his voice sounding a mixture of compassion and anger.

"I'm sorry," Abbie said. "Sorry for this woman but also sorry I can't help you. Do you have any idea how many homeless women there are in this city? And most of them have no contact with support agencies whatsoever. In any case the people we support are younger women, many of them teenagers still."

Page shook his head, feigning disbelief. "What a society we live in. A society where you can be homeless before you've even grown up and left home. How did we ever end up like this?"

Abbie gave him a supportive look. "For many of our clients you might argue that being homeless is better than staying at home: a home where at best you live in constant fear and are regularly exposed to domestic violence between your parents, or at worst where you are actually the victim of violence or sexual abuse yourself."

"I know. And the work you do here is admirable but who helps my homeless friend, late of this parish?" Page asked sarcastically and rhetorically really.

"Many older homeless people are unable to adapt to hostel life, even if enough hostel spaces existed," Abbie continued. "By the time they are on the streets they are living chaotic lifestyles, often complicated by alcohol or drug dependency and once there they are written off, ignored and blamed for the predicament they find themselves in. But they are real people like you and me. They all have a lifetime of experiences, memories, secrets, hopes and fears that they are carrying around with them. And how did they find themselves middle-aged and homeless? Redundancy, relationship breakdown, mental health issues or just plain bad luck."

Page nodded. "And there but for the grace of God go you or I." He realised that once again he had been too quick to judge. This young woman who he had initially thought was dressed more for a day off than a day in the office was actually wise beyond her years. Clearly compassionate and a credible champion for the disadvantaged and dispossessed. He was impressed and a little embarrassed. "I'm sorry I've wasted your time," he apologised. "I always knew it was unlikely that you would be able to help, but I had to start somewhere."

"That's no problem. I really hope that you can find out who she was."

"Thanks, and keep up the good work," he said as he stood up, and then worried that she might think he was being facetious quickly added: "I sincerely mean that. You really are making a difference, and that's all that any of us can hope for in the end."

"Thank you," she said, her face reddening a little, "I'll show you out."

As he retraced his steps back through the shopping centre and on to Bridewell Police Station his conversation with Abbie kept going round and round inside his head, and he felt himself slowly getting angrier and angrier. The odds were that his mystery woman wouldn't be known to any of the homeless agencies. She would have spent the last few years of her life wandering the streets of Bristol by day begging for money to buy tea or coffee to warm herself up or alcohol to help her forget the realities of her existence. At night she might have slept on a grubby sofa in a squat somewhere if she were lucky, otherwise she would have been huddled in a shop doorway, wrapped in cardboard, trying to balance the need for sleep with the need to stay awake to protect herself from violence or worse.

The homeless were like a zombie army defeated by the iniquity of capitalism but left to roam the streets of our cities as a visible deterrent to anyone else thinking of challenging the status quo. 'It's all about political choice and power,' he thought to himself, 'and we are all of us only a pawn in their game.'

Little Lies

"Sorry to have kept you waiting Mr Wilson but DI Page has been delayed so I will now be conducting this interview," Connor explained as she pulled the chair out from under the desk.

In fact Page had returned from wherever he had been that morning and gone straight into his office. When reminded about the interview with Wilson he had told her he had phone calls to make and suggested she carry on without him. So here she was.

Sitting herself down and opening a pale blue cardboard folder she looked across at Sean Wilson. "Thanks for coming in to talk to us. As I explained earlier your attendance is on a voluntary basis, and just to remind you, you are not under arrest."

"I wouldn't call it 'voluntarily' but get on with it," Wilson retorted as impatiently as when he had spoken to her and Page the previous day.

"Do you know why you are here Mr Wilson?"

"No. But I am sure you are going to tell me."

"You are here because a number of things you told us yesterday don't appear to be true."

"And that makes me a murderer does it?"

"Not necessarily, but it does make people like me wonder just what it might be that you are trying to hide."

"Ask away," he said sitting back in the chair and folding his arms across his chest.

"Let's start with why you didn't tell us that you were in dispute with Clare and that she had threatened to seek legal advice on her contractual position."

Wilson shook his head. "It was hardly a contractual dispute. The last few weeks the till has been short whenever Clare's been working and the number of breakages and amount of wastage was getting beyond a joke. I didn't want to sack her, so told her I'd be stopping some of her wages until the situation improved. That's all. A caring employer I'd call it."

"So nothing to do with the fact that you had been bothering her, despite her asking you to stop?"

"What do you mean bothering her?"

"I mean that you were unhappy that she was refusing your sexual advances."

"Look here," Wilson said, for the first time appearing to lose the couldn't-care-less attitude he had adopted at the outset. "I wasn't forcing myself on anyone, and I certainly wouldn't waste my time on a prick-teaser like her."

"That's strange Mr Wilson. Yesterday you told us you thought she was a lesbian and today…"

"You know what I mean," he said, just starting to raise his voice.

"I think I do Mr Wilson. I think you are unable to cope with rejection, and unable to comprehend how the combination of your masculine allure and your position of power don't instantly render you irresistible."

"What sort of question is that?" he demanded angrily.

"It's not a question Mr Wilson. Just an observation." Connor wondered whether she had gone too far and decided to change tack. "Remind me what time you arrived at the pub yesterday morning."

"I told you. I don't remember."

Connor looked at the paperwork in front of her and ran a finger down the page searching for a specific section. "But that's not what you told us. You said you didn't know the exact time but that you had returned from your mate's flat, and I quote, 'sometime between ten and half past eleven to find the alley swarming with police'."

"I don't know," Wilson said, quite calmly now. "If I said it was then, then it was then."

"Except it wasn't, was it?" Connor said after a slight pause. "You got to the pub around half past eight, and there were no police there then were there."

"I don't know," Wilson said again, now refusing to make eye contact with Connor.

"If you saw Clare's body why didn't you report it?" Connor waited, but no answer came. "And if you didn't see it, why not? It was right outside the door." Wilson still said nothing. "So where had you gone, if not to the pub as you had told Mr Green when he dropped you off?" Silence. Connor watched as Wilson seemed to be weighing up his options, running his hands through his hair and grimacing like a man in pain.

After half a minute or so Wilson broke his silence: "I'd like to go now, or speak to a lawyer."

"That's up to you," Connor said, tidying the paperwork on the desk and closing the file cover around it. "If you were somewhere else then tell me where and you can go, otherwise you probably will need a lawyer."

Wilson was now rubbing his eyes. After another long pause he finally admitted: "I wasn't at the pub."

"I never thought you were," Connor confirmed. From the very first time she had spoken to Wilson she was convinced that he was only being vague about the timings because he hadn't been there at all. "When did you get to the pub?" she asked, as much for her own benefit as for the record.

"Literally a few minutes before you did. I got a text message from one of my casual staff asking what the police were doing at the pub, and I thought I ought to get down there ASAP. They'd just let me in and I'd just lit up a cigarette when you and your mate arrived."

"And where had you been?" Connor asked, not sure whether or not she would get an answer.

"I was having coffee with a couple of mates. Trying to tap them up for some money. I've got the odd cash-flow problem right now."

"A serious problem?"

"Sort of. I owe a bit of money, not a lot, but the people I owe it to aren't very nice. And they want their money back."

"I'm not overly interested in your financial affairs Mr Wilson, unless you think it has any bearing on the death of Clare Harding."

"It doesn't. They might be thugs but they aren't deranged killers."

"And your friends will confirm that you met for coffee, and be able to tell me what you talked about?" Connor asked hoping to draw the conversation to a close.

"Yes, I'm sure they will."

"In that case I think we're done Mr Wilson," she said as she pushed the chair back and got to her feet. "Apart from one thing. When we met earlier you indicated that you would have no objection to providing a DNA sample. Is that still the case?" Wilson nodded without saying a word. "Right then. If you sit there for just a few minutes more I'll send somebody in to take a mouth swab, and then you'll be free to go."

Connor closed the door to the interview room behind her and stood in the corridor holding the pale blue folder to her chest. Her instinct told her that Wilson hadn't killed Clare but she needed hard evidence to prove this. For what it was worth, she didn't believe a word he'd said about meeting his friends to ask them for money. Once again he'd kept things vague and hadn't volunteered any names for his friends or even mentioned where they had all met. He had been up to no good. She might not believe that he was capable of murder but she had no doubts that deep down he really was a nasty piece of work.

The soft soles of her shoes squeaked as she walked along the corridor towards the stairs. In her head she was already preparing herself for the debriefing with DI Page.

Parklife

He tried not to drink during the week before a Wednesday. Wednesdays were 'crib night', although not much cribbage was played these days. Friday evenings were usually his drinking night, four or five pints and a takeaway pizza. Shifts and workloads allowing of course. But here he was two pints in on a Tuesday night and still only a few hundred yards from the office. The evening briefing had indeed been brief, even by his standards. Certainly short but not very sweet. It seemed they were getting absolutely nowhere. They now had a name for Dick from the Seven Stars: Stuart Land. From what they could tell he was a heavy drinker who could often become aggressive and sometimes violent. He was now a person of interest they wanted to speak to, but he had gone to ground. And then their initial prime suspect, Sean Wilson, had been sent on his way by DC Connor. Not that Page really believed he was their man, but he needed something to help him believe that they were making progress and not just running around in the dark

"Another one Jim?" the barman asked as he cleared and wiped the table next to him.

"No thanks. Quick wee then I'll be on my way," but Page knew there was nothing quick about having a wee in the White Lion. Before you could reach the Gents you had to negotiate the very narrow, steep and winding metal staircase that took you down below the bar. The very same staircase that was originally to be found in Bristol's old Victorian gaol. At least these days having successfully made it all the way down to the bottom you knew it would only be a matter of minutes before you were on your way back up again.

Outside it was starting to get dark. Page glanced fleetingly at his watch, more out of habit than the need to be anywhere at any specific time, and then set off on his walk to the bus stop. As he crossed the road, about to walk past St James's Park above him, he heard the loud voices of the rough sleepers jostling for the best positions and arguing over whose filthy blanket was whose. He hesitated before turning up the narrow entranceway to the churchyard. The large uneven slabs beneath his feet were difficult enough to walk on during the day but in the dark they could be treacherous. It wasn't fully dark yet but the walkway was unlit, and the high stone walls on either side only made it more difficult to see exactly where he was stepping. Perhaps that wasn't a bad thing he thought, given the strong smell of urine emanating from the ivy growing on the walls it might be better not to know. At the top he turned right and went into the park, but couldn't shake off the feeling that he was being followed. He had looked back a couple of times but not seen anybody. In front of him on the benches around the grassed area he could make out figures huddled together and slowly he walked towards them. As he got closer to them, dressed as he was in his work suit, he became increasingly aware of how conspicuous he must look. "Hi," he said, reaching into his pocket for the picture of the homeless woman, but he didn't have the chance to get it out.

"Piss off," a lone voice shouted, and then more responded in drunken unison: "Yeah - piss off."

One of the figures on the bench stood up and pushed Page gently in the chest. He stepped back deliberately to prevent himself from stumbling but before he could regain his balance fully he found himself confronted by five or six individuals. "Look," he said, "I'm just trying to find out some information about somebody you might know."

"Who are you - a copper?" the apparent ringleader asked with equally apparent suspicion.

Page wasn't sure whether it was a good idea or not to reveal his identity. Would coming clean about being a police officer calm or enflame things? He quickly concluded that what was going to happen was going to happen regardless. "Yes, I'm a detective, but I'm on your side. I'm just trying to work out what happened to this woman," he explained as calmly as he could, pulling her picture from out of his pocket.

They all crowded round to have a look but there was a lot of head shaking going on. "We can't really see it," one of them said.

Page got his phone out, turned on the torch and held it over the picture. "Does that help?"

"Not really," somebody replied and a small round of laughter and coughing rippled through the group.

"OK, not to worry," Page said, turning his phone off and putting the picture away. "It was just a long shot."

As he was turning around to go one of the men at the front grabbed his arm. "I used to know her, if that's who I think it is."

Page tried to pull the man closer to him and away from the others, but by now the rest were intent only on returning to their benches. Letting go of the man he asked: "Who do you think it is?"

"It looks a bit like Shirley," the man said, before adding: "but she's not from around here."

Page's initial optimism had gone and he asked himself why he had been prepared to put any store at all by the word of this homeless alcoholic. Well meaning no doubt but clearly too eager to please. "So where is she from?" he enquired, wondering what exotic location the man would come up with.

"Temple Meads."

"Temple Meads?" Page repeated in surprise. "You mean Temple Meads train station?"

"Yeah. She doesn't come or sleep around here. She stays down there. Around the station and the Feeder canal."

"And how do you know this?" Page asked, still not expecting a fully rational answer.

"When I first came to Bristol that's where I stayed for a while, until I came up here to Broadmead. But Shirley was mental. Really mental. Always walking around talking to herself. In the end it does your head in."

"And when did you last see her?"

The man looked at Page, or more precisely looked through him, wrinkling his nose and squinting as if desperately trying to get his memory to cooperate. Finally admitting defeat he shook his head and said: "I don't know."

Page wasn't surprised at this, but overall he was very pleased with what he had just learned. The first real bit of progress today. "Here," he said taking a £10 note from his wallet and passing it to the man with the sleight of hand usually reserved for tipping hotel porters or waiting staff on your way out the door. "Spend it wisely."

He walked back towards the park entrance, his hand lightly tapping the outside of his jacket pocket that contained the woman's picture: Shirley's picture perhaps. He hadn't quite reached the entrance when he heard a rustling behind him. Before he could look round he felt the sudden blow to the back of his head and he fell forward. He put an arm out to break his fall but his face still hit the cold, hard stone pathway. He felt his cheek slide across the ground. At first the side of his face felt warm, then wet, and then this sensation gave way to a burning pain from the ear up to his temple. From the corner of his eye he saw a sudden movement and less than a second later felt the sickening thud of a kick to his ribs.

"Back off," a voice growled somewhere above him, and then another kick, less powerful than the first, hit him on the side of his head.

He closed his eyes, waiting for the next blow, but instead he heard another shadowy voice shout: "That's enough," and then it all went quiet.

He hadn't been in a fight for a long time, a very long time, but he couldn't remember ever having been felled quite so easily. He needed to get his breath back but he also needed to get back on his feet, not least for his own sense of pride. He could feel the dampness from the ground coming through his clothes and he was starting to shiver. He looked around to see if anybody was watching but in the gloom he couldn't make anything out. All he could do was remain lying on the floor, not sure which part of him hurt the most, and wondering how on earth he was going to summon the strength to actually get up.

Over two hours he had been waiting for his name to be called and then before he could get to his feet the doctor had disappeared back down the corridor from where she had first appeared. After a few false starts he had found the examination room, been told to sit down on the couch and after ten minutes of prodding and poking had been given three days' worth of strong painkillers and told to go home.

He was now sat in the reception area of the Bristol Royal Infirmary waiting for his lift home. Not up to a bus journey at this time of the night he had rung the station and explained what had happened. Every time the sliding entrance doors opened he looked up expectantly, but so far it had just been more walking wounded arriving, not yet knowing that it would now be tomorrow before they would be seen by a doctor. It was half past eleven when the doors parted and he looked up to see DC Connor staring at him. His heart sank.

"Oh my God," she exclaimed. "What do you look like?"

"I don't know and I don't care. Just take me home."

"Are you alright?" she asked, sitting down next to him.

"Yes. Badly bruised but nothing broken apparently."

"What happened?"

"Not here. Let's talk in the car."

As it was he didn't feel like talking in the car. It might have been the seatbelt holding him firm but each time he breathed in he suffered a sharp pain across his rib cage. And his head was thumping. Some hangover this was going to be.

He hadn't intended asking Connor in. In fact he hadn't. She had insisted that she see him in and make him comfortable with a drink before she left him. 'Duty of care' she had called it.

Over a coffee he explained to her how he had gone into St James's Park, spoken to the homeless group and been given Shirley's name.

"What possessed you to do that on your own?" she asked as he held the mug in both hands with his nose to the rim, literally smelling the coffee.

"I needed to try and find out about our mystery woman. And I did."

"But at some cost to yourself," she said, shaking her head. "And then they turned on you. What did you expect?"

"What do you mean?" Page asked, quickly looking up at her.

"As soon as your back was turned they attacked you."

"Who do you think attacked me?" Page asked, his eyes narrowing as he looked at her.

"Who do I think attacked you? Well the homeless lot obviously."

Page grimaced. He put his coffee down and sat forward, wincing as the pain again ran around his ribs. "It wasn't the homeless guys."

"Well who else do you think it was then?"

"I don't really know," he admitted. "But it wasn't them."

"How do you know? Did you get a look at your attackers?"

Page shook his head. "No. I didn't see much at all. Just their feet. And that's how I know." Connor looked at him quizzically but before she could ask the obvious question he continued: "It was the shoes. They weren't the shoes of a homeless man: the only pair he owns, the same pair he wears every day of the week whatever the weather, the pair of shoes he walks and sleeps and lives and dies in. It was another pair of shoes." He shut his eyes. His head was hurting so much and he just wanted to be left alone. "You've done your Good Samaritan bit Connor. You can go now." She stood up and went to collect the empty coffee mugs but Page stopped her. "Leave those. I'll do them in the morning."

"OK. I'll pick you up tomorrow around eight. Sleep well," she said, walked into the hallway and let herself out of the house.

Page thought he might put some music on to help himself relax. He went to stand up but nothing happened. He waited a second or two and then made another big effort to get out of the chair but the pain was too much and he sank back into the soft upholstery. The thought of a third attempt at getting up was just too much. His body clearly wasn't going to cooperate and for once in his life he decided to listen to what his body was telling him. He would stay put. He closed his eyes and before long he managed to drop off. A temporary reprieve at least from the nagging pain that was dominating his every thought.

BLACK AND BLUE

Page was in the bay window, his mobile phone to his ear waiting for the call to connect. He hadn't slept properly. He had been asleep on and off but had finally given up the pretence around half past six. The painkillers were at last starting to work. His headache had gone and his ribs only hurt when he moved, but now he felt nauseous. He'd splashed some water on his face, enough to feel a little more refreshed but nowhere near enough to clean the congealed blood away. As he'd gently patted his face dry he'd noticed the black shadow spreading under one of his eyes. A spray of his best eau de cologne, a clean shirt and he was ready for whatever the new day might bring.

The ringing in his ear stopped and without waiting for any answer he launched straight in: "Charlotte, it's Jim."

"Good morning Jim. Thanks for asking, I'm doing very well, and you?"

"Are you in your office or still at home?" he continued, oblivious to his colleague's sarcasm.

"I'm in the office. Is that the answer you wanted?"

"Great. Can you have a look at the post mortem report for our homeless woman. When you sent your summary findings over there was no mention of drugs. Did you do a toxicology test?" He could hear Dr James sighing and the rustle of papers being leafed through as she obviously looked for the case file.

"Here it is," she said. "Just give me a second."

Outside Page saw DC Connor pull up and as she opened the car door he gesticulated at her and pointed to the phone by his ear in an attempt to tell her to stay where she was and explain that he would come out when he was finished. The elaborate charade seemed to have been successful as Connor waved back and made no attempt to get out of the car.

Dr James' voice brought him back to the business in hand. "Yes. There were traces of some psychoactive substances in the blood stream, but this would not have contributed to her death and therefore would not have been included in our summary findings…"

"No worries," he interrupted. "There's no complaints about the information you've provided. I just wanted to know whether or not she was a drug user."

"Well she certainly used legal highs," Dr James confirmed.

"Or illegal highs as they have been since the introduction of the Psychoactive Substances Act 2016," Page corrected her.

"You're prickly this morning Jim. What did you have for breakfast?"

Page wasn't sure whether she was joking or whether his pedantry had really irked her. "Nothing at all," he said. "I've had nothing for breakfast but that's another story."

"You should look after yourself better," she said in a genuinely warm way before again adopting her business voice. "By the way, the DNA sample you sent over from Sean Wilson does not match the DNA found at the scene. Good news for Mr Wilson, but not for you if he was your prime suspect."

"Early days yet," Page said dismissively. He reached between the blinds, knocked on the window and put his thumb up to DC Connor to indicate he was on his way. "I've got to go. Thanks for your help as always Dr James," and without waiting for any response he ended the call.

When Page walked into the office all heads turned to greet him. He knew they already knew what had happened the night before; he knew they were all looking at his bloodied face and black eye; and he also knew that nobody would be brave enough to mention it. But he knew he had to. Walking to the middle of the room he slowly turned around once and with the biggest smile he could muster said: "Go on - all have a good look. And if you think this is bad, you should see the other bloke!" A loud, knowing cheer went up and with that the matter had been fully addressed and put to bed.

He hadn't even reached his desk but he could already see the folded yellow piece of paper waiting for his arrival. Without sitting down he picked it up. It was a handwritten message from PC Sharma advising him that the Chief Superintendent wanted to see him at eleven o' clock. He screwed the message into a ball and threw it towards the waste paper basket in the corner. Not even bothering to see whether it had gone in or not he returned to the main office and looked for Connor.

She was in the kitchen area and looked up when he came in. "Do you want a coffee?"

"Yes please." He sat down at one of the small circular tables. "I've been invited to see the Chief Super at eleven, so how about you pay Sean Wilson another visit. Give him the good news that he's off the hook, but let him know we are still interested in finding out what he is really up to. Without threatening or harassing him you understand."

"Message understood," she said as she placed his coffee in front of him, turned and walked away towards her desk.

"And meet me for lunch later," he called after her. "Make it one o' clock. I'll give you a ring and let you know where I will be." He honestly didn't yet know where he might end up for lunch but he already knew that he would need cheering up after the morning he was going to have.

'And meet me for lunch later.' Connor presumed that was an instruction not an invitation. Not that it made a great deal of difference but she did wonder to herself why Page was sometimes so direct. She was starting to think that deep down he might be a caring person but it was difficult to recognise the genuine man from the world weary detective he played for all to see.

The door to the Seven Stars was locked but Connor could hear movement inside. She gave the door three loud knocks and stood back.

"We're shut," Sean Wilson shouted.

"Police," Connor shouted back.

"Hang on." After a few seconds she heard the sound of bolts being drawn back before the door opened. Wilson, standing out of sight and holding it open said: "Come in."

Connor walked straight to the bar. She heard the door being closed behind her and the bolts being put back into place. Wilson took up a position behind the bar but not directly opposite her. Despite this Connor had no difficulty immediately seeing what it was he was trying to hide. "What's happened to you?" she asked, unable to take her eyes from his bloodied and beaten face.

"A bit of a misunderstanding last night."

"It looks like a lot of a misunderstanding to me. What happened?"

"I went out to check the tables last night ready to close up and these two guys jumped me. Slammed me into the wall and literally rubbed my face in it."

"Did you recognise these guys?"

"No."

"Well there's a surprise," she said before adding: "What did they want?"

Wilson shrugged his shoulders. "Probably something to do with my money problems."

"So why would you jump to that conclusion if they didn't say anything or didn't even give you a clue why they were doing it?" He shook his head and shrugged his shoulders again. "And will you be reporting this assault?"

"No. Probably best to keep you lot out of this," he answered, clearly having been helped to reach this decision.

"If you change your mind then let me know." Connor smiled at him. "Now the real reason I'm here is to confirm to you that the DNA sample you gave us does not match with that found on Clare's body."

"So you'll be leaving me alone now," he said, more as a statement than a question.

"We do not believe that you were directly involved in Clare's death, but as somebody closely linked to the deceased and unable, or unwilling, to fully explain their movements around this time, we wouldn't want you leaving the country Mr Wilson."

"What do you mean? I've already told you what I was doing."

"Indeed you have but that doesn't mean that you're telling us the truth."

"What do you think I've been up to then?"

"I have no idea, but I'm going to make it my business to find out. You will soon be fed up with the sight of me."

He looked rattled. "If that's all for now I'll let you out."

"Thank you very much," Connor answered over-politely as she turned and followed him. "And if I were you I'd get somebody to take a look at that face of yours. You don't want to lose your good looks I'm sure."

The room was brightly lit. So bright in fact that he could feel it in his retinas. Page was standing over the handbasin staring at the reflection of his face, mottled with dry blood and blue bruises and dominated by a large black eye. He had hoped, without any real belief, that he would now be looking more presentable than first thing this morning. With all such hopes dashed he turned on the tap, bent forward and filled one hand with water. Sucking it into his mouth he used the other hand to pop in two painkillers before standing up and swallowing them in one gulp. He rubbed the wet hand through his thinning hair and turned to the hand dryer. He winced as the motor started up with a ridiculously loud, high-pitched whine that sounded like a plane taking off.

Detective Chief Superintendent Charles Tanner had his office on the fourth floor. He was not one to easily mix with the rank and file but if he was ever forced into a social situation he would always fall back on his standard attempt at informality: 'Call me Chas, we're off duty after all.' He rarely left his office. Individuals were only invited to see him for one of two reasons: to be congratulated for a job well done or chastised for the failure to do a job well.

Warm furries or cold pricklies were the names Page had given to these two distinct types of meetings. Suffice to say he was rarely afforded a warm furry, and today he was fully expecting another cold prickly. "Good morning Julie," Page said as he approached the desk outside DCS Tanner's office, checking the time on his watch and on the large white faced clock on the wall.

"My God Jim what happened to your face?"

"Don't ask. Is he ready for me?"

"Yes. Go on in."

Page took two large strides to the door and gave it the kind of knock you do when you know you are expected.

"Come in," was the answer he got, and that was the answer he was expecting. He walked into the room. Tanner was typing on a laptop and without looking up said: "Take a seat." Hitting the enter key with the flourish of a concert pianist he turned to look at Page. "My God man. What have you done to your face?"

"Got into a scrape Sir. Last night."

"I can see. Hopefully not off duty."

"Strictly speaking Sir, off duty, but work related."

"Nothing I should be concerned about I hope?"

"No Sir. Absolutely not."

Tanner didn't look overly reassured but he clearly didn't want to be distracted from the main purpose of the meeting. "Look here Page, I won't beat about the bush. I hear we are making no progress at all on this pub killing."

"We are making some progress Sir," Page tentatively suggested whilst knowing full well that it wasn't the progress that DCS Tanner wanted to talk about. "We have been able to rule out our initial suspect and we have now identified another person of interest…"

"You might have identified them," Tanner interrupted, "but you don't know where they are, do you?"

Page knew this was one of Tanner's rhetorical questions that he didn't want you to answer but expected you to respond to. He tried to choose his words carefully. "Sir, what we are…"

Tanner didn't wait to hear what Page was going to say. "What you need to do is find out who is running around town stripping and murdering young women. That's what you need to do." The volume of his voice went up as he warmed to his theme. "And what you don't need to do is spend your time investigating the death of some homeless person when no crime has even been committed. Do I make myself clear?"

Page recognised that this was a question he did need to answer. "Yes Sir. Absolutely clear. Thank you."

"And another thing," Tanner continued: "It might be helpful if you managed to keep yourself out of trouble on an evening."

"Yes Sir." Page was hoping that this would be the end of the audience. It was.

"Thank you DI Page. Close the door behind you."

Page stood up trying not to show the pain he was in. He nodded his head to acknowledge his superior officer, but DCS Tanner had already turned away, back to his laptop where he was once again beating out a staccato rhythm on the keyboard.

Page shut the door behind him as quietly as he could and smiled at Julie, Tanner's PA, not knowing how much she had heard. "Well, that didn't go too badly," he volunteered and walked straight on towards the stairwell, holding his ribs with his right hand and thinking to himself: 'Not too badly at all for a cold prickly.'

Station To Station

He didn't like talking on the phone whilst we has walking so he had stopped in an office doorway. As he was waiting for her to answer he turned towards the glass door and once again was presented with the less than flattering image of his face. He moved his head from side to side in an attempt to see whether or not his black eye was getting worse but the reflection wasn't good enough to help him decide.

"Good afternoon," Connor's voice chirped in his ear.

"Hi. It's Page." He didn't know why but he always announced himself at the start of phone conversations even though he knew full well that his Caller ID would already have given this information to the recipient. "How was Mr Wilson this morning?" he continued.

"Well funny you should ask. He seems to have got into a bit of a scrape last night and his face looks very similar to yours."

Page instinctively looked at his reflection again in the glass door. "What do you mean, 'a bit of a scrape'?"

"He says he was attacked late last night by two men outside the pub. He was clearly targeted, just like you. Now that can't be a coincidence surely?"

"It could be of course, but I don't believe it is. I would say that somebody knows Mr Wilson has been talking to us."

"Yes, but talking to me mainly, so where do you fit into this?" Connor asked.

"I don't know. Perhaps they think we have more of a lead on this murder than we actually do. And perhaps these thugs are really gentlemen and their warped code of honour means they would never hit a woman." Connor didn't answer. His irony might have been missed but it seemed more likely to him that they had been cut off. "Are you still there?" he asked. After a brief wait and no response Page redialled.

"Hi," Connor greeted him again before adding: "I don't know what happened there."

"Not to worry. Listen Connor, change of plan," he announced returning to the main purpose for his call. "No need to meet me for lunch now. I've already eaten and I've got things to be getting on with."

"OK. How did your meeting with the Chief Super go?"

"As expected really. He wants me to put more effort into solving this murder enquiry and to forget about our homeless woman."

"So that's what you're going to do, right?"

"Don't ask, but I want you to find out everything you can about Stuart Land. And I mean everything. Where he lives, what he looks like, who is friends are, what he does all day. We need to find him Connor. He's all we've got. We'll talk in the morning." And once again the conversation was over without the usual concluding pleasantries.

Crossing the road his spirits were lifted, as they always were, when he saw the cathedral like tower rising above the iron and glass canopies that afford pedestrians protection from the elements as they approach the station entrance. He always thought that this view of Temple Meads was one of the best architectural displays Bristol had to offer. The original station had been built around 1840 and had been designed by local hero Isambard Kingdom Brunel. The first of many subsequent alterations and expansions had already taken place by the 1870s and Page often wondered, thinking of Trigger's broom in the TV sitcom Only Fools and Horses, how much of today's station could actually still be attributed to Mr I. K. Brunel.

Once inside however, grandeur soon gave way to gloom. The roof structure over the platforms was either covered with scaffolding and ripped polythene sheeting or covered in black soot and pigeon shit. The consequence of both was that daylight could not easily pass through the glass roof panels and so whatever the weather or time of day it always felt like late afternoon on a foggy autumnal day.

Page showed his warrant card at the ticket barrier and was let through to the platform. He turned right and walked down the steps to the underpass area that linked all the platforms. Lined with advertising posters and containing a few coffee shops, pasty stands and other concessions this area was bathed in bright, artificial light. There were however, one or two dark areas hidden away in corners not easily seen when walking along the main thoroughfare. Here, if you looked, you might find individuals sleeping or at least discover empty sleeping bags temporarily discarded like pupae once the butterfly has emerged and flown. Page knew that these 'butterflies' would be back later to sleep but for now they would be flitting between the platforms in search of food or money. And it was here that he had been led to believe Shirley, his mystery homeless woman, had based herself.

He went into one of the coffee shops and paid for his drink with a £20 note, asking for as much small change as possible. He understood that any help he might get wouldn't come for free. On his way out of the shop he was approached by a dishevelled man, anywhere between twenty and forty years old, with a dirty blue hospital blanket draped over one shoulder like a child carrying its comfort blanket.

"Can you spare some change?" he asked in a voice clearly resigned to routine rejection.

"Yes. Come over here a minute," Page answered walking to a ledge where he could balance his cup of coffee. He took a pound coin from his trouser pocket and showed it to the other man as a magician would before making it disappear again. Then taking the picture of Shirley from his jacket pocket he passed it to the man along with the pound coin. "Do you recognise this woman?"

The man held the coin tightly in his closed hand and studied the picture before saying "No. Sorry."

Page took the photo and put it back into his pocket. Before he could pick up his coffee and turn around the man had shuffled away and almost immediately Page heard his voice again, this time asking somebody else: "Can you spare some change?"

For nearly an hour Page walked the platforms. He was surprised and saddened at just how many individuals there were busily trying to get money from travellers by one means or another. Some positioned themselves outside the retail units hoping to shame people coming out with food and drinks for their journey. Some sat quietly in the middle of the platform with a handwritten sign telling their story and avoiding eye contact at all cost. Others dashed from arriving trains to departing trains with stories of lost tickets and urgent travel needs where cash was always the only solution. He spoke to them all but not one person admitted to knowing Shirley. Time to call it a day he thought to himself and started to walk back to the underpass.

As he approached the bottom of the stairs leading back up to the main exit he glanced to his right and in the dark recess he saw the figure of an elderly looking man sat on a flattened cardboard box, back against the wall with his knees drawn up to his chest. By his side was an empty bottle of red wine. Page had no loose change left but still decided to walk over and talk to the man. "Are you alright?" he enquired, solely as a means of getting a conversation going.

"As right as I'll ever be," the old man responded.

"Is this where you stay every day?" Page continued, not really sure what he meant by that exactly.

"Nowhere else to go, and can't go very far anyway."

"So you sit here every day?"

"Already said I can't go far. Not like the youngsters walking round all day. But some of them look out for us older ones if they can."

Page considered sitting down next to the man but if the thought of not easily being able to get back up again wasn't enough to put him off the idea then the pain in his ribs as he tried to bend forward certainly was. He held his breath as he reached down and offered the now tattered and torn picture to the old man. "Do you recognise this woman?"

"That's Shirley," the man said without hesitation. "Not seen her for a few days. You'll be telling me she's dead next."

"What makes you say that?" Page asked, genuinely surprised by the comment.

"Because that's what you policemen do isn't it. Do nothing to help us when we're alive and then harass us when we're dead."

For a second Page wanted to ask him how he knew he was a Police Officer, but then wasn't sure he wanted to hear the answer. "I'm not here to harass you, I'm here to help Shirley. To help find out who her family might be so that I can talk to them and tell them what's happened."

"She never spoke about family. Never spoke much at all. Apart from to herself. But that will be those drugs."

"What drugs?" Page asked, and then immediately regretted the question. He was starting to sound like a policeman harassing a dead woman.

"I don't know, but I told her no good would come from it. But she didn't listen. Didn't want to listen."

Page realised that Shirley and this man might have been close. "You cared about Shirley didn't you?" he suggested.

"I liked her and we got on most of the time."

"And what's your name? What should I call you?" Page asked.

"They all call me Paddy."

"Can I call you Paddy?"

"I don't care if you do or don't."

"OK. Paddy it is. Do you know where Shirley got the drugs from?"

"No, not really, but not from around here. She used to go up towards town and meet them there somewhere."

"Who did she meet there Paddy? Last question, I promise."

"I don't know. Some blokes I guess. I never met them. Never went with her."

Page felt in his pockets and pulled out the last of his money: a £5 note. Taking another deep breath he bent down and squeezed the man's hand as he gave it to him. "Thanks for your help Paddy. I do appreciate it. And I'm sorry about Shirley, I really am." As he slowly stood up he smiled as best he could and added: "I'll come back and see you soon. Let you know how I'm getting on with finding Shirley's family." He turned to go.

"You've forgotten this," the old man called after him, holding out the photocopied picture of Shirley.

"No, that's alright. It's yours Paddy. You keep it."

Setting Sun

He looked at the picture on his desk and smiled. He knew what he had to do, and he knew that this evening he would do it.

He glanced up at the pinboard cleared of all the usual clippings and confusion, now displaying just the picture of the naked woman with the yellow star above her head. This lone picture was positioned in the very centre of the board.

Looking back down again at the picture on the desk his eyes were drawn to the yellow halo behind the man's head, and he smiled to himself again. Another angel, he thought. But this time the halo was at the bottom of the picture. The figure was upside down and the yellow disc seemed to be slipping out of the picture like the setting sun disappearing below the horizon.

He stood up and reaching down to the desk he nudged the picture with the index finger from each of his hands, first left then right, then up and down, until it sat absolutely straight in the very centre of the desk. He looked one last time at the picture. His preparations were over. Now it was time for action.

In The Cage

Wednesdays were 'crib-night' and had been for nearly twenty years. The Cribbage League had finally given up the ghost about five years ago but the fixture had remained in their diaries. They both still called Wednesday nights 'crib night' but these days Page saw it as a way of supporting his friend, giving him something to look forward to and offering him some respite from the domestic responsibilities that normally burdened him. But tonight it was Page who needed some support from his old friend.

Page could walk from home to the Annexe in less than five minutes. It was a real community pub. A real ale pub, unlike the Sportsman to which it was joined, that Page always rather sniffily called a pool and lager bar. Situated a few hundred yards from the Gloucestershire County Cricket ground and within easy walking distance of the Memorial Stadium, home of Bristol Rovers Football Club, the Annexe was a pub to avoid on match days. Unless of course you were going to the match! As a local a Wednesday evening was the ideal time to go, when you could be assured of a seat and a quiet corner where you could drink your beer and hear yourself talk. Or play cribbage if the fancy took you.

As he walked through the door he saw that his friend was already sitting with a pint in 'the cage'. The cage was a small snug area separated from the main bar by waist high wooden base panels and then iron work up to the ceiling featuring large curved patterns in the shape of ears, a design normally seen on a smaller scale atop metal gates on 1960s' housing estates. Having bought himself a beer Page walked into the cage and joined his friend at the table. "Hi Frank. How are you doing?"

Frank was nearly twenty years older than Page. Although fitter than most men of his age he was noticeably slowing down of late. He was a big man, tall but not fat. He had a shock of snowy white hair and whatever the weather he always wore a shirt and tie, covered by either a jumper or a zip-up cardigan. He had a tie for every occasion. "Evening Jim, not doing too badly at all thank you. Same old same old, but still breathing."

Page took a large mouthful of beer and reached across to the neighbouring table for a beer mat before he placed his glass carefully back down. "Anything exciting been happening in your world?" he asked.

"Not since I saw you last Wednesday. Although I did find a DVD boxset of The Prisoner in Oxfam on the weekend."

"That'll keep you busy for a few nights. Well a number of nights probably."

"It will, but remember: 'I am not a number'."

Page laughed: "I'll set them up, you nod them in."

Both men took a sip of their drinks before Frank asked: "And how about you Jim - busy as always?"

"Yes, got a lot on right now."

"And your face, what happened to that?"

Page smiled. He knew Frank had spotted his injuries as soon as he had walked in. Even as he had emerged from the darkness of the doorway. "Got done over last night around St James Barton."

"Robbery?"

"No, just assault and battery." He waited for a second but Frank didn't pick up on the Genesis song title so he let it go. "Probably connected to a case I'm working on."

"That murder down by the Seven Stars?" Frank asked, adding: "I saw about that in the Evening Post."

"Don't believe everything you read in the Evening Post Frank." Both men looked at each other for a brief second before Page continued: "I'm also working on another case Frank, and it's getting to me. I'm starting to lose perspective, I know I am, but I can't do anything about it. I got a bollocking this morning from my Chief Super, he told me to let it go, but I can't." He drained the last mouthful from his glass. "It's brought it all back Frank."

His friend stood up. "You seem to be thirsty. Let me get us another beer and we'll talk about it."

Page watched his friend ordering the drinks at the bar. He couldn't hear what was being said but he could guarantee that Frank was making sure he got his OAP discount of 20p off each pint. He smiled to himself. He didn't have many friends but Frank was a good friend.

"There you are," Frank said as he returned with two fresh pints and put them down on the table.

"Cheers," Page said, raising the full glass and taking a swig before putting it down again. He waited for Frank to sit down and get himself sorted, to put his wallet away and refold his coat on the bench seat next to him. Once done Frank looked up at Page as much as to say: 'ready, whenever you are.' Page took another mouthful of beer, another shot of courage to steady himself before he began. "We've found this homeless woman. Dead. But we don't know who she is. She was probably in her early sixties. Homeless - I've said that already, sorry. Almost certainly had mental health problems." He paused. "And I know it isn't. Know it can't be. But I just keep thinking it's my mother. How stupid is that?"

Frank shook his head slowly in an encouraging way. "It's not stupid Jim. These thoughts and feelings never go away."

"But I was ten years old when she disappeared. That's nearly fifty years ago for God's sake!"

"And that's the point Jim. It's not how long ago it was, but how young you were. How can a child ever reconcile their mother walking out on them?"

Page sighed. "I've tried to rationalise it over the years. Told myself that with hindsight she probably had severe mental health problems and didn't know what she was doing. I've convinced myself that she's still alive, even though no-one has ever seen her and the chances of her having taken her own life somewhere soon after she disappeared are high. I've always worked on the basis that dead bodies are usually found and identified, and subscribed to the view that if you don't want to be found then the best plan of action is to hide in plain sight." Page stopped to catch his breath and to slow down the beating of his heart that was starting to make his ribcage hurt again. He took a sip of beer and continued. "All these homeless people on our streets, we see them everyday but they remain invisible. We look through them and walk past them and never give a thought to the person they used to be or of the life they used to lead. But this is how I prefer to think of my mother. Alive somewhere but invisible, because that is better than thinking of her as dead." Frank said nothing. Page picked up his beer but this time he changed his mind and without bringing it to his lips he put it straight back down again. "The uncertainty is what most people can't cope with, but for me it was the uncertainty that kept her alive in my mind. And then on Monday morning we find this homeless woman dead in Castle Park, her cloak of invisibility suddenly removed and her frailty revealed. And in that moment I saw my mother. And for the first time ever I was certain that she too was dead."

Frank looked at Page and waited a while longer before comforting his friend. "I'm sorry Jim, that's a heavy load to bear. I can't imagine how you must be feeling." Page stared at the drink in front of him. "Have you spoken to anybody about this?" Frank asked.

"I'm speaking to you about it right now."

"I know, but I mean have you spoken to anybody at work. Your Chief Super for instance?"

"No," Page answered slowly. "I've not told anyone at work. If I did they'd probably pack me off to see the Force shrink or start asking me again whether I've thought anymore about retiring, even though I've never thought about retiring."

"Well, perhaps you should. Talk to somebody I mean, not retire. It might help."

"It might, but it probably won't. What I need to do is find out who this woman is. Find out who she was and how she lived before she ended up sleeping rough on the streets of Bristol. I need to do it for her, to give her back some of what she once had; and I need to do it for me, to finally lay my mother to rest."

Frank looked at his friend. "And if you can't identify her, what then?"

"I don't know. I've not thought of that," Page replied, and a forced smile flickered across his face.

"Do you think you should even be trying? You've already said that your boss has warned you off."

"I have to try Frank. Doing nothing is not an option."

"Whatever the cost?"

"Whatever the cost."

Frank smiled at Page. "Once you've got something into your head nobody's going to make you change your mind, I know that, so I'm not going to try, but be careful and look after yourself."

Page returned the smile. "I will. Thanks for listening Frank. And thanks for understanding." He'd said enough for now. Time to change the conversation. "How's that lad of yours these days?" he asked. "I've not seen him for a few years."

"Oh - he's fine. Growing up. You'd hardly recognise him."

"You should bring him down one Wednesday night. It would be good for us all to catch up again."

Frank nodded enthusiastically. "That's a great idea. I'll suggest it to him."

Page stood up and gestured towards Frank's almost empty glass. "Let me get us another beer and then you can tell me all about this model railway club that you were thinking of joining."

Page was looking at the glass of beer in his hand, not sure he could manage to drink any more. He couldn't think why he'd opened it. He didn't normally drink at home and he'd already had enough with Frank earlier.

He'd left the Annexe around half-nine but hadn't come straight home. Bearing his soul had made him restless and despite his aches and pains he'd needed to clear his head before returning home. He'd got in around eleven, poured himself a beer and retired to the living room.

Sat in his chair he put the beer down and felt around for the remote control. It had slipped down beside him. Having spoken about it with Frank he'd got in and put on Dark Side of the Moon. The introductory, drawn out organ notes to the song Us and Them were slowly building. He pointed the remote at the stereo and turned the volume up. He closed his eyes and tried to let the music wash over him but the pain from his ribs was getting worse. He'd probably over done things. He waited for the track to end and then stabbing at the remote with his finger he stopped the CD even though the album wasn't yet finished. He must be feeling unwell. The thought of going upstairs and getting undressed was too much, so he decided not to bother. For the second consecutive night he would try and get some rest here in his chair.

Strange Fruit

The noise woke him, and at first he couldn't place it. He knew it wasn't his alarm clock but he still looked around trying to find it. He then noticed his mobile phone beside him on the arm of the chair and could see the screen illuminated with an incoming call. Raising himself up and leaning over he could just make out who it was that was calling at this time of the morning: DC Connor. He let himself fall back into the chair. "Bollocks," he grunted, an exclamation brought on both by being woken when he had only just got to sleep and the sharp pain he could feel in his ribs as a result of leaning back again so suddenly. The phone stopped ringing but he knew it would only be a matter of seconds before it started again. He used this time to slowly sit up and steady his legs on the floor. Sat upright on the edge of the chair he reached back to pick up his mobile just as the ringing started again and the screen announced the imminent arrival of DC Conner. He swiped the screen: "Hello. Page here."

"Good morning Sir. DC Connor here…"

"Yes I know," he said impatiently.

"Sorry to ring so early Sir but we've got another death."

"Where?"

"Brandon Hill. A hanging apparently."

Page ran his fingers through his hair in frustration and tried his best not to take it out on Connor. Don't shoot the messenger and all that. "Since when do we get called out to suicides? That's not our bloody jobs!"

"I know Sir, but we've been tasked to attend. I'll pick you up in twenty minutes."

When Connor had arrived Page was already dressed and waiting in the bay window. He hadn't had time to make himself a drink and so had instructed Connor to stop at one of the bakeries on the Gloucester Road that sells takeaway coffee. They were now sat in traffic in Stokes Croft. The start of the rush hour.

Page took a sip of his coffee, which was still a little too hot to drink as quickly as he wanted to. He looked out of the passenger window and then turned back to look at his colleague. "Did you do anything nice last night then Connor?"

"Last night?" she said, clearly stalling for time. "Yes. I went to a meditation session."

"A meditation session. What's that? Where you all sit around crossed legged and naked humming 'Om' while some guy in orange robes burns joss sticks smelling of patchouli and prays to Hare Krishna?"

Connor stared straight ahead, keeping her eyes on the car in front. "Is that what you really think it is?"

"No - not really. I was pulling your leg. I don't expect you were naked at all."

At this Connor did turn to look at him and she could see the broad smile fixed to his face. "You can mock, but you should try it sometime. Get in touch with your inner feelings and clear your mind of negative thoughts. It's like a massage for the soul."

"Perhaps I should," Page said, "but it all sounds a little too touchy-feely for my liking." He took another sip of his coffee and looked away. The thought then struck him that perhaps he had in fact been getting in touch with his inner feelings last night too. With Frank over a few pints of beer and a packet of crisps. The thought made him feel uncomfortable. He turned back to Connor. "Don't you know a quicker way that will avoid all this traffic?"

Connor had parked the car in Great George Street as she had when she visited Jeremy Green earlier in the week. She was now trying to catch up with Page who had walked ahead and was already at the entrance to Brandon Hill.

The uniformed officer at the gate glanced at Page's warrant card and stood aside for him to pass through. "Good morning Sir. You'll need to turn left here and take the path down to the southern end of the park."

Page didn't respond. He could see Charlotte James sat on a bench a few hundred yards further on down the path. Next to the bench was the silver briefcase that she always had by her side whenever she was required to turn up and pronounce on the dead. "Charlotte," he called out, still some way from the bench.

She stood up and greeted him. "Good morning Jim. And before you ask, I haven't got a clue. I haven't had a close look at the body yet."

"Why not?" he asked impatiently.

"Because I've been waiting for you."

"What on earth is going on here?" His impatience was starting to turn to annoyance. "First of all I get woken up and then get dragged down here to have a look at some bloody suicide, and then when I get here the pathologist is having a sit down and hasn't even had a look at the body."

"I've had a look at the body Jim, but I've not examined it yet." Her voice sounded almost as annoyed as he felt. "And it's not a suicide," she added. "That's why I waited for you to see the scene first."

"What makes you think it's not a suicide? Hangings normally are."

"Well not this one." Dr James bent down to pick up her case, turned and started to walk away. She looked back at Page who had now been joined by DC Connor. "Walk this way," the pathologist said leaving the pathway and heading across the open grass area towards a group of trees. Page could see that a cordon had been set up around the trees and Dr James was waiting for him there. As soon as he reached her side she lifted the tape barrier above his head and stretched out her other arm in front of him. "Have a look for yourself."

Page walked slowly into the small grove, Connor by his side. His eyes were drawn to three trees set slightly aside from the rest, but it was the middle one that grabbed his attention. He stopped in his tracks and shook his head in disbelief.

Connor remained silent. Her eyes too had been drawn to the tree from which the young man was hanging. His head was close to the floor. He was hanging upside down, suspended by just one foot. His arms were tied behind his back but his free leg had come to rest in the most unnatural and ungainly position imaginable.

"See what I mean?" Dr James had joined the two detectives without either of them noticing.

"I think you might be right Charlotte, probably not suicide, but we will need a post mortem just to make absolutely sure." He smiled at her to make sure that she knew he was joking.

She smiled back. "So that's an apology Jim?"

"As close as you are going to get."

"I'll take it," she said, smiling again. "If you're done here we'll get him down, have a preliminary look in situ and then take him in and do a PM later this afternoon."

"Sounds good," Page confirmed, before adding: "Thanks Charlotte. And thanks for not asking what happened to my face."

"I look after the dead not the living," she called back over her shoulder. She was already bent down above her opened silver case putting on a pair of surgical gloves.

Once out of the trees and back on the pathway Page looked at his watch. Breakfast time. Connor was stood next to him, looking bewildered and waiting it seemed to be told what to do. So he told her. "Find out from the uniforms who it was that reported this, and then go and speak to them. And see if Dr James turns up any ID for our dead man, and if she does then make a start on that."

"Of course," DC Connor said but her look seemed to be saying: 'And what will you be doing?'

He felt he owed her an explanation of sorts. "I need to get something to eat, and then there's something I need to do.

Probably best that I do that on my own. We'll catch up later, is that OK?"

"Yes, fine."

And with that Page walked off towards College Green.

Connor was angry. Angry with Page for leaving her to do all the legwork when he was off doing goodness knows what. And angry with herself for once again having given him the opportunity to laugh at her. Telling him she'd been at a meditation session. What on earth had she been thinking of? 'Too touchy-feely' was what he had said. Touchy-feely indeed! She might not go around getting herself beaten up but she was the one doing all the hard work here. What little progress they had made so far was down to her, but then no doubt in the end it would be Page who took all the glory. Having said that Page hadn't covered himself in much glory of late. A thought worth hanging on to perhaps.

She looked up from the bench where she was sitting, up to the top of the hill where the red sandstone tower was rising into the blue sky like a rocket. Cabot Tower, one of Bristol's most famous landmarks built to celebrate the achievements of one of the city's most famous adopted sons. Construction of the tower had started in 1897 to mark the 400th anniversary of John Cabot setting sail from Bristol and discovering Newfoundland. It was a story all local school children had been taught back in the day and Connor remembered many visits to the tower as a child, climbing the spiral staircase to reach the viewing platform nearly 100ft from the ground. From the top of the tower the views of the city and beyond were spectacular. Now sat at the bottom of the tower looking up she wondered whether John Cabot's exploits were still of interest to today's kids, and then for the first time ever she noticed the stone figure atop the tower. From where she was sitting it looked like an angel. She could just about see the wings pointing upward but no other features were discernible from such a distance.

"On your own?"

Connor turned to find Dr James standing there, silver case in hand. "Yes. DI Page had to go... Had to go."

"Not to worry. I'm done for now. We'll know more once we've done the PM but it looks as though he was dead before he was left swinging from the tree. Strangulation." The pathologist held out a clear plastic evidence bag. "You might want this. The few things we found in his pockets."

Connor took the bag. "Thanks."

"Are you OK?" Charlotte James asked. "You look deep in thought there."

"Yes, I'm alright. Just trying to second guess what DI Page expects of me."

The pathologist laughed. "When you find out perhaps you could let me know too."

Connor forced a smile in reply. Dr James set off back up the hill towards the tower and the entrance where she had parked her car. Connor studied the evidence bag she had been given. There wasn't much to see. Some loose change and a door key. And a white access card on a grey lanyard. Connor looked for a name on either side of the credit card sized piece of plastic but there was nothing other than a very small line of blue lettering which she could only read with difficulty:

18421918-TurmSol Ltd. Not much help, it was the name of the security card manufacturer. Her disappointment lasted only a matter of seconds. As she straightened the plastic bag she had a better view of the lanyard and there in black ink, repeated regularly a number of times along its length, were the words: The Three Tuns. She took out her phone and googled The Three Tuns. It was a pub. Opening her map app she entered the pub's name and selected the Get Directions option using her current location as the starting point. She pressed Go and was surprised when almost immediately the route appeared on her screen. It was just a three minute walk away: out of the park at the next entrance, down some steps and she should be able to see it at the end of York Place. Her next move had literally been mapped out for her. She smiled to herself and wondered what the intrepid explorer John Cabot would have made of SatNav.

Front Page News

Page was angry. Angry with himself and angry with everybody else. This was not the start to the day he wanted. Not after yesterday.

Having left Connor on Brandon Hill he had gone to Woodes at the bottom of Park Street for brunch and then made his way once again to Temple Meads station. He wanted to speak to Paddy again and find out more about these trips Shirley used to make to Broadmead to buy her drugs. This time he knew exactly where he was going and once through the ticket barrier he had gone straight down the stairs to the underpass. There in the corner wrapped in an old anorak was Paddy, exactly where he had left him the previous day. The hood of the anorak was pulled over his head and halfway down his face. His chin was wresting on his chest as if he were asleep, but as soon as Page had got close to him he had raised his head and looked straight at him. Even in this dark corner of the underpass Page couldn't fail to instantly see the swollen eye, the split lip and the bloodied face. Less than an hour. Less than an hour between him leaving the old man yesterday and this happening. Page knew this wasn't coincidence and he was angry with himself for having brought this upon poor old Paddy. He'd spent most of the day cleaning him up and making him more comfortable and then persuading the Transport Police to increase the frequency of their visits to the underpass for the next day or two.

And then this morning, before he had even got into the office, his day had already been ruined. Connor had spoken to him the previous afternoon and passed on Dr James' initial thoughts about the hanged man's cause of death. Initial thoughts. Nothing more. Nothing certain and nothing confirmed. And yet when he'd stopped to buy a coffee on his way to work that morning, there on one of the tables was a copy of the Bristol Post, the front page headline screaming: 'THE BRISTOL STRANGLER - City's second strangulation. Is there a serial killer on the loose?' Page hated tabloid newspapers and how they worked. The use of capital letters and strings of alliteration. And then the most preposterous and usually unfounded suggestions presented as questions. No need to have any evidence if you are just asking a question, but the seeds of the idea have already been sown in the readers' minds. Page was getting angry just thinking about it.

The piles of paper that usually sat on the desk had been removed and were now stacked on the floor, propped against the glass partition. The telephone handset had been repositioned in the middle of the desktop and Page and Connor were sat facing each other, both leaning forward, heads bent down like chickens fighting over some corn.

Dr James' voice was coming from the speaker between them, the telephone having been set to hands-free mode. "The deceased died as a result of asphyxiation. The hanging was a post-mortem event that in no way contributed to the death.

Its significance however, is something that will no doubt interest you more than me. The time of death is difficult to determine precisely but I would estimate it to be sometime between 10pm and midnight."

"OK. Thanks Charlotte," Page said, lowering his head even closer to the speaker.

"And just one final thing that you need to know." Page looked up and caught Connor's eye. Together, heads almost touching, they waited to hear what Dr James had to say. "We managed to recover a significant amount of DNA from around the deceased's neck. These samples are an exact match to the DNA found at the scene of Clare Harding's murder."

Page sat back in his chair. "Shit. So we are dealing with a serial killer."

"Over to you Jim. Best of luck. Speak soon." There was a click and Dr James was gone.

Page moved the phone back to its usual position and Connor shuffled her chair a little farther away from the desk. "Brilliant. Absolutely brilliant," he said sarcastically, putting his head into his hands. "We haven't even got started on the first murder and then we get a second. Some nut-job running around strangling strangers for fun." He looked at Connor. "Well - do we have anything to go on? Anything at all?"

She hesitated. "Well yes in a way. We now have more than we had yesterday."

"Go on Connor, enlighten me."

"Bear with me," she said, leaning forward, resting her elbows on the desk and putting her hands together. "The body yesterday was that of Callum Roberts, a twenty year old student who worked behind the bar in the Three Tuns.

He was probably killed at the end of his shift and his body was discovered very close to the pub where he worked. Clare Harding worked behind the bar in the Seven Stars, was probably killed at the end of her shift and her body was found very close to the pub where she worked." Connor stopped and looked at Page.

"Go on," he said.

"Well, we now know that both victims were killed by the same person, and that they were both strangled. Early enquiries would lead us to believe that the victims were not known to each other."

"But why strip them or hang them?" Page interrupted.

"I don't know, but let's stay positive and focus on what we do know. We know both victims worked in a pub. We know both killings happened between 10pm and midnight. We know they were both strangled and by the same person."

Page now leant forward, nodding his head slowly. "Yes, you might be right Connor. All of this helps us know what we don't know. Our known-unknowns as Mr Rumsfeld called them. For starters we need to establish whether or not the fact they both worked in pubs was the reason why they were killed. Or is it just that our killer happens to hang around in bars?" Page sat back in his seat and continued in a soft voice, almost as if to himself: "And similarly we might deduce that the strangulation is not the motivating factor here. It might simply be the means to an end. The way in which the bodies can be posed…" He stopped short. "Bloody hell, I'm starting to sound like Sherlock Holmes now."

Connor laughed. "But I think you are right. What this tells us is that we need to concentrate on the killer, not on the victims. The victims have no significance in their own right."

"Just in the wrong place at the wrong time," Page muttered to himself before asking: "So what do we know, or not know, about our killer then?"

Connor sat back in her chair. "Not much really. We know it is a man. We know he is unknown to us. We know he seems to be familiar with pubs around the city, and we know he is out at night. The murders have both been around closing time, so perhaps our killer has somewhere to go shortly afterwards."

"What do you mean, somewhere to go?"

"Well, somewhere like work. Perhaps he works in the early hours. A security guard, a baker, a postman, or a…"

Before Connor could finish Page interrupted her and in a quiet voice continued: "…or a policeman." The thought didn't bear thinking about.

"But Sir, all police officers go through biometric testing before they are appointed, so we would have found a match on the DNA database if that were the case."

Page didn't look convinced. "Yes, that's what is supposed to happen, but who knows?"

"I think it's very unlikely myself," Connor replied. "And I'm not sure we should let this distract us from far more likely explanations."

"For the second time in a few minutes Connor I think you are right. But let's not discount it completely. Not just yet."

Connor nodded in agreement, before sitting forward again. "One positive thing, well interesting at least, is that witnesses who were in the Three Tuns late last night remember seeing a man, a regular visitor apparently whose name they don't know, but whose description fits the one that we have for Stuart Land."

"And how did they describe him then?" Page asked.

"Tall, well built, long black hair and thick stubble. Drinks a lot and can get aggressive quite easily."

"And who seems to frequent different pubs the same night as people get themselves killed," Page added, only half joking.

"Yes, as I said, interesting."

"And we still don't know where this Stuart Land fellow lives?" Page asked, although he knew the answer to the question.

"No, but we do know that he is not known to us and that he is not a serving police officer."

"Progress at least," Page said somewhat sarcastically, before stating the blindingly obvious: "but we need to track him down as soon as possible."

Connor smiled at Page. A smile that seemed to say 'and you think I don't know that?' She moved her chair back and started to stand up but Page quickly put out his hand and said: "Sit down. There's something I need to tell you." He waited for her to sit back down again. Then he put his hands together softly before resting them both on the edge of the desk. "Look Connor, for reasons I won't go into, these last few days I've been making enquiries about our homeless woman. That's where I've been and that's what I've been doing. I think I've found out her name, it was Shirley, and I've found somebody who knew her quite well. Another homeless guy.

But that's not the point. The point is that I was just trying to find out who she was. But…"

He hesitated and Connor stepped in encouragingly. "But what?"

"I was just trying to find out who she was," he continued, "but my enquiries seem to have upset certain people. Really upset them. So much so that all three of us - me, Paddy, that's my homeless contact at Temple Meads, and Sean Wilson, well we've all ended up black and blue. But that can't simply be because I am trying to find out the identity of a dead homeless woman can it. There must be more to it than that."

"Like what?"

"Like drugs. Shirley was buying some psychoactive substances or something from somebody, and I reckon that's just the pretty soft end of what they peddle. Anyway, I'm beginning to suspect that these dealers think I'm on to them. Which I'm not. Well, I wasn't."

"And you think they are trying to warn you off and discourage others from talking to you?"

"Yes," Page said forcefully. "It would make sense, wouldn't it." Connor didn't respond. "So we are investigating a gang of drug dealers, not just the identity of a homeless woman."

Connor looked nervously at Page. "But Sir, we are also investigating a serial killer."

"You think I don't know that," he said, pushing a copy of the Bristol Post across the desk towards her. "Have you seen this? The whole bloody world now knows we are investigating a serial killer."

She only glanced at the front page. "Oh dear."

"Oh dear indeed. So I know full well that this case takes priority, but we can do both." Again Connor didn't answer but she raised her eyes at him. "Don't look at me like that," he said, trying to smile at the same time. And then to reassure her he added: "But you are right. Today we need to try and track down Stuart Land."

"And where are we going to start?" she asked.

"In the pub. Tonight," he announced. "I've been listening to what you were saying and we need to be in and around the pubs this evening at closing time."

She now looked a little disappointed. "But it's Friday night tonight."

"Yes it is Connor, but serial killers don't take weekends off you know."

"But I need to be at home for Aaron."

"Who's Aaron?" he asked.

"My son. I can't just leave him at home alone."

"Well, get off early this afternoon and sort something out. Put your feet up and pick me up about eight o'clock." Connor looked a little disgruntled with him. He tried to be sympathetic. "It's not ideal I know, but as you said, it's imperative that we find this Stuart Land sooner rather than later."

Parents

It was nearly seven hours ago that he had said it, but still it irked her. 'Serial killers don't take weekends off you know.' Bastard. And she'd thought she had done so well up to then that morning.

'Go home this afternoon,' he'd said, 'put your feet up and pick me up about eight o'clock.' Put her feet up? Fat chance! In fact she'd spent most of the afternoon rearranging her Friday night. Firstly she'd had to ring and cancel her massage and treatment session. No chance of swapping it to this afternoon at such short notice. And then she'd had to ring around her friends until one of their daughters, obviously with boyfriend in tow, agreed to come over and child-mind Aaron, her fourteen year old son. Childminding on a Friday night doesn't come cheap and in addition to the negotiated fee there was the need to provide the extra incentives of some drink, pizza, dips, crisps and nuts. Finally she'd had to draft a list of instructions of what Aaron was allowed to watch on the TV, how long it was he could spend in his room on the Playstation and what the absolute latest time was by which he must be in bed.

Aaron was only four when his father had left them. They had married young but her husband had never been able to grow up. The responsibility of having a child seemed to pass him by completely. Having to cope with a wife working shifts and irregular hours was just too much for him. He wasn't able to make the changes needed to make the marriage work. And so he left. Went to live on his own, where all he had to worry about was himself. And that seemed to suit him. These last ten years he had had little to do with his son. He kept making promises to take him out or come over to see him, but more often than not these arrangements changed at the last minute. Something always cropped up unexpectedly that he was unable to deal with. Life, she called it. And yet despite all of this she harboured no great animosity towards him, just a huge frustration at his inability to function as a normal person or parent. It was Aaron she felt most sorry for, and everything he had missed because of the shortcomings of his father. And at times she felt guilty herself that she wasn't able to give Aaron the time she wanted to or he needed. She felt guilty about working, and about enjoying the work she did. But she was doing her best for him, doing her best to provide for him. But she couldn't do it alone. Without the support and help from her mother she wouldn't have been able to cope, and still couldn't. She would certainly have said goodbye to the police force a long time ago.

Right now she was sat down in the kitchen with a mug of tea and a biscuit but already she knew that in less than an hour-and-a-half she needed to be showered, changed and on her way to pick up Page. She was pleased that finally he seemed to be taking the case seriously but she did wonder how long that would last. How long it might be before his homeless woman or this drug dealing cartel turned his head once again. One thing she was pretty sure of was that tonight's efforts would probably be in vain and not be very enjoyable to boot. The chances of finding Stuart Land in the two or three pubs they could visit between nine and eleven o'clock were slim to say the least. And as for the thought of spending her Friday night out with DI Page, then that was simply too much to dwell on. She finished her tea and put the mug into the dishwasher before going upstairs. She tapped lightly on Aaron's door.

"What do you want?"

"Can I come in?"

"Yeah." She pushed the door ajar and put her head into the room. Aaron, games controller in hand, was looking at her impatiently. "Did you want something?"

"No. Just reminding you that I am going out this evening and Lizzie will be here in a minute if you need anything."

"OK."

Pointing at the television Connor said: "This goes off at nine mind, and I want you in bed by ten thirty. I've told Lizzie that's what needs to happen."

Aaron was already turning back to the screen and unpausing the game. "OK," he confirmed.

"See you in the morning," she said, but her son didn't answer. He couldn't. He was engrossed in a full scale military attack that required his undivided attention. She pulled the door to and smiled to herself. Kids - who'd have them?

Moving Pictures

It had been two days ago already and now it was time to update the gallery. Reaching up to the board he moved the picture of the naked woman slightly to the left. Then from the desk he picked up the picture of the hanged man and pinned it next to the other one, so close that they were almost touching. Almost like one picture of two people on its own in the middle of the board.

He stood back and looked at his efforts, smiling to himself. And his efforts were being rewarded. On the desk under the pin-board was the front page story from that morning's Bristol Post, carefully cut out and already pasted onto a piece of card. The Bristol Strangler. Not a name he would have chosen for himself but at least people were starting to pay him some attention now. He opened the drawer that was built into the frame of the desk and carefully slid the mounted newspaper clipping into place on top of the pile of other pieces of paper and card already in there.

He shut the drawer, locked it and put the key back in its hiding place. He could relax now. It was Friday night. He would have something to eat and then he would decide what it was he wanted to do and where he wanted to go.

Drinks After Work

It was only a short walk from the Bridewell office where Connor had parked the car to the Bank Tavern. Tucked away in a small lane the pub found itself sandwiched between 1970s concrete office blocks and the fourteenth century St John on the Wall church, built over the only remaining gateway to the original walled city. A small, one-bar pub Page had deliberately chosen the Bank as a starting point so that they could talk to each other with relative ease before moving onto the city centre.

It was half past eight when they got to the pub and whilst Page was at the bar buying the drinks a table became free near the door. He turned round with a pint of beer in one hand and large glass of tonic water in the other to see that Connor was already sitting down and waiting for him to join her. "Cheers," he said putting the drinks on the table before sitting down. "Well, don't we look like a couple out for a night on the town!" He looked at Connor and smiled but she didn't smile back. But that had been the plan. What they had agreed that morning. That if they were going to learn anything that evening they had to make an effort to look and act just like any other couple and not like a couple of off duty plain clothed police officers. "You're looking very nice," he said, and he meant it.

Connor seemed to understand that. "Thank you," she said.

He took a mouthful of beer and smiled at her again. "Cheer up. I'm sure this isn't the Friday night either of us would have chosen, but it's only for a few hours. And I'm not such bad company, honestly."

She did smile at this. "So what would you normally be doing on a Friday night?"

He laughed. "I'd be in the pub drinking. But in my local, in some scruffy old clothes and talking bollocks with a few other grumpy old men. And you?"

"I would have had a massage tonight, gone home, cooked something to eat and then spent the evening watching rubbish on the telly with my son."

"And that's Aaron."

"Yes, he's fourteen. Have you got kids?"

"Good God, no!" Page almost choked on his beer. He swallowed loudly. "Never been married. Never wanted a wife nor children." Connor nodded her head and smiled. Page wondered what conclusions she was coming to. "I'm not gay," he announced.

"I didn't think… It wouldn't matter…" Connor was clearly flustered and that hadn't been Page's intention.

"No, that's alright," he reassured her. "I'm just saying: I'm not gay. I know some people at work think I am, guessed you might have heard it mentioned and here we are sitting in a gay bar."

"I'd not heard that particular rumour," she confirmed.

"Good. For the record I live on my own and I am happy with the situation. I'm not lonely either. Just set in my ways."

Even in a lively and increasingly loud pub the silence that followed felt embarrassing. "Sorry, I didn't mean to pry.

I don't know what to say now." Connor looked awkwardly across to her boss.

"You don't need to say anything. You've not offended me, honestly. Let's move on. Literally. Drink up and we'll move on."

Emerging from St John's Gate Page was intending to turn left and walk towards the Centre, and maybe the White Lion, before heading towards King Street and the pubs along the waterfront. But there on the corner opposite were two men, clearly at the end of a difficult conversation.

"Please, just until tomorrow night," the smaller of the two men was pleading. "Please, help me Stu. Just until tomorrow night."

"No way. No money, no gear," and the tall, well-built man with long black hair strode away.

Page looked at Connor. They didn't need to say a word. Both knew this was Stuart Land. They set off to follow him, as quickly as they could without making him suspicious. When Land reached the pedestrian crossing over the two carriageways and four lanes of traffic he didn't wait. He stepped straight out and made a weaving course between the cars, intent on reaching the other side. Page and Connor were not going to let him slip away so soon. Land had already slowed the traffic and the pair of them steered the course he had set, following in his wake. Once on the far side Land hesitated a second before heading towards the courtyard area at the bottom of Christmas Steps. By the time they arrived there was no obvious sign of Land.

Looking towards the top of the long, steep flight of steps Page could just make out a figure. As he prepared for the long climb he called out to Connor: "You go into the pub and have a good look around for him in there. I'm going up."

The ascent wasn't easy at the best of times. A narrow medieval street climbing steeply with a number of flights of well worn stone steps interspersed with short, uneven, flagstoned landings. Whilst offering some respite from the steps themselves these still sloping areas brought their own challenges, not least walking at speed without slipping or tripping. It was on one of these slopes about halfway up that Page paused for just a second to catch his breath. He wasn't sure whether the pain in his chest was due to his injured ribs or the start of a heart attack brought on by his exertions. With no time to dwell he continued upward but when he reached the top where the narrow stairway opens up to the street there was no sign of Land at all. Or of anyone else for that matter. Page felt dizzy and sat himself down in one of the stone alcoves provided precisely for that purpose.

He'd been there around ten minutes before Connor climbed the last few steps and joined him. "Are you alright?" she asked, looking quite concerned.

"I am now," Page wheezed, still struggling for breath.

"He wasn't in the pub," Connor confirmed.

"I know. It was him at the top of the steps, but by the time I got here he was long gone. Get on to Control. I want every car and copper in the Centre to be looking out for him."

After she'd made the call Connor wandered back towards Page but this time she sat down next to him. "On a positive note," she started, "he's probably seen us, knows we are onto him and won't do anything stupid. Not tonight at least."

Page didn't respond immediately. He was still holding his arm across his chest with his hand tucked under his armpit, grimacing slightly. "On a less positive note," he finally said, "what do you reckon the chances are of us walking out of the Bank and bumping straight into our man?" Connor looked at him quizzically. He continued, "I mean, of all the pubs in all of Bristol, he's waiting outside of ours, so to speak."

"What do you mean?" Connor asked, still looking confused.

"With my cynical head on I am beginning to wonder who was actually following who. And right now it feels like we've been given the run around."

Connor looked away but she didn't contradict him. Perhaps she was thinking. Then she asked: "So what now?"

"Now DC Connor, we are off duty. So let's go and have a drink before we head off home."

The White Lion was busy but they had managed to find two stools and were perched at the long, high counter top looking out of the window onto the Centre. Three unkempt young men were on the steps of the Cenotaph deep in conversation bordering on disagreement. One was standing and pointing a metal crutch accusingly at the two who were seated, who in return were waving their arms and gesticulating. Smartly dressed couples, arm in arm, walked past this sideshow paying it no attention at all. Either oblivious to what was going on or not wishing to get involved.

"Wonder what that's all about," Page commented, nodding towards the Cenotaph.

"Who knows," Connor answered.

Inside, the pub was full of loud voices and laughter but it was possible to speak and be heard without too much effort. Page turned towards his colleague. "So not a complete waste of time this evening."

"No. We now know Stuart Land hasn't gone to ground."

Page nodded in agreement. "But we also know he always seems to be on the go. Here one minute, there the next. From the brief conversation we overheard outside the Bank it would seem that he could be involved in some drug dealing of sorts. Which would explain his erratic movements and why he can always be found outside pubs." Connor was staring at him, vacantly. "You don't agree?" he asked.

"Sorry. What?"

"You don't agree that Land might be dealing drugs?"

"Yes. Sorry, I was thinking." Connor seemed to be trying to get herself back into the moment. "We agreed this morning that there was no obvious link between the two victims. That they were not known to each other. And that might still be true, but what if they were both known to Stuart Land? Not close friends or associates, but simply customers."

Page shifted on the stool and felt a sharp pain in his chest. "You might have something there," he admitted. "Customers who couldn't pay, or who knew too much?"

"I don't know," she countered. "It seems a big step from a small drug debt to a ritualistic killing, but it is a link we need to eliminate at the very least."

Page agreed. "But our post mortem reports would have told us that."

Connor looked concerned. "I don't remember reading anything about toxicology results do you?"

"No," Page confessed. "We were either too easily satisfied with both causes of death being strangulation that we didn't read on, or a full toxicology report wasn't commissioned or provided. Either way that's something we need to check out or put right first thing on Monday morning." He lifted his glass and drained the last mouthful of beer. "I need something to eat. Let's walk over to the chip van by the Watershed and get ourselves some real soul food."

Connor looked less than eager. "Do they do anything a bit healthier, like salad?"

Page wasn't sure whether or not she was joking. He presumed she was. "If I have a burger with my chips then you can have the lettuce," he suggested.

She laughed. "You know how to spoil a girl on a night out don't you!"

WAIT

The weekend hadn't gone as well as he had wanted it to.

On Friday evening he had gone out but couldn't shake off this strange feeling: a feeling that somebody was watching him. Following him almost. In the end he had abandoned his activities, taken a short cut, doubled back on himself and returned home.

Saturday hadn't been much better. He couldn't summon up any enthusiasm to go out and so had spent the day thinking. But thinking wasn't the same as planning, and he knew he needed a plan. The harder he had tried the worse it had got until early on Saturday afternoon such a headache had come on that he had finally given up trying to do anything.

Sunday morning had been spent recovering and although he hadn't been able to formulate his plan he had managed to come to terms with things. He'd realised that there was no rush. Things could wait.

It was now Sunday afternoon. He was looking at the picture lying in the middle of his desk. 'It can wait, there's no rush,' he reaffirmed to himself, picked the picture up and put it away in the drawer, out of sight and out of mind.

Tempest

The front of the table was dominated by microphones topped with brightly coloured covers bearing the printed logos of the various news outlets. The two police officers were sitting behind the desk with their names and rank displayed on folded pieces of white card placed in front of each of them. Behind them was a blue coloured screen featuring an overly large representation of the force crest.

DCS Charles Tanner had just finished the formal briefing and had agreed to take some questions from the floor. "Yes, the gentleman in the front row," Tanner said, pointing a finger.

"Thank you. Matt Hall from the Bristol Post. It's now a week since the first murder. It's all well and good giving advice to the public on how to stay safe but what exactly are you doing to catch this killer?"

Tanner turned to look at the officer next to him.

"Tosser. You absolute tosser," Page shouted at the reporter, but of course nobody on the TV screen could hear him.

Tanner was looking at DC Connor, waiting for her to respond. "As you would expect," she tried to explain, "this is not a straight forward investigation…"

Page picked up the remote and turned the television off. Tanner had told him that morning about the news conference and the fact that he wanted DC Connor to accompany him.

'It's no reflection on you Page but we simply cannot alienate half the population by having a news conference run by two white, middle-aged men. Those days are long gone. Our equality commitment, and of course common sense, says that we need a woman at the top table.' Page hadn't argued. There wouldn't have been any point, but in his mind you should send the person best suited to the job. Poor old Connor didn't have any experience of news conferences as far as he knew, and she had very little information that could add much to this particular one, but at least she would make DCS Tanner and the constabulary in general look inclusive and forward thinking.

When she arrived back at the office Page didn't let on that he hadn't watched all of the news conference. "Well done Connor," he said. "Never an easy thing to do."

"I don't know why I was there really. DCS Tanner had told me to say the bare minimum and leave it to him wherever possible. And then he dropped me in it from a great height."

Page spared her the thought that she had been there simply to tick a box and to make Tanner look good. "Don't worry. You did really well," he said instead. "Grab yourself a coffee and pop into my office."

"What do you think it achieved?" she asked as she came through the door with a mug of coffee in each hand. "I brought you one too," she clarified, nodding her head at the coffees.

"Probably not a lot, but it needed to be done. The world now knows that we have a DNA profile of the killer, and that we have a prime suspect." Page reached for his coffee and took a sip before putting it down on the desk. "Equally, the world also now knows," he continued, "that we have no idea who the killer actually is or even where they are."

"Damage limitation. Or expectation management. Or both," she suggested.

"Bloody hell Connor, have you been on a Public Relations seminar or something?" They both laughed. "It is what it is," he reflected before changing the subject completely. "Look I need you to do me a favour." Connor stared at him but before she could say anything he continued: "I've had a call from one of the British Transport Police I know down at Temple Meads. Apparently Paddy, my homeless mate, has something for me. Something to do with Shirley."

"And?" she asked.

"Tanner told me in no uncertain terms that I had to forget about the homeless woman. There is no way I can turn up at Temple Meads this afternoon. Not after his news conference earlier. The one he didn't want me to attend because apparently he would rather see me getting on with catching our killer."

"I'm not sure I like where this might be going."

Page could see that she knew exactly where this was going. "Tanner said I had to drop it but he never said that you couldn't carry on in the meantime." From the lack of any tell tale expression on his face it wasn't clear whether Page actually believed what he was saying or not. "And whilst you are at Temple Meads," he continued, "I can be here working hard to find out exactly where the bloody hell Stuart Land might be."

Connor sighed. "With respect Sir…"

"Oh please don't 'with respect Sir' me Connor. Are you going to help or not?" They looked at each other without a word being said. He stared hard into her eyes but got nothing in return. He tried smiling at her encouragingly but still she sat there poker faced. "Call it a late lunch if you want," he suggested, before finally saying: "Please."

The drive back to Bridewell was slow. The rush hour had already started and it was only half past four. She had done as Page had suggested and taken a late lunch: a sit-in sandwich and hot drink which was an unusual treat for her on a busy working day. Over her sandwich she had tried to think exactly what it was that had made her agree to run Page's errand for him, but she couldn't decide: couldn't decide whether it was because she felt sorry for him or because she felt she had no other option. She just didn't know. What she did know however, was that somehow or other, either sooner or later, she would probably come to regret it.

In reality it hadn't taken up much of her time at all, and nobody else in the office knew where she was going. The trip to Temple Meads and the brief conversation with David Miller, Page's contact within the Transport Police, had taken less than thirty minutes, and surprisingly had been quite interesting. It was the traffic on the way back that was now eating into her time and starting to annoy her.

Forty minutes later she knocked on Page's door. He was leafing through an open file on his desk. He looked up. "Ah, the wanderer returns," he said, closing the file.

She decided to let this remark go. Smiling she said: "Yes. It all took a little longer than I expected, and the traffic out there didn't help."

He motioned for her to sit down. "Not to worry. Now what have you got for me?"

"First things first - David sends his regards," she said as she took off her coat and sat down.

"Oh good. He's not a bad sort. A good copper actually, just a bit of a train spotter."

"Then he must enjoy his work," Connor added. Page laughed, and this made her wonder why he might be in such a good mood. She continued: "David told me that Paddy's not been doing too well these last few days. He's missing Shirley it seems and that beating he had has really knocked him for six. But interestingly, David has an idea of who might have been responsible for the attack."

"Anyone we know?" Page asked.

"He has no names if that is what you mean, but on the day of the attack he recognised somebody hanging around the underpass who he had seen once before talking to Shirley. He didn't get a good look but he remembered the man from his build and his long black hair."

"How interesting," Page responded before asking: "But how did David Miller know we were looking for Stuart Land? Tanner was very careful at the press conference not to give anything away about our suspect."

"He didn't know about Land and still doesn't," Connor confirmed. "He mentioned all of this in passing simply because he thought you might be worried about Paddy. When he mentioned Land's description I tried to look interested without giving the impression that this information was potentially of importance to us."

"Well done," Page said, nodding his head in approval. "So that was what he wanted to tell me?"

"No." Conner said, reaching into her coat pocket. "That was just something that came up in conversation. He wanted to give you this." She withdrew her hand from her pocket and handed Page a small rectangular piece of paper. "Apparently, Paddy found this in some of Shirley's things."

Page took it from her. It was a photograph. A small, colour photograph of two young boys sat together, smiling out of the picture. The elder boy had his arm draped protectively around the other boy's shoulder. From the same haircuts and similar crooked smiles it was obvious that they were brothers. He studied it carefully and then looked up at Connor, but she had never seen that look on his face or in his eyes before. If she hadn't have known him as well as she did then she might have said that there was the start of a tear in his eye. In silence he looked back down at the photograph. He gave a big sigh and turned the photo over, glancing quickly at the reverse side. His eyes seemed to suddenly light up. "Have you seen this?" he asked. Before she could answer he went on, almost excitedly: "This could be Shirley's sons and if so we now know where to start looking for them." He slid the photograph towards her, face down, tapping the small black printed text as he did so.

She already knew what it said. Just like Page the detective in her had instinctively made her turn the picture over when David Miller had given it to her, but unlike Page the parent in her had immediately recognised the name of the photographic studio: H Tempest Ltd - St Ives. She knew that she was going to disappoint him and probably spoil the good mood he seemed to be in. "I don't think it tells you that," she started. "It tells you that the photograph was produced in St Ives but it could have been taken anywhere in the country." Page looked at her blankly as she took a deep breath. "Tempest are responsible for taking nearly every school photograph. At least they were back when this was probably taken. They employ a network of local photographers but the processing and admin is all done centrally in Cornwall."

Page indeed looked disappointed. He turned his gaze back to the photograph, held it up and squinted at it. Under his breath he said: "There's no name on the badge."

"No, there isn't," Connor concurred. "You can see a crest on the jumpers but no name."

Page threw the photograph down onto the desk. "Bollocks. What an absolute waste of time."

Connor waited. She had an idea but wasn't sure how well it would go down. "This might be a long shot," she ventured, "but through a friend of a friend I know one of the photographers who used to take school photos for Tempest in the West Country and I could ask him to have a look."

"Long shot's the word," Page muttered, not looking too impressed with the suggestion.

"Long shot or not it's better than nothing." She sat back and waited, not wanting to poke the hornets' nest unnecessarily.

"Yeah, go on then. It can't do any harm," Page conceded.

Connor looked at him closely and for once he didn't seem angry, just crestfallen. He looked lost and right now she felt sorry for him and wanted to help. She picked the picture up from the desk and put it back into her coat pocket. Standing up she said: "I'm off home. Do you want a lift?"

"No thanks. I've got some more reading to do and I've got a murder to solve." He gave her a smile. "You get off. I'll see you in the morning."

As she walked back to her desk she also smiled to herself and shook her head slowly. Despite all her earlier misgivings, here she was getting herself more embroiled in Page's clandestine investigations. She might still ultimately regret it but right now she was happy to lend a hand. For whatever reason it was clearly very important to him, and for her it seemed like the right thing to do. The only worry she had was that perhaps for different reasons they were both letting their hearts rule their heads. Perhaps, but then again who knew that Jim Page had a heart?

Incommunicado

Page was getting restless. He didn't like being in cars at the best of times but just sitting here, waiting, going nowhere was intolerable. He kept thinking of everything else he could be doing. Anything, except for this. Not for the first time he asked Connor impatiently: "What exactly are we waiting for?"

"We are waiting for the two support units to get into position, to cover all potential exits and escape routes before we go in."

Page knew this of course. He looked out of the passenger side window and then turned back towards Connor. "What's this for?" he asked pointing at the dream-catcher hanging from the rear view mirror.

"It's a dream-catcher," Connor answered without any further clarification.

"A what?"

"A dream-catcher. A Native American charm to protect you from harm or evil spirits."

"So is this standard issue now for police vehicles? Part of the wide range of Personal Protective Equipment modern coppers can't do without?"

"Of course not," Connor countered. "It's a personal thing."

"Ah - so you believe in this then? Believe that this bit of net and a few manky feathers will keep you safe?"

"Yes and no. I know that it probably won't help in a specific way but hope that it might make a difference more generally."

Page laughed quietly. "Oh Connor. The triumph of hope and belief over science and empiricism. The foundation stone of religion and the gateway to mysticism."

"So you don't believe in anything?" she asked, not looking at him.

"I believe in the irrefutable," he responded, before adding: "The unexplained is exactly that, unexplained, and I don't need any comforting or convenient answers to its mysteries."

"It must be nice to be so sure about everything," Connor retorted a little sarcastically.

"I'm not sure it is actually," he mused. "When people look for ways to cope with uncertainty, however untenable their resolutions might be, I think they at least find hope. When you don't feel the need to seek answers you are sometimes left with nothing but despair. And that can be hard to live with."

He looked out of the side window and drummed his fingers on the arm rest. "That won't make things happen any quicker you know," Connor said, still smiling.

It was only a matter of seconds later that the radio receiver lit up and a voice announced: "All in position. Ready to go on your command."

Page glanced at Connor and as they both opened their doors he reached for the handheld microphone, squeezed the talk button and yelled: "Go, go, go."

By the time they reached the short garden path the battering ram, or big red key as it was known, had done its job and five police officers dressed in body armour and what looked like dark blue crash helmets were streaming into the property. Shouts of 'Police - don't move' could be heard from inside the house along with the banging of internal doors. Page and Connor stood outside the front door, waiting for the all-clear to go in. They didn't have to wait long.

As they stepped into the dark hallway one of the armoured officers shouted from the first room on the right, "In here Sir."

Page entered the room. There was little furniture to be seen but clutter everywhere. Old newspapers, empty silver take away food trays and cans of extra-strong cider lay scattered across the floor. The only curtains at the window were ripped and badly discoloured net curtains. So discoloured in fact that very little natural light could get in. Stood in the middle of the room handcuffed and flanked by two support unit officers was a tall, well built man with long black hair. "We meet at last, and what a pleasure it is," Page said sardonically, walking towards him. Once they were face to face Page dispensed with the mocking pleasantries. "Stuart Land, I am arresting you on suspicion of the murders of Clare Harding and Callum Roberts. You do not have to say anything, but it may harm your defence if you do not mention when questioned something that you later rely on in Court. Anything you do say may be given in evidence."

"Are you mad?" Land snarled through gritted teeth. "I ain't killed nobody."

"Take him in," Page ordered, stepping aside so that his support unit colleagues could lead Land to the white custody van already waiting at the kerbside. "Right, let's get to work and have a good look around," Page instructed the uniformed team that had now entered the house.

"What do you want to do - go back and speak to Land?" Connor asked.

"No. Let him stew. We can…" but before Page could even start to explain his thoughts there was a shout from the team searching the kitchen. When he got there one of the uniformed officers was holding up a large, clear plastic bag, the size of a normal supermarket carrier bag. Inside were smaller plastic sachets the size of cigarette packets, each containing dozens of small white round tablets. The tablets were deeper than they were round and resembled watch batteries. "What have we got here then?" Page asked.

"Not sure Sir, but there are another three large bags like this in the other cupboards."

"What, just in the cupboards, not even hidden?"

"No Sir."

Page looked at Connor. "What do you reckon?"

"Probably not aspirins," she suggested.

"It would be some bloody headache if they were," he quipped. Turning back to the search team he pointed at the contents of the open kitchen units: "Get this stuff into evidence bags and have some samples sent off to the lab. And mark it 'Urgent' please." He looked around the kitchen which was as dark, damp and dismal as the front room. "Let's have a look upstairs," he said to Connor.

Page led the way up the uncarpeted staircase and onto a dark and narrow landing. The lights didn't work when he tried the switches. Probably had the electricity cut off he thought to himself. The two bedrooms were that in name only, as neither contained a bed. Two dirty mattresses had been left on the floor. No sheets were to be seen, just piles of crumpled clothes strewn everywhere. As unappealing as these rooms were nothing could prepare them for what they would find in the bathroom. The bath itself could hardly be seen, covered as it was by the shower curtain and broken rail hanging from the wall. The handbasin tap was running very slowly leaving a hard, shiny trail across the dust encrusted surface. The lid to the cistern was missing and the toilet seat was snapped in two. There was very little water in the WC pan and it was hard to tell whether the thick brown staining under the waterline was limescale residue or something worse. There was no doubt however, that the dark deposits above the waterline and all over the back wall was indeed something worse.

"Who lives in a house like this?" Page asked, trying to make light of the situation.

"Animals," Connor gagged. "No better than animals."

He laughed and shooed her out of the room back onto the landing, making pig-snorting noises behind her as they went back down the stairs. In the hallway he shouted out to the uniformed team still searching through the kitchen: "We're off now. Secure the place when you're done and somebody can update me later."

Somebody heard him because a muffled "OK Gov" came from somewhere.

Stepping back out into the fresh air he turned to his colleague. "Come on Connor, let's go and get a coffee, and if all this hasn't spoilt your appetite, perhaps something to eat as well."

It was only a short walk from Suart Land's place in Grosvenor Road to The Social, where Page had suggested they could get breakfast. It was probably just beyond what most people would call Stokes Croft, on the Cheltenham Road. If giving directions Page would say it was on the Gloucester Road but that was only because he never really knew exactly how far up it was that Cheltenham Road became Gloucester Road. He liked The Social because the breakfasts were good and they served beer. Today of course he would have to content himself with coffee.

"Do you come here often?" Connor asked without any obvious hint of irony.

"No, not often but it is on my list of good breakfast haunts if ever I find myself on this side of the city at this time of the day."

They had already finished eating and were now halfway through their second cups of coffee. "What do you make of Stuart Land?" Connor asked Page.

"Not sure really, but there's definitely something about him. Stood next to him just now I realised we'd met before, and I don't mean Friday night when we followed him up Christmas Steps. Standing so close to him I could smell him, and I recognised that smell. I'm pretty sure it was Mr Land who I met in the park last week and who put me in A&E."

"So at the very least he's a dangerous thug with something to hide," Connor suggested.

"He's certainly that, and now we just need to find out exactly what it is he is hiding. Although he's not very good at hiding his drug stash is he?" Page joked. As if on cue his mobile rang. "Page," he barked, looking at Connor before silently mouthing to her "Sharma." This was enough to allow her to stay seated and glean what she could from the conversation.

"Morning Sir, just an update."

"Go on then. I suppose it's not good news or you would have waited for me to get back to the station."

"Sir, just to let you know that Land has been processed and is refusing to speak to anybody until his solicitor is present."

"As is always the case," Page pointed out impatiently. He knew instinctively that this wasn't what Sharma was trying to tell him.

"I know Sir, but his solicitor won't be available until tomorrow afternoon."

"And his solicitor is?" Page asked, not sure he really wanted to hear the answer.

"Simon Ravell from Holly & Bloom."

"Simon Ravell," Page repeated. Connor shrugged as if the name meant nothing to her. He continued: "So we just have to wait until tomorrow afternoon before we can interview Land, is that right?"

"Yes Sir. DCS Tanner has instructed me to tell you that nothing is to happen until then."

"Has he indeed."

"Yes Sir. On the basis that Mr Ravell will not oppose any application to hold Land without charge for up to 36 hours."

"Really? I wonder what they need to sort out in the meantime?"

"Don't know Sir, but DCS Tanner also told me to say: 'Well done for getting your man so quickly'."

"Did he. Let's not count our chickens just yet. Anything else for me Sharma?"

"No, I don't…" but Page had already ended the call.

He put his phone back in his jacket pocket and looked across at Connor opposite him. "Well, well, well. We seem to have caught ourselves a big fish Connor."

"In what sense?" she asked, still looking a little uncertain.

"Our Mr Land is not just a thug. It seems he is a very well connected thug, who has Simon Ravell as his lawyer."

"Should I know Simon Ravell?" Connor asked hesitantly.

"Not really. Most of the scrotes we nick can't afford Mr Ravell's services. He's probably the best defence lawyer this end of the M4." Connor looked impressed and concerned at the same time. "But what's more surprising," Page continued, "is that Mr Ravell is prepared to let us keep his client locked up incommunicado for nearly two days rather than rushing straight down to the station, demanding his rights and getting him bailed before lunchtime."

"I wonder why that is?" Connor queried, almost to herself.

"That, Connor, is the $64,000 question. It seems somebody needs to put an awful lot of ducks in a very long row before Mr Land is allowed to open his mouth."

"And in the meantime, what do we do?" Connor asked.

"Not a lot. The Chief-Super has warned me off until tomorrow, and in any case we won't have any DNA or forensics back until then at the earliest." Page could see that Connor was disappointed. "Don't worry," he tried to reassure her. "Tomorrow afternoon will soon be here and I suspect it will all kick-off then."

"So this is the lull before the storm so to speak," she reflected.

"Something like that," Page acknowledged with a broad smile across his face. "Anyway, you've got things to be getting on with. Don't you need to speak to a man about a photograph?"

"Yes, it's all in hand. I'm meeting him tonight."

"Good work. You managed to track him down quickly."

"Yes," she confirmed, a little evasively, and then added: "You'll make a detective out of me yet."

Page laughed, but then wished he hadn't. He wasn't sure she had intended the comment to be funny, and even if she had, was she was poking fun at him or herself? Worried he was now starting to overthink the situation he smiled at her and before the moment was lost said: "Thanks for arranging it so quickly. I really appreciate it."

"No problem," she responded, returning his smile. "Let's hope it's all worth it."

"I'm sure it will be." Page looked into his coffee cup but it was empty. "Better not have another one," he reasoned, "or I'll either be hyper for the rest of the morning or needing the loo every ten minutes, neither of which would be very conducive to us making progress on our case would it now." Connor didn't answer. She was looking for something in her handbag. Standing up he said: "Let's make a move," and then after a measured pause he continued as casually as he could: "I was thinking perhaps we could go to the office via Temple Meads." Again Connor didn't say a word but this time she gave him a look, an unmistakable look. He pulled a face, the kind of face a child pulls when they've been caught red handed doing something they shouldn't be. Through a broad grin he conceded: "OK, you're right. It was only a suggestion."

Table For Two

It was big and busy. Big, busy and noisy. Not the sort of place she would normally choose to eat but she had chosen it nonetheless. She didn't come across to this side of town very often and didn't know many other places to suggest. In any case a large chain restaurant adjacent to a cinema complex couldn't be misconstrued as anything other than a place to meet and eat. She had gone home early that afternoon. She had wanted to make sure Aaron had something substantial for dinner before her mother arrived, and then she wanted to have a shower and change before going out. She wanted to feel relaxed and look her best. Look her best for herself that was, and to feel comfortable and in control. That was why she was sat here alone, early, so that she could be the host and receive her guest. She had to keep reminding herself she was only doing this for Page. It was simply work and certainly not pleasure.

She saw him come through the door and hesitate briefly as he scanned the large room. She smiled to herself. He had clearly made an effort just as she had. His tall, thin frame was looking as trim as ever, set off by a pair of dark designer jeans and a black polo neck shirt. It was the sort of thing he wore when he needed the smart-casual look. In fact, it was what he always wore when he needed the smart-casual look. When he looked in her direction she raised her arm and gave a little wave. He waved back and strode purposefully to where she was sitting. Once at the table he sat straight down.

"Hello Louise, how are you?"

"I'm good thanks. How are you?"

"Not bad. Very busy. You look very nice."

Usually this would have made her feel uncomfortable but tonight it played into her hands. "Thank you. That's the second time this week I've been paid the same compliment." It worked. He looked taken aback. She continued: "I was out for a drink with somebody on Friday evening, and he said exactly the same thing."

She deliberately said nothing else and enjoyed the brief silence that followed before he asked: "How's Aaron?"

"He's fine. I told him I was meeting you this evening and he wanted me to remind you that you still haven't arranged his birthday trip as you promised."

"I know. I've been busy."

"We're all busy Mark, but he's your son." She had to remember not to start a row. Not this evening. "Make sure you give him a call. Have a chat and arrange a date."

"I will," he said. She knew he wouldn't.

The young lad waiting tables was hovering. She made eye contact to indicate that they were ready to order. Mark hadn't had time to properly look at the menu but she knew already what he would choose: lasagne, coleslaw and then after some deliberation chips instead of salad. The waiter picked up their menus and wandered off.

Before any small talk could begin Connor got straight down to business. "I don't know whether or not you still do school work for Tempest but could you have a look at this?"

She offered him the old school photograph. "Would you or any of your associates recognise the badge on their jumpers?"

He took the photograph from her. He held it up and tilted it, looking closely at the small area of the picture towards the bottom right of the frame. "It looks like a shield to me. There is no name, but there is some writing - BTA I think it says."

"But you don't recognise it?"

"No, I don't. I guess this is work related," he surmised, clearly beginning to understand the real reason for the dinner invitation.

"Yes it is."

"Can I keep this for now? I can show it to Chris. He does all the admin for us."

She felt uneasy. She knew this was the only chance they had but wasn't sure Page would want to let go of the picture. "This is evidence Mark. Take a picture of it on your phone and that way I can keep the original." She was pleased with the suggestion.

"Of course," he said taking his mobile phone from his jeans pocket.

"And another thing," she added, "Don't say where you got this from or why you want to know which school it is."

"I won't," he said. She believed him. He was unreliable in so many ways but he had never compromised her professional integrity.

She was putting the photograph back in her handbag when their food arrived. Great timing. She could now eat and let Mark do most of the talking. He liked talking, and liked talking about himself. Tonight he talked about the gym membership he had recently taken up that she knew he would never use; about the problems he was having with his car and the difficulties associated with buying a new one these days; about redecorating his living room that he hadn't started yet but really needed to; about needing some new interests but not having enough time to commit to anything. She tried to look interested and to respond sympathetically in all the right places but she had heard it all before. Not these specific stories but the same excruciating excuses. He hadn't changed at all, and never would. He was still the Mark she knew and didn't love anymore: a man forever paralysed by his own incessant procrastination.

When the waiter came to take their plates Connor declined to look at the dessert menu. The trick now was to bring the evening to a close without seeming impatient, or indeed ungrateful. She made a show of looking at her watch. "I'm sorry Mark, but I need to be getting off. Early start in the morning."

"Of course. Well this has been nice. Not just work but pleasure too I hope."

She tried to choose her words carefully. "It was good to see you looking so well, and to hear how busy you are."

"Yes. You too. I'll sort the bill out."

"Thank you."

"Perhaps we can do this again some time soon," he suggested.

She caught the look in his eye and knew he was being serious. "I'm not sure that's a good idea Mark. That boat has already sailed a long time ago." He looked disappointed but not surprised. "It would be nice though if you came round for tea one weekend and got to spend some time with Aaron."

"Yes, I'll do that. I'll sort out a date and let you know."

"Well make sure you do. You can only let him down so many times you know." She stood to leave. She was starting to sound like his mother, and that had always been the problem. Deep down he was just a big kid disguised as an adult.

He jumped up from the table but didn't seem sure what he should do. "I'll let you know if I have any luck with that photo." He looked at her and smiled, warmly. "And I'll be in touch to arrange my visit for tea and cakes."

"Thanks," she said again and briefly squeezed his arm that was dangling by his side. She gave him a big smile, a reassuring maternal smile, before walking away, leaving him stood at the table looking confused and forlorn.

As she opened the restaurant door and stepped into the darkness she let out a big sigh of relief and thought to herself: 'So there you are DI Page. I hope it was all worth it.'

Monkey Man

He was folding the crisp packet into an origami style triangle and pushing it into the empty cardboard sandwich container when she walked into his office.

"Another meal-deal bites the dust," she observed.

"Why is it that the sandwiches always look good until you eat them and then they are totally underwhelming?" he asked grumpily.

"Additives, cheap ingredients and crap bread," she answered authoritatively.

"You're right, but we still buy them. The curse of the desk-bound lunch break." He threw the sandwich packaging and empty Coke bottle into the waste bin by the side of his desk. No time or inclination to take them to the recycling bins in the kitchen area. "Right then Connor, before we start. We've got the lab results back. Stuart Land isn't our killer. The DNA doesn't match, but we won't let him know that straight away. The slightly better news is that he won't be going anywhere. The tablets we took from his place were Ritalin: prescription only drugs."

"So, back to square one with our murder investigation then."

"So it seems. Although Mr Land appears to have been at both crime scenes. We need to find out if that is just coincidence or bad luck."

"Maybe not the perpetrator but an accessory perhaps?" she suggested.

"Could well be," Page agreed. "Are we ready?" he asked, getting to his feet. She nodded. "Right, let's do it then."

When they entered the interview room Land was already sitting at the table with his solicitor by his side. Page tried hard not to show his dislike for the lawyer. Simon Ravell was around forty years old, with a mop of blonde, curly hair. He was wearing a bright blue checkered windowpane suit with a yellow waistcoat over a white shirt. The blue bow tie was the icing on the cake for Page. "Sorry to keep you waiting," he said, but he didn't mean it.

"Quite understandable," Ravell answered with a smile. "One clearly wanted to have the DNA results to hand before commencing battle, so to speak." Page looked at Connor as they both sat down. Ravell continued: "So with no match confirmed I posit that my client is fully exonerated."

Page already on the back foot, and disliking Ravell more each time he said anything, had to work hard to keep his feelings in check. "Mr Ravell, you are quite right that there is no evidence of your client being directly involved in the two murders, but he was seen at both of the locations on the nights in question, and we wonder why that might be."

Ravell looked unperturbed by Page's efforts. "The question is rather why he shouldn't have been at the two hostelries in question. After all it is not against the law to drink in more than one licensed establishment in the same city on any given evening as far as I am aware."

"The point I am making is that whilst your client might not himself be involved in these two murders, his presence at both locations means he may be able to help us with our enquires."

"Now that's a different proposition altogether Detective Inspector Page and my client would be very pleased to 'help you with your enquires' as you put it."

Page was struggling to conceal his impatience. He looked at Land who until this point had simply sat opposite him with a self-satisfied grin on his face. "Mr Land, tell me, when you were in the pubs on the nights of the murders did you see anything that, with hindsight, now strikes you as odd or significant?"

Stuart Land didn't move. He remained leant back in his chair looking relaxed. "I guess the thing that caught my attention most, thinking about it, was that on those evenings I saw the same man drinking in both the pubs."

"And do you know this man, or would you at least recognise him?" Page asked.

Land looked at Ravell before answering: "I don't know him but I know of him. It was Lenny Rhodes."

Page looked at Land in disbelief. "Lenny Rhodes?"

"Yes. Lenny Rhodes."

Before Page could properly process this revelation Ravell had again started to speak. "There you are Detective Inspector Page, enquiries assisted to the fullest possible extent." Page turned to look at Ravell, who continued: "So in the circumstances there is no longer any justification for you to detain my client in relation to these matters."

"Indeed there isn't and consequently your client is no longer under arrest for the suspected murders of the two persons previously identified." Page paused, waiting for a reaction from either of the men opposite but none came. He glanced quickly at Connor before playing his trump card. "However, Stuart Land, I am arresting you on suspicion of the possession of methylphenidate, a controlled class B substance, with the intent to supply. You do not have to say anything, but it may harm your defence if you do not mention when questioned something that you later rely on in Court. Anything you do say may be given in evidence."

Land didn't react at all. Instead Ravell responded. "Detective Inspector Page, my client absolutely and robustly refutes the allegation that he is in any way involved with enterprises linked to the supply of controlled substances. With regards to possession there is no evidence at all that my client had knowledge that these items were secreted within his property."

Page could contain himself no longer. "Mr Ravell these drugs were not 'secreted' within your client's property. They were filling his kitchen cupboards. I suspect your client would have been more surprised to find boxes of Weetabix in there rather than the industrial quantities of prescription drugs on open display."

"Detective Inspector Page, your attempt at humour does not disguise what still amounts to little more than uninformed supposition. As you well know my client was not present at the property when these 'controlled substances' were allegedly discovered. Now I am not in anyway suggesting…"

Page lurched forward and banged the table but before he could say anything Connor intervened. "Gentlemen, let's not get carried away. Mr Land, can you explain how such a large quantity of drugs came to be in your possession?"

Instantly Ravell came back at her. "The drugs in question were not in my client's possession, they were in his property, and therein lies a significant distinction. Now, given the absence of evidence to the contrary, it seems my client may have been the unwitting victim of a deception by persons as yet unknown."

"Victim?" Page spat out. "Your client is no victim. Given the amount of drugs we found I'd say he's looking at somewhere between five and fourteen years."

"But you are not the judge in this case Detective Inspector Page, you are the investigating officer, and may I say it, one who has still to find any evidence whatsoever linking my client to these drugs. I appreciate you need to discover how they found their way into his home but whilst you do this there is no reason whatsoever for my client to be detained any longer."

"Your client will be detained as long as I say he will." Page was now staring directly into the lawyer's eyes, who in turn simply smiled back at him. Connor leant towards Page as if she were going to say something but he spoke to her first. "Get the custody officer in here."

She leant over the intercom and pushed the button for the custody suite. When the light turned green she simply said: "We're done in here."

Ravell had stopped smiling but still looking at Page asked: "No further questions Detective Inspector Page?"

"Not for today," Page confirmed gruffly, now avoiding eye contact completely. They sat in silence as Ravell packed the stack of paperwork that he hadn't even used back into his leather satchel. All the time Land was sat back in his chair grinning. The door opened and as the custody officer was entering the room Page bellowed: "Bail him."

Land and Ravell followed the clerk out and into the corridor but on the way the lawyer stopped briefly in the doorway and turned to Page and Connor. "Thank you both. As always, an absolute pleasure."

Connor shut the door of the interview room behind them and turned back to Page. "Count to ten," she cautioned but Page was already out of his seat and pacing up and down.

"Absolute pleasure. Who does the bastard think he is - Perry bloody Mason?" Connor didn't move from the door. Page stopped his pacing and sank into one of the chairs. "That really couldn't have gone any worse. They were taking the absolute piss. Ravell was one step ahead of us all the way. He knew about the DNA results and he was fully prepared for the drugs charge; and all the time Land just sat there playing the nodding monkey to his over-dressed and over-paid organ grinder." Page looked at Connor but before she could say anything he added angrily: "And how the bloody hell didn't we know that Lenny Rhodes was back on the streets?"

Connor sat down opposite Page. "I'm sorry if this is a stupid question, but who is Lenny Rhodes?"

Her naivety was disarming and he could feel the anger start to subside within him. "Lenny Rhodes is a maniac, in the strictest definition of the word. As far as I knew he was still inside for the kidnapping and torture of two members of a local third division crime syndicate. He didn't kill them but he might as well have."

"Could he be our man?" she asked genuinely.

"Murder's not normally his prime motive but as a by-product of perverted, physical humiliation then quite possibly."

Connor's eyes lit up. "Presumably his DNA is on file and it will just be a matter of cross-checking his with that of our killer's."

Page didn't look as convinced. "Of course on a basic level that's all we have to do, but it all seems just a bit too easy doesn't it." Connor looked confused. He continued: "Ravell couldn't wait to feed us with Rhodes' name. At the earliest opportunity he had Land tell us, just as they had rehearsed."

"But that doesn't alter the fact that the DNA will confirm whether or not Lenny Rhodes is our man," she insisted.

"I know, but I suspect whatever the result might be it will only be the start of our problems and not the end. Simon Ravell and Lenny Rhodes really are unlikely and unpredictable bedfellows."

"Shall I check the DNA records then?" Connor persisted.

Page nodded but in a resigned way. "Yes of course, although I am sure that like any good lawyer worth their salt Mr Ravell already knows the answer."

Poison

The evening was drawing in. The light was gradually fading but there was still at least an hour before it would be fully dark. He knew where they lived. He regularly saw them playing together in the park. Importantly they knew him too. Trusted him. Persuading them to come away with him however, might be the difficult part.

He waited opposite the house, sat on a wall behind a parked car, hopefully out of sight. He hadn't been there more than ten minutes before the front door opened and a man stepped out. At the garden gate the man turned back to the open door and shouted: "Come on girls, keep up with Daddy please."

He followed them from the other side of the street until they reached the end of the road and then turned left towards the rank of shops. He crossed over but waited on the corner, watching their every step. When the man went into the mini-market he made his move. He walked quickly towards the shops calling out: "Hello girls, it's me. Do you remember me?" At first they just looked at him but as he got nearer they clearly recognised him. Both of their tails started wagging and one of the dogs ran up to him excitedly, taking the biscuit he was now holding out. It wasn't long before the second one joined him and he bent over rubbing both of them on the back of their necks. "Come on then," he instructed cheerfully, walking away and holding a biscuit out at chest height. Both of the dogs bundled after him, jumping up and down trying to snatch the biscuit from his hand that he made sure was always just out of reach. With the two dogs dancing and leaping into the air like a circus act he led them to the park.

The dogs ran and played and chased the stick he kept throwing until it was almost completely dark. It was then he stood up and called them to him. When he walked towards the road they followed him, not wanting to be left behind. They kept close to him in the dim light, brushing against his legs throughout the short walk to the Golden Hill allotments, as if making sure he was still there. They followed him along the narrow grassed pathways until he reached the boundary hedge and a wooden shed. He opened the door and encouraged them inside. "Come on girls. See what I've got for you." In the middle of the shed floor were two bowls overflowing with dog food. The two dogs smelled their meals before they could see them and bounded into the warmth and apparent safety of the shed. He immediately shut the door behind them and swung the hasp over the loop before securing it with the combination padlock he had brought with him.

He knew what would happen next but he didn't want to think about it. He wouldn't be there to witness it, but once the two dogs had eaten the poisoned food they would start shaking uncontrollably before the vomiting started. The difficulty breathing would come next before the coma, and then ultimately the sweet release of death. By tomorrow morning it would all be over.

Missing

Half past eleven and still Page hadn't put in an appearance. She'd spoken to him on the phone first thing that morning and that was when he told her he wouldn't be in first thing. He'd had a late night. Later than Wednesday crib nights usually were, apparently. He'd sounded a bit agitated to her but she had fully expected to see him by mid morning. At this rate it would be gone lunchtime and she wasn't sure how much longer she could keep DCS Tanner at bay.

The phone call from Julie had come around nine o'clock. 'First thing' for the Chief Super. "Hi Louise, Julie here. I was looking for Jim."

"Hi, sorry, he's not in just yet."

"I didn't think so. I've tried his phone a couple of times and got no answer. DCS Tanner wants a word with him. When will he be in, do you know?"

"He won't be long," she'd offered, fully believing that to be the case.

The visit from DCS Tanner himself had come around ten o'clock. Coffee time. As awkward as ever he tried to make small talk with anyone at their desk on his way through the office. As he approached her she smiled. "Good morning Sir."

"Morning. How are you?"

She noticed how he had avoided using her name. "I'm well Sir, thank you."

"Is DI Page in yet?"

"No Sir. He's following up some information on the drug case we're dealing with." She didn't know why she had said this and more to the point didn't know what she would say if pressed further on it.

Luckily DCS Tanner didn't want any more information. "Good. It can wait. Carry on," he instructed but from the way he walked back across the office it was clear to her that it couldn't wait much longer. She picked up her phone and sent Page a WhatsApp message: 'Tanner wanting to see you. He's getting impatient. Doesn't look good.'

She'd then gone to the kitchen area and made herself a cup of coffee. Walking back to her desk she saw her phone light up and recognised the WhatsApp banner announcing that she'd received a message. Behind that was another notification that she had missed a call. Picking up the phone she was surprised to see that the call and message hadn't been from Page but from Mark. 'Hi. Tried calling you. Didn't want to leave a voice message. Give me a call.'

Back in the kitchen area she'd shut the door behind her before returning Mark's call. Within two rings he'd answered.

"Hi. How are you?"

"Busy, but I presume this is work related."

"Of course, but it was nice seeing you the other night, and having dinner."

"It was nice but it was business Mark." The silence that followed wasn't unexpected.

"Anyway," he said, clearly choosing not to take the matter further, "Chris has come up trumps with your missing school kids."

She didn't correct him. The less he or indeed anyone knew about this extracurricular activity the better, especially with Tanner snooping around again. "Go on," she said with her pen poised above a scrap of paper ready to make some notes.

"I was wrong. The letters in the shield weren't BTA." He sounded excited to be helping. "Chris looked at it and straight away saw the T in the middle as a cross, or a cruciform as he called it. After a bit of checking he's pretty sure it's the badge of St Mary's primary school in Bradford Abbas. That's what the B and A stand for either side of the cross."

She was more pleased with this information than she thought she would be. "Any ideas where Bradford Abbas might be?" she asked.

"No, sorry. I didn't think to ask that." Mark sounded disappointed, as if he had only done half the job.

"Not to worry, it'll only take a few seconds to find out," she tried to reassure him. She was genuinely grateful to him for this and Page would be over the moon. "Thanks for this Mark. This could be the breakthrough we've been looking for." And then just to make sure that he didn't get the wrong idea again she closed the conversation in her normal manner with: "And don't forget to give Aaron a call."

Back at her desk she'd googled Bradford Abbas and discovered it was a small village in Dorset, between Yeovil and Sherborne, and more importantly only a two hour drive south of Bristol. Bradford Abbas had at first sounded to her like one of the fictitious villages featured on Midsomer Murders, but she wouldn't be sharing that with DI Page.

The second phone call from Julie had come around eleven o'clock. "Hello Louise. Is Jim there?" No niceties this time.

"No. I'm not sure where he is." No excuses this time either.

"Can you give him a call? Probably best coming from you rather than from me. A bit less informal."

"Yes of course." She picked up her mobile and first checked that she hadn't missed any calls or messages from him. Nothing. She selected his number and waited. It went straight through to voicemail. He hasn't even got his phone switched on she thought to herself, and decided not to leave a message. That way at least he couldn't be accused of having ignored it.

It was now half past eleven and still no word from him. He was on his own now. She had things to be getting on with. She pulled the keyboard closer to her and logged herself onto the offender database. She only had the basic information to hand but in her experience the search function was generally very good. She clicked on the identity tab and waited for the enquiry screen to load. In the box next to SURNAME she typed: 'Rhodes'. She skipped the next box, FIRST NAME, and headed for the field marked KNOWN AS. Here she put in 'Lenny' and pressed the return key hoping that would be enough. Almost instantly the search form was replaced with a formatted document with a colour picture in the top right hand corner. Her eye was drawn to the picture before any of the printed information beneath it. Staring at her from her computer screen was a bald man somewhere between forty and sixty she guessed. His nose was twisted and he had a scar under his left eye; the right eye as she looked at it. From the background she was almost certain that the picture had been taken whilst he was in custody somewhere. The printed information added some detail to the basic snapshot: 'Rhodes, Lenny - d.o.b. 09 July 1979.' She read on. He had convictions for shoplifting as a minor; driving whilst disqualified; possession of cannabis; violent assault; and most recently, Grievous Bodily Harm. The final section titled Custody Status contained just two words: 'On Licence.'

At the bottom of the page were the words Background Documentation presented as a blue coloured hyperlink. Connor clicked on the link and waited while the long list of individual document hyperlinks loaded. She moved the mouse, sliding the cursor down the page until she reached DNA Profile. As she selected it she looked up and saw Page sauntering across the office. She shook her head at him as if to say 'Where the hell have you been?' He responded with a stupid grin and a shrug of the shoulders, clearly understanding her meaning. She looked back to her screen and was surprised to see an error message: Unable to Load - Error Code: 2691. She reloaded the list of documents available and reselected the DNA option. Again after about ten seconds she was presented with the same message: Unable to Load - Error Code: 2691.

By now Page was standing beside her and from the frustrated look on her face he couldn't fail to notice something was wrong. "Problems?" he asked.

She pointed to the screen. "I'm trying to access Lenny Rhodes' DNA profile and keep getting this."

Page leaned in closer and squinted at the screen. "Strange. His DNA will be on the database. Don't worry about it. Give IT a call and see what this error code means."

"OK. Did you get my message? Tanner wants to see you. Urgently."

"Yes, thanks," he confirmed with very little urgency on his part it seemed. "I'll go up and see him now."

She hated contacting the IT team. They were always so unhelpful and did everything they possibly could to avoid personal contact. She punched in the number for the IT Helpdesk and waited for the hostilities to start.

"Helpdesk," somebody sang into her ear.

"Hi, it's DC Connor here. I'm having trouble accessing a DNA record on the offender database. I keep getting an error code."

"Have you logged this with the Helpdesk?"

The reference to the Helpdesk in the third person annoyed her immediately. 'You are the Helpdesk' she muttered under her breath but still responded a little angrily: "That's what I'm trying to do right now."

"Sorry. You have to complete the autofill form on the intranet. Once sent you will get a job number and you can then track this on your desktop."

"Look I just need to know what the Error Code: 2691 means. It's important."

"I understand that, but the email logging system for IT faults allows us to prioritise jobs and then advise you what priority has been assigned to it and let you know when you can expect to have the issue resolved."

At this point Connor normally gave in. There was no use arguing with the architects and overseers of automated bureaucracy, but today she had already had enough. "This information relates to a dangerous individual and at this very moment DI Page is in with DCS Tanner." She waited and could almost hear the Helpdesk colleague conflating these two unrelated statements, just as she had intended.

"Code 2691 you say. On the DNA database."

"Yes, name of Rhodes, Lenny Rhodes."

"I'll have a look and drop you an email DC Connor. It'll take about ten minutes."

Connor was still waiting for the response when Page reappeared from his audience with Tanner. "Everything alright?" she asked, as much out of curiosity as compassion.

"Yes," he laughed. "He wanted to know, now that we had spent a week tracking down the wrong man, when precisely we might start going after the right one." Page paused and then added a little more seriously: "And he also dropped in that if I wasn't up to the job then he would find somebody that was."

There was nothing Connor could say to that, and luckily she was saved by the email alert on her desktop. "It's from IT," she announced. "I'll read it out: "DC Connor I logged your query about the DNA database error code and the job number assigned was 05/9544. This job is now showing as completed." She shook her head in disbelief. They always win in the end she thought. She continued reading aloud: "Code 2691 is rarely used but in relation to DNA or fingerprints it means the record has been deleted due to concerns raised around the validity of the original sample."

She stopped reading and looked at Page. It was him now shaking his head. "Read that again," he said. "The last bit."

"The record has been deleted due to concerns raised around the validity of the original sample."

"There's something not right here," he said screwing his face up. "There's something fishy going on. I can smell it."

"So what do we do now?" Connor asked.

"Not a lot we can do is there. We probably need to track Lenny Rhodes down and have a word with him."

Page set off for his office. "Sir," she called after him, waiting for him to turn around. "There's some things I need to update you about. Can I do that now?"

"Yes. Let's do it over a coffee."

"Great," Connor responded, knowing full well that this meant she had to go and make the coffees herself and then deliver them to his office.

Private Investigations

The train had been stopped at Keynsham for what seemed like an eternity. Only seven minutes into the journey, this was not the start he wanted.

When Connor had told him yesterday that the school photo had probably been taken at Bradford Abbas he could think of little else. Overnight he had decided to make the trip today, but had only let Connor know first thing that morning. It was when she rang, as she always did, to see if he wanted picking up that he'd told her. "I'm going to take today off. I'm probably owed a day and don't want to wind Tanner up anymore."

"Is everything alright?" she'd asked.

"Yup. Just taking a trip down to Bradford Abbas." He hadn't been surprised by the silence that followed, but he had been expecting more of a subsequent reaction than the one he'd got.

"OK. Is that wise?"

"I need to do it Connor. I'll be back in touch tomorrow. In the meantime, see if you can track down Rhodes' whereabouts, but don't do anything without speaking to me first. Understand?"

"Yes Gov." She rarely called him Gov and it had sounded to him that the familiarity of the address was being used to hide her frustration. She was trying to sound comfortable with the situation when that was probably far from the truth. He understood that and did feel a little guilty about it all if he were to be honest.

The train started to move at last. Page looked around the carriage and wondered where all these people were going. He presumed a lot of them would be getting off at Bath Spa for a day's shopping interspersed with some food and drink. As for the others where would they be travelling to on a Friday morning? What was it that might be luring them to Trowbridge, Dorchester or Weymouth? Not to mention Yeovil Pen Mill, which was his destination, or station-stop as the train manager infuriatingly insisted on calling it. 'We are now approaching Oldfield Park. Oldfield Park your next station-stop.'

Despite how busy trains were these days, and how dirty they were, and how late they could be, he still enjoyed travelling by train. Not that there was much choice for him on long distance journeys. Coaches were too claustrophobic, they made him feel sick and they were too susceptible to being held up in traffic. He had never driven. Never felt the urge or the need. Being in control of a vehicle was not a responsibility he had ever wanted to assume. He wasn't sure he could trust himself. He had always been frightened and intrigued by just how easy it would be to deliberately steer into the path of an oncoming lorry or bus. He knew deep down that somedays the temptation might be too much.

Because he had only decided to make the trip late last night he hadn't made any arrangements in advance. He had over breakfast checked the website of St Mary's School and discovered that the headteacher was a young woman called

Erin Welch. From the small picture accompanying her résumé he would estimate her to be in her mid thirties. He wasn't really sure what headteachers did but he couldn't imagine that they would be so busy that they couldn't make time to help the police with their enquiries. He smiled to himself, wondering what exactly it was that he was doing here. Was it a police enquiry or just a private investigation? He'd decided to wear his suit and to bring along his warrant card to help any difficult conversations along a little. So perhaps it was a bit of both.

The taxi ride from the station to Bradford Abbas had taken just five minutes. His phone app had estimated a journey time of ten minutes but clearly hadn't accounted for the fact that Uber seemed to employ ex-Formula 1 racing drivers down here. The taxi stopped in Church Road as he had asked it to and on getting out of the car he found himself directly opposite the church of St Mary the Virgin. To the right of the church was an attractive, stone faced building with one very tall chimney dominating the front elevation. The Rose & Crown as it was now had been occupying this site in one guise or another since the fourteenth century. Page looked from one building to the other. Strange how often it was that in English villages you found the pub right next door to the church, and it wasn't coincidence either he thought. It was just another way for the landowners and clergy to keep the workers, or should that be peasants, in their place. On a Sunday they would be threatened with Hell whilst being promised a place in Heaven. And then they would be brought back down to earth with beer, plenty of it in fact, enough to keep them poor and happy, enough to prevent them organising themselves and rising up against their exploitation. The working class had never chosen to drink of their own accord, they had cynically been led to this temptation by those with vested interest. And not much has changed he thought to himself. Every weekend the pubs were still full of people drinking to forget the week they'd had and steeling themselves for the one ahead. Page was no different. So much then for free will.

He turned and walked the few hundred yards into Mill Lane, and there was the entrance to St Mary's Church of England Primary School. 'Get them while they're young,' he muttered as he entered the playground. He was surprised to find that the main entrance door was locked but then saw that it was equipped with one those new camera doorbells. He pressed the button, smiled and waited, conscious that he was being observed.

"Hello, can I help you?" a woman's voice enquired.

"I hope so. I'm Detective Inspector Page," he explained, holding his warrant card up to the camera. "I need some help identifying a couple of children."

"Are they in trouble? Is there a problem?" she asked, sounding concerned.

"No. Sorry, nothing like that. It's an historical case I'm working on."

"And have you made an appointment with the school?"

"No. I was in the area and thought you might be able to spare me a few minutes."

"I can give you five minutes."

That sounded like a final offer to Page so he took it. "Thank you very much," he said, trying his best to sound grateful. When the door opened he was taken aback to see Erin Welch the headteacher. He had assumed he was talking to the school secretary. Perhaps schools didn't have secretaries any more. Yet another consequence of budget cuts.

"Detective Inspector Page, good morning. I'm Erin Welch, headteacher here."

Page resisted the temptation to say that he knew, that he'd seen her picture and read about her. Instead he said: "Good morning. Thanks for seeing me at such short notice Ms Welch."

She showed him into the corridor and pointed to two soft chairs close to the door. "Please do sit down." This meeting was clearly not going to last more than the allotted five minutes. "How can I help you?"

He took the old school photograph from his pocket and handed it to her. "I believe these two boys attended St Mary's, possibly thirty-five, forty years ago."

The headteacher looked at the picture briefly and handed it back to him. "I don't recognise them. Sorry."

"Would any of the other teachers or school staff know them?" he asked, desperate to keep the conversation going.

"No, I don't think so. None of us was here back then."

"I realise that, but this is a village school, embedded in the local community. Somebody might recognise them."

"I'm sorry Detective Inspector Page. We are a young teaching team here and we don't necessarily live in the area. I'm sorry I can't be of any more help." She stood up and walked to the door. As she opened it she said: "I do hope you find what you are looking for. Good luck."

He smiled and managed a "Thank you" as he walked past her back out into the playground, still holding the photograph in his hand. He didn't bother to look around but he heard the door click closed behind him. A brief but not very enlightening encounter. Personally he was disappointed. He had hoped the school would hold all the answers. Professionally he was curious. Curious why Erin Welch had asked no questions. She hadn't asked why Page was looking for the boy's identities, hadn't asked if he had any ideas who they might be. Why was that he wondered. Did she recognise who they were and not want to tell him? Or was it that she didn't know them and didn't really care about something that had happened before she had probably even been born! He was inclined to believe it was the latter.

Not wanting to waste his day off completely he thought he would exercise what little free will he did have by visiting the Rose & Crown for a pint and a spot of lunch. He found a table by the window, chose a pint of local real ale and ordered a cheese and onion doorstep sandwich with a side of thick cut chips. If this was his heavenly reward for today's futile endeavours then he could live with it.

The middle-aged woman who had taken his order behind the bar came over to him carrying some cutlery and condiments. She placed them on the table, smiled at him and said: "Your food won't be long. Are you OK for drinks?"

He looked at his glass which was already half empty. "Go on then. Another pint please."

When she returned with his drink she asked: "So, is this business or pleasure today?"

He recognised it immediately as a leading question and decided to come clean. "A bit of both really. I'm a police officer and it's my day off, but you're never really off-duty are you."

"I thought so," she said, looking pleased with herself. "I hope there is nothing bad afoot in the village."

"No, nothing to worry about," he confirmed. "Just an old case I'm working on." She turned to go back to the bar but he stopped her. "Are you local, have you been here a long time?"

"No and yes. I'm not from the village but I'm a Dorset girl. I've had the pub here just over twenty years now."

"You might be able to help me then," he said, withdrawing the photograph from his jacket once again. "Do you recognise these boys? They went to St Mary's school about thirty years ago."

She took the photograph and looked at it. "No, sorry. I've never had anything to do with the school. With the kids I mean, and this was probably before my time anyway." She handed him back the photograph. And then as matter of factly as you like she came out with it. "You want to speak to the vicar."

Page's eyes lit up. "The vicar at St Mary's here?"

"Yes - no," she answered. "I mean the old vicar, Reverend Howell. He was here when I came to the pub. Retired about fifteen years ago but he was such a lovely man we stayed in touch."

"And he still lives in the village?" Page asked excitedly.

"Oh no. He's in a care home now in Yeovil. He can't get out and about anymore."

"And you're still in touch with him you say?"

"Yes. I call in and see him from time to time."

"Do you think he would see me?"

"If it meant talking about the village I'm sure he would, but he's not too well these days. I tell you what, I'll grab your food and bring it over, and while you're eating I will give the care home a call."

"Splendid. Thanks." Page drained the remainder of his first pint and arranged the cutlery in front of him ready to start eating when his lunch arrived. He sighed contentedly and thought to himself: 'Perhaps there is a God after all.'

From the outside Grovelands Care Home looked impressive. He had been expecting a 1960s formerly council owned type design but instead was greeted by a modern, turn of the twenty-first century building, complete with a Georgian style portico. Inside the welcome was equally pleasant. The duty manager had been expecting him and once the signing-in formalities had been completed he was escorted up to the first floor.

The door to room 206 was ajar and the manager gave a knock. "Hello Ken. I've brought your visitor up to see you." Some acknowledgement that Page couldn't hear must have been received because the staff member said to him: "You can go in. I'll see you back downstairs when you leave."

He entered the room and there sat in a very comfortable looking arm chair with a novel in his hands was a white haired man, wearing dark trousers and a grey cardigan. Page noticed that he wasn't wearing a clerical collar. Perhaps retired clergymen didn't wear them. He'd never really thought about it. "Good afternoon Reverend Howell, I'm Detective Inspector Jim Page." As he introduced himself he saw the old man instinctively go to stand. "Oh please, don't get up on my part," he quickly implored him.

The man smiled at him. "Thank you, how kind, and please call me Ken. Jenny rang and said you might be coming." He pointed to the empty arm chair opposite him. "Please, sit yourself down." Once Page was settled the vicar said with obvious delight: "How exciting. A visit from a policeman. Or should I say, an Inspector calls."

Page understood the reference to the J. B. Priestly play and laughed with genuine affection. "Yes, very good."

Before he could continue the old man interjected: "I've not lost my marbles yet you know. My mind is still sound. It's the body that's weak. You'd expect me to say this as a vicar but I've never been frightened of dying. My biggest fear has always been of growing old."

Page wasn't sure how to follow that so he went for the safe option. "But you are looking very well, I must say."

"Thank you. You know how to flatter me. Now, how can I help you?"

"It's a long story, or rather a story from a long time ago," Page started to explain. "I have a photograph of two young boys, taken at St Mary's Primary School in Bradford Abbas I believe. I don't know when the photograph was taken. I'm guessing it could be somewhere between thirty or forty years ago."

"And you have the photograph with you?" the old man asked. Page nodded. "Let me have a look then," he said eagerly. Page leant forward and handed him the school photograph. He stared at it and started nodding his head. Without looking up he whispered: "So sad."

Page waited before asking the question he could hardly wait to ask. "You recognise them?"

"Yes. So sad. The Herring boys. Joshua and Jacob. Why do you have this photograph Inspector Page?"

"I think it might have belonged to their mother."

"You mean Shirley. You've found Shirley?"

Page took a deep breath. "There's no easy way of saying this, but we found a woman's body two weeks ago. We think it might be Shirley but we've not been able to positively identify her."

"How sad. And you found this photograph?"

"Yes amongst her belongings, and I had a hunch it might be her sons."

"And your hunch was right. So very sad." Reverend Howell took another long look at the photograph before handing it back to Page. "A deeply troubled family. So sad."

"Can you tell me about it?" Page asked.

"Where to start. Alan and Shirley were devoted to each other but unable to cope with things even before the boys came along. Alan was an alcoholic and after the second child was born Shirley suffered with severe post natal depression. When the boys were about six and eight she disappeared one day and has never been seen since. Rumours around the village were that Alan had somehow killed her and disposed of the body. But you only had to look at Alan to know that

that couldn't possibly true. Not two years later, just after that photo was taken I would say, the youngest boy, Joshua, was killed in a hit and run incident one evening. Alan was in the pub at the time and had left the boys alone at home. That was that. The older brother, Jacob, was put into care." He paused, and then went on: "But it doesn't end there. Within a year Alan was dead. He took his own life. And that just left poor old Jacob who one way or another has never really managed to free himself from his own institutionalisation."

Page sat in silence letting the full horror of the story sink in. "And do you know where Jacob is now?" he asked after a while.

"No, but I'm sure you will be able to find him." Page looked questioningly at the old man who then clarified: "He's in prison. Lincolnshire or somewhere in the North East I think."

"That is sad. Thank you. That's been really helpful and I'm so sorry you've had to relive this tragic tale all over again."

Reverend Howell smiled. "But that's our jobs - yours and mine. The priest's and the policeman's lot is not a happy one. Our interventions are usually only required once the worst has already happened and then we must deal with people's trespasses as kindly as we can and deliver those poor souls for judgement in a higher place."

"I've never thought of it like that," Page admitted. "I've often thought being a police officer was a bit like being a surrogate social worker, but I've never seen myself as a man of the cloth."

The priest smiled. "How you see yourself is one thing, but how others see you is more important."

"This is getting very deep and philosophical," Page joked, "and I'm not sure I've got the intellect to contribute much to such conversations."

"Don't judge yourself so harshly Inspector Page."

They both laughed. Page stood up. "One thing I do know for sure is that unfortunately I don't have time for such discourse today."

His intellectual sparring partner looked disappointed. "Are you going already?".

"Sadly I am. I need to catch a train but I could keep you updated about Shirley and Jacob if you would like me to."

"Yes please. And thank you Inspector Page, even at this late stage, for taking the time and effort to reunite a lost mother with her son. I can think of no worse an estrangement."

From his seated position the old man extended his hand. Page leaned forward and took it and very quietly said: "Nor can I."

Dogs

He couldn't believe it. It was hardly light and here he was stood in the bay window, cup of coffee in hand waiting for Connor to pick him up. He'd got back from his trip to Somerset and Dorset around half-six yesterday evening, had quickly changed and walked to the Drapers Arms for a few pints. A celebration of sorts. It had been a good day's work. A day off well spent. When the Drapers closed at nine-thirty he'd walked back towards home calling in at the Annexe for a night cap or two. He hadn't expected to be back on duty quite so soon.

The headlights dazzled him momentarily as Connor pulled across the road. From his sentry post he acknowledged her, downed the last mouthful of coffee and leaving the dirty cup on the windowsill left for work.

"Good morning Connor," he said, climbing into the front passenger seat.

"Good morning Sir. How was yesterday's trip?"

"Fine. Mighty fine. I'll tell you all about it later. But first, remind me why we are being called out at the crack of dawn on a Saturday morning."

"All I know is that we have an 'unusual situation' at the Full Moon in Stokes Croft."

"An 'unusual situation'. What the hell does that mean?"

"I don't know. That was the message I received from dispatch."

"And why do they need us to attend? I mean specifically you and me Connor."

"I don't know that either, other than it is another incident related to a city centre pub, which seems to be our speciality these days."

Page had no more questions for now. He sat in silence. They were already halfway down the Gloucester Road. When they reached the old carriage-works he started to get restless again. "This had better be good. A good use of my time I mean."

Connor ignored him. As she approached the Full Moon she indicated and steered the car up onto the wide pavement. In front of the entrance to the pub's beer garden they could see that a blue forensic tent had already been erected. A uniformed police officer was standing alongside it.

"Nobody told us this was a murder scene," Page complained to the officer on duty, waving his warrant card at her.

"I'm not sure its is a murder scene Sir," she answered hesitantly.

"Then what the bloody hell is it?" he countered.

"Perhaps you should take a look yourself Sir," she suggested, moving to unfasten the entrance flap.

Page stooped slightly as he entered the tent, then stood bolt upright. He could hardly believe his eyes. On the ground in front of him were the bodies of two dogs, both clearly dead. They had been positioned on their sides so that their noses and both their front and back paws were touching. It reminded him of the folded ink blot pictures he used to make as a child. Perfect symmetry. He turned and stepped out of the tent. "Have a look in there," he said to Connor, "and tell me what the hell you think is going on." Connor disappeared into the tent and was only in there for less than a minute before re-emerging. "Well?" he asked.

"I haven't got a clue," she admitted.

"Who the hell do they think we are - the bloody RSPCA?" He stormed back towards the car.

Connor pressed the remote to unlock the doors and followed him. Once in the car she turned to him. "Don't bite my head off but this might not be about the dogs."

"Then what is it about?" he demanded.

"We have already discussed this and come to the conclusion that the victims themselves might have no particular significance. If that's true then it doesn't matter whether they are male, female or dogs."

"Or cats," he added sarcastically.

She continued undeterred: "You yourself suggested that for our killer, posing the bodies post mortem was probably more important than the actual killings. Well this bizarre scene is just that: a contrived tableau."

Page looked at her. He wasn't sure what surprised him the most. That she had words like 'tableau' in her vocabulary or that she could see beyond the immediate distraction and focus her thoughts on a broader explanation. Either way he was quietly impressed.

There was a knock on his window. The uniformed officer was saying something he couldn't hear. Connor put the key into the ignition so that he could lower the window. "Will you be wanting a word with the witness, the one that called this in?" the uniformed colleague asked him. "She's in the pub waiting."

"Yes. Tell her we'll be there in a few minutes." He closed the window and looked back at Connor. "Give Scenes of Crime a ring. Let's see if our animal assassin has left any clues behind."

As they walked into the bar they could see two women at the far end, sat at a table drinking tea or coffee from large china mugs. It was the police officer that noticed them first. She shot up, almost knocking the drinks off the table. "PC Bhavsar Sir. I've been talking to Ros and keeping her company."

Page motioned for her to sit down. "We'll join you, if that's OK."

"Would either of you like a drink?" the other woman asked.

He was ready for another coffee but more keen to get this over and done with. "No thanks. We're fine," he said, speaking for Connor too.

"This is Rosalind Sharp, she's the manager here," PC Bhavsar explained.

"Call me Ros. Everybody else does, apart from my mum."

"Ros it is then," he confirmed before launching straight in with his questions. "And it was you that found the bodies? The dogs' bodies, if you know what I mean."

If she did know what he meant then she didn't let on. "No. I didn't actually find them. It was me that called the police."

"So who did find them?"

"I'm not sure exactly. They were a large group. The last to leave, around two o'clock. I saw them start to leave the premises and then I heard a lot of shouting. I went over to the door to ask them to keep the noise down and that's when I saw them all crowded around the two dogs."

"And nobody else had noticed anything untoward before?" Connor asked.

"No." Ros went quiet.

Page picked up on Connor's line of enquiry. "I presume you have door-staff working on a weekend. Didn't they see anything?"

"No. They would have said if they did." Page looked at her, inviting her to elaborate, and it worked. "Our last admission is at eleven. Once things are tidied up outside the door-staff come in and then they stay in and help people leave in an orderly and considerate fashion."

"And last night, or this morning as it seems to have been, how did that work?" Page kept pressing.

"What do you mean: 'how did that work'?"

"I mean, what were the timings. When did the door-staff come in and when did people leave? I'm trying to build a chronology."

Ros looked taken aback at his directness. PC Bhavsar stepped in to help her. "I know you're very tired Ros, but we need to understand when it was that this happened. That will help us find who it was that did this."

Page looked less than impressed but Bhavsar's intervention had the desired effect. Ros perked up a little and explained: "As I've said we shut the doors at eleven and last night the staff were all inside before half eleven. That's actually earlier than normal. Anyway, last night was a little unusual. Most of the people in belonged to the large group and so by midnight all the casual punters had left."

"Meaning?" Page asked.

"Meaning," Connor answered, "that between midnight and two-am there were no comings or goings."

"A window of opportunity," Page reflected, but then he turned to Ros again. "Do you have CCTV cameras at the entrance?"

"Yes, we do."

"And do they cover the pavement area outside?"

"Yes, they do, but they don't always work."

"Brilliant," Page responded sarcastically, "hardly worth bothering with then." Conscious that he had let his impatience show he turned to PC Bhavsar and tried to sound a little more conciliatory. "If Ros can give you whatever video footage they might have then perhaps you can help make sure that she gets home safely."

Bhavsar responded positively and looked pleased with the responsibility she had been given. "Yes Sir. Thank you."

With any unpleasantness seemingly averted Page stood up. "Thank you for your time Ros," he said and gave her a quick, tight smile. Then looking at Connor he issued his next instruction: "Come on, it's breakfast time."

It had only been Tuesday morning since they were last there, but here they were again at The Social for breakfast. Connor had ordered poached eggs on toast with fruit juice. Page needed something stronger after last night's exploits and had opted for a large black coffee and a full-English.

Despite having no milk to mix Page was staring intently at his mug whilst trancelike stirring the coffee round and round. Finally he withdrew the spoon and placed it in the saucer. He looked up at Connor. "Vis-à-vis this morning's discovery we will have to wait for the forensics and then see whether or not the video surveillance comes up with anything. But right now it seems to have been a complete waste of our time." He paused but wasn't expecting her to comment. He changed the subject. "How did you get on yesterday with your search for Mr Rhodes?"

"It was less of a search, more desktop research to be honest. The standard licence conditions require him to register at an address as you know. This seems to be a flat in St Judes owned by the council. I thought I would wait for you before making any unannounced visits."

Page nodded. He had told her not to go rushing in. "Go on."

Connor took a sip of her juice and continued as instructed. "His probation officer is Josie Hughes-Green…"

"God help us," Page interrupted.

"Do you know her?"

"No. It's just that all social workers and probation officers these days have names like Josie Hughes-Green. They've all got degrees in social anthropology and not an ounce of common sense. The triumph of education over experience." Connor looked at him and shook her head. Page smiled back at her. "Anyway, I'm sure she speaks just as highly of me. Carry on."

Connor hesitated as if trying to remember what she had been saying before she was interrupted. "His probation officer is Josie Hughes-Green," she repeated, "and I've got a call booked with her this afternoon to find out if there are any extra licence conditions that have been attached to his release."

Page nodded again. "Great. So all being well we should be able to pay Lenny a visit tomorrow morning, assuming he's not at church."

Their breakfasts arrived. Connor waited until Page had salted his meal and liberally applied a film of brown sauce to his fried eggs. "How did yesterday go?" she enquired.

"Very well," he teased before putting a large piece of hash brown into his mouth. He made her wait even longer while he scooped some beans onto his fork and ate them too. Then wiping his mouth with the white paper napkin he said: "It was Shirley's boys in the photo. Jacob and Joshua their names. She disappeared a couple of years before that photo was even taken and she's never been seen since." Page took another mouthful of breakfast and became conscious of Connor looking at him. "What's wrong. Am I dribbling?" he asked through his half chewed breakfast.

"No. Nothing like that. It's what you just said."

"What did I just say?"

"You said that Shirley disappeared a couple of years before that photo was taken and that she hadn't been seen since. So how did she get to have that photo?"

Page put his knife and fork down and wiped his mouth again, just in case. "That's a very good point. I hadn't thought of that."

"What makes you think that Shirley had disappeared before that photo was taken?" Connor queried.

"Because that's what the old vicar in the care home told me." He took a sip of coffee and a few moments before concluding: "So either the old boy's got his timings mixed up or somebody did see her again after she'd left."

"Sounds to me like your star witness might be getting a bit forgetful," Connor suggested.

Page gently shook his head. "I'm not so sure, he seemed pretty switched on to me, but we'll find out. Anyway that's not the important bit." He waved a finger at Connor to say 'give me a second' and loaded his fork with a generous helping of sausage, beans and egg. Whilst he ate the remainder of his breakfast he recounted, between mouthfuls, the tragic story of the Herring family.

Connor sat and listened without saying a word. Still chewing the last mouthful he put his knife and fork down together onto the plate and pushed it to the middle of the table to demonstrate that he had finally finished eating. After wiping his mouth one last time he screwed the paper napkin into a loose ball and tossed that onto the plate too. "All I need to do now," he said, bringing things back to the present, "is run Jacob Herring through the offender database and off we go."

"Off we go, where?" Connor asked warily.

"Off to visit him. Break the bad news to him. Somebody's got to."

"Yes, but does that need to be you? Surely somebody from the local force or the Prison Service could do it?"

Page looked into his coffee mug. It was empty. "I think it would be better coming from me."

"You mean because you are the police officer investigating her death?"

Page looked at Connor. For a split second he thought about telling her the truth, the whole truth, but he couldn't. Not yet. He leant forward. "Partly because it's my case," he said quietly, "and partly because I promised the priest I would."

Connor looked at him, almost in disbelief. She simply shook her head. "I hope you haven't been making promises you can't keep. How on earth will you square it with Tanner?" she asked, clearly in no doubt that somehow or other he would manage it.

A broad smile crossed his face. "We'll think of something, won't we Connor."

Rumours

He'd tried to ignore it, but he couldn't. He could have shut the office door but he hadn't. He didn't like working alone behind a closed door, separated from the team. It gave the wrong impression. But enough was enough. He couldn't concentrate with that monotone droning burrowing into his ears. He got up from his desk, walked to the doorway and then shouted to no-one in particular: "Do we have to have this racket on?"

The responses were immediate: "Rovers are playing" and "It's Saturday afternoon Gov."

He wasn't sure who had made the comments but he fired straight back: "Then go and find something to do near the Rovers ground and watch it for yourselves."

"But they are away at Burton Albion Gov."

"I don't care. Turn it off, or it will be your radio that's going for a Burton."

This was met with a few sarcastic whoops and a brief refrain of "Shit-head, Shit-head" that was jokingly intended to imply that Page was a Bristol City supporter. The joys of living in a two team town, he thought to himself, where everybody assumes you support one or the other and nobody believes that you have no interest in either. The radio commentator was cut off mid-sentence and calm was restored to the room.

Page returned to his desk and sat down. He nudged the mouse to bring the screen back to life and then groaned when he had to re-enter his password to unlock the security screen. He clicked on the offender database icon on the desktop and when prompted put in Jacob Herring's details. He waited as the cover page loaded and suddenly there he was, looking out at him from whatever institution it might be. There was a crest on the prison issue jumper but Page couldn't make it out. How ironic. His hair was darker now but just like in the old school photograph it was still collar-length, parted in the middle and covering his ears. Page glanced quickly at the identity details: 'Herring, Jacob (Alan) - d.o.b. 12 November 1982.' Page looked back at the picture on the screen whilst he did the maths in his head. 'That makes him forty-one, so the school picture was taken about thirty years ago, which means his mother went missing around 1990 or 1991.' There was no mistake. The man in the prison jumper was the boy in the school photograph. It was all there to see. All that was missing was the childhood he never had. Page moved his eyes down the screen looking for the final piece of the jigsaw. There it was. Custody Status: HMP Lincoln - Three Years Burglary (Sentenced/2021).

The knocking took him by surprise. He looked up to see Connor stood in the doorway. "Is this a good time or a bad time?" she asked.

"Good time," he confirmed. "Come on in and meet Jacob Herring." He pointed to his computer screen.

Connor walked round the desk and stood by his side. "Wow. You've found him."

"Yes. Safely locked up in Lincoln prison. Currently serving three years for yet another domestic burglary. That seems to be his main line of work although given how often he ends up inside I'd say he's either not very good at it or he's developed a special liking for prison food." Connor laughed. "Anyway, how can I help you?" he asked.

She walked back to the other side of the desk and sat down. "I've just spoken to Josie, our friendly, neighbourhood Probation Officer, and…"

"Do I detect a note of cynicism creeping in there Connor?"

She laughed again. "Obviously I'm not one to cast aspersions on other members of the sisterhood but just this once your uncharitable characterisation might be spot on."

Page was amused. "Just this once," he repeated.

"Yes. Just this once," she insisted. She took a deep breath, as if to draw a line under this levity and help her get back to the business in hand. "Josie was very nice but she didn't tell me much that we don't already know. She was able to confirm that Rhodes is living in Haviland House, Lamb Street, and that she has visited him there. Interestingly she also told me that an additional condition of Rhodes' release is that he does not enter or remain upon any licensed premises between 18:00 and 11:00 hours. Meaning he's restricted to daytime drinking."

Page sat back in his chair. "Meaning that he's either breaching his licence conditions already, which I doubt very much, or Stuart Land and his stuck up lawyer are lying to us, and that I can believe." He leaned forward again, putting his hands on the desk. "So Josie had nothing else for us?"

"No," Connor replied, giggling to herself. "Other than she did tell me that Lenny Rhodes wants to make a fresh go of things and that he has put his past behind him and that with his new council flat…"

"Stop. Connor, please stop. You're making me laugh and it still hurts a bit." The two of them looked at each other and Page shook his head in mock disbelief. He was about to send Connor off to get a coffee, a decent take-away coffee, when his mobile phone started ringing. He looked at the screen but it was a number he didn't recognise. He swiped to accept the call and putting the phone to his ear he grunted: "Page."

"Detective Inspector Page?" the man's voice queried.

"Who's this?" Page asked in a less than friendly manner. Connor stood up to leave.

"DI Page, this is Matt Hall from the Bristol Post."

Page motioned at Connor, moving his arm in circles and mouthing at her in an attempt to get her to close the door and rejoin him. "Hang on," he said into the phone and then taking it from his ear he tried a second time to explain to Connor what it was he was trying to say. She understood, shut the door and sat back down again. Page put his finger to his mouth and she nodded. He then put the phone down onto the desk and hit the hands free icon. "You still there?"

"Yes. Good afternoon DI Page."

Page quickly scribbled something onto a piece of paper and turned it round for Connor to see. 'Matt Hall - Evening Post.' She grimaced. "How did you get my number?" Page asked angrily.

"Not too hard. Us detectives and journalists are good at finding things out."

"What do you want?"

"Just wanted to give you a heads up really, and ask a few questions."

"About what?"

"Let's start with the curious incident of the dogs last night, can we?"

"What about it?" Page liked the literary allusion but wasn't going to let on.

"What can you tell me about it?"

"Look Mr Hall, It's not my job to give out confidential or classified information. It's not really my job to answer your questions but I'm happy to humour you, providing they are closed questions. You remember the old game, you ask a question and I can only answer yes or no." He shot a glance at Connor who made a movement with her open hands as if to say 'calm down a little.'

There was a brief pause then the journalist started again. "OK. From the pictures I've seen I would say that those two dogs didn't just happen to die there on the pavement. They appear to have been arranged, 'posed' is probably a better word. Would you agree?"

Page looked at Connor again and gave her an ironic smile. "OK Mr Hall. I seem to have been hoisted by my own petard. How about we start again. Can we agree to have a chat off the record and then agree what it is that you will print?"

"That sounds a sensible way to proceed DI Page. And please, call me Matt."

"So you have pictures Matt?"

"Yes. Most of the group that stumbled upon the scene last night took photos on their phones. Given that there are no identities that need to be protected and the pictures were taken on a public highway or thoroughfare then there seems to be no prohibition to their publication."

"Agreed. No prohibitions but where's the public interest grounds for publishing such pictures?"

"I think the angle is more likely to be around the supernatural and animal sacrifice."

"You what?" Page could hardly contain his incredulity. "You must be joking. You're a local hack writing for the Evening Post, not the bloody Daily Mail."

The journalist seemed rather pleased with this analysis and not at all offended. Laughing he said: "Times have changed DI Page. It's the Bristol Post not the Evening Post anymore. We are now part of a nationally owned group, and as we are speaking 'off the record' I can tell you, it's all about click-bait and adverts these days."

Page didn't argue. "So the link to the occult is? Please enlighten me."

Again the journalist seemed only too pleased to explain. "The pub. The dogs were found outside the Full Moon, and on Friday night there was a full moon."

Page groaned out loud. "Good luck with that. I'm sure the question mark after the headline 'Full Moon Sacrifice?' will do all the heavy lifting required."

"Very good DI Page. We'll make a journalist out of you yet."

"Very droll. So was that it?"

The silence that ensued worried Page. He sat there fearing the worst, waiting to hear more. "Actually there is something else. I wanted to ask you about the other two murders, the two strangulations. Are you linking these to last night's events?"

This time the silence probably told Matt Hall all he wanted to know. "And why might we be doing that?" Page asked, clearly avoiding the question and playing for time.

"Because I understand that in both of your murders the bodies were left in unnatural positions. Posed. There's that word again."

Page paused and took a breath. He would need to choose his words carefully. "Matt, you know that I can't talk to you about that, and you also know that any information you think you might have about this is sub judice and can't be published."

"Of course. I'm well aware of that. I was just asking the question."

"And to be clear I didn't answer your question. I didn't confirm or deny it. That's as helpful as I can be."

"Thanks. I appreciate that."

Connor pulled a face as much as to ask 'why did you say that?' Page responded by raising a hand before continuing with the conversation. "Matt. It's my turn to ask some questions. Have you seen photographs of the crime scenes?"

The response came immediately and Page seemed to be back on the front foot. "No. Good God, no. Honestly. I haven't."

"That's probably best for both of us then," Page acknowledged. "Now, what have you heard on the grapevine?"

"Rumours. Just rumours really. Rumblings on a couple of local chat-sites that the murders might not be as straight forward as the police are letting on. Nothing mainstream, these sites are on the edge of the web, and they're often the source of anti-establishment conspiracy theories, but I'm led to believe that some of the 'evidence' being put forward by them in this case is uncharacteristically persuasive."

"Have you seen any of these posts yourself?"

"No. I'm just aware of them. Keeping a listening brief as a good journalist should."

Page had heard enough. He wanted to draw the conversation to a close but he needed to keep Matt Hall on side. "Thanks for that Matt, and thanks for calling. Sorry we got off on the wrong foot, but it was a very useful chat. Hopefully it was for you too. I'd like to stay in touch if we can. Maybe a coffee some time. And if you hear anything else of interest on the dark web then give me a bell."

"I will. I've got your number, so to speak."

Page laughed. He'd give the young man of words that one. "Thanks again, and good luck with your double-devil-dog story." Niceties over, Page touched the End-Call icon. He waited for the display to return to his home screen and then waited a further four or five seconds. "Well, well, well."

Connor was staring at him, open mouthed, as if she couldn't believe what she had just heard or been part of. "Where do they get all this information?" she asked.

"I don't know, but it's probably good for us right now to know what they know; and for them to know that we know what they know, if you know what I mean."

She smiled. "Yes. I think so."

He continued, thinking aloud really: "No real damage done. Both sides better informed and no immediate risk of any sensitive information being published. We could have done without the devil-worshipping speculation until we knew for certain what we were dealing with, but we were always going to struggle to keep those bloody dogs under wraps. Figuratively speaking of course."

"Do you think there is anything in it?" Connor asked, moving around in her chair after having been so still and so silent for so long.

"Anything in what?" Page queried.

"In the full moon thing. Don't you think it's strange that this happened on the night of a full moon outside a pub called the Full Moon. It can't be coincidence can it."

Page tried hard to not let his impatience show but he couldn't help himself. "I don't know what it is Connor, but I do know it has nothing to do with black magic or werewolves or any other such nonsense. We are dealing with a straight forward nutter here not the Prince of Darkness." Connor sat still again and said nothing. Page picked up his mobile and put it back into his jacket pocket. "What I also know is that somebody has been leaking details of our crime scenes. The simplest possibility is that it is one of the people who discovered one of our bodies, the other possibility is far less palatable." He stood up, put his jacket on and walked around the desk. He'd had enough for today. "Can you pick me up tomorrow morning? We'll pay Lenny Rhodes a visit."

"Yeah. No problem."

"And Connor, can you get me the contact details and interview notes of the people who found the bodies. And can you chase up the lab for whatever it is they might have got from our canine friends." She nodded, looking a little fed up. "Thanks," he said, smiling, "I know it's hard. It's a dog's life."

Bark At The Moon

The last few days had taken their toll, both mentally and physically. The sight of the two dogs dead in the shed had almost broken his heart. It felt as though he had betrayed them. Betrayed the trust that animals give us humans so unconditionally. Killing the others had been much easier. No pangs of guilt there, just a sense of retribution. Not that those particular individuals had ever done him any harm, but they were essentially no different to the others. To the others who looked at him and couldn't see beyond his social awkwardness.

But it was done now. He looked at the picture on his desk. The two dogs facing each other, their heads raised, barking at the moon. And the moon looking back at them and showering them with light like miniature halos. He reached up to the pinboard and moved the two pictures already displayed there to the left. He took the picture from the desk and pinned it next to the other two, this time leaving a small gap between each of them to create a triptych effect.

There was no going back now. He was doing the right thing, he knew that, but soon others would see it too. See him in a different light. See him for who he really was, what he could do and what he was really worth.

Days Like This

He hadn't been expecting the knock on the door. He knew he was running a little late, but not that late he thought. He opened the door and there was Connor. Before he could apologise for being late, she apologised for being early. "Sorry I'm a bit early. Had to get some fuel so allowed plenty of time, which as it turned out I didn't need."

"Don't worry. Come in. I'm nearly ready." He showed her into the lounge. "Have a seat. Do you want a tea or coffee?"

"No, I'm fine thanks."

"Give me a minute then, and I'll be with you." He went into the kitchen and put his cereal bowl into the sink. He'd do the washing up later. He added a splash of milk to his coffee and put the milk away in the fridge. He would have to give his toast a miss today. Mug in hand he walked back along the hallway and into the lounge. "Everything alright?" he asked.

Connor looked up from her phone. "Yes fine. The lab managed to get some samples and they are going to do a couple of final tests this morning and we should have some provisional information by this afternoon."

"Great stuff," Page said, carefully putting his lips to the hot coffee and making a quiet slurping sound.

"I also went back to the witness statements as you asked."

Her voice seemed to trail off towards the end of the sentence. "And?" Page asked, sensing there was more to come.

"Callum Roberts was found by a dog walker the morning after his death: Emily Chivers. I interviewed her that morning. The notes are on your desk. She's late thirties and works for one of the big audit companies in those glass offices behind Temple Meads. She didn't strike me as somebody that frequents seedy internet chat rooms but you can have a look for yourself and make up your own mind."

He took another tentative sip of coffee. "Thanks. And our first victim?"

"That's where we seem to have a problem." She paused, probably expecting Page to explode, but he had already realised there was a twist to this tale and said nothing. She continued. "If I remember rightly Clare Harding's body was also found the next morning by a dog walker but no witness statement seems to have been taken."

Page put his mug down. "Don't tell me it was the same dog walker."

Connor now looked slightly nervous. "No. Well I presume not, but we don't know."

"We don't know," Page repeated slowly, emphasising every word.

"No. The cover sheet of the case file hasn't been completed. There is no reference to who took the original report, who called it in or who was detailed to attend. Nothing."

"Bloody control room cock-up again," Page muttered. "Why am I not surprised. Those bloody desk jockeys have got just one job to do and even then…" He didn't finish. He didn't need to. He'd sort it out tomorrow. He looked over at Connor. "I'll have a word with Sharma in the morning. There will be a log of the call on the comms system, and in any case, the wooden-top that attended and secured the scene should have the information we need in their notebook." Connor looked relieved that he was taking it so well. Page stood up. "Come on. Cock-ups I can cope with, it's corruption that concerns me more."

Haviland House was a large, imposing block of council flats probably built in the early 1960s. It was hard to tell from looking at it due to the cream and pink cladding that had recently been added and that now hid the original exterior. Not a high-rise in the usual sense, it contained around ten storeys, but with external deck access to the maisonettes only on every other level the block seemed much longer than it was tall. Page had always thought it resembled a battleship. Despite its size this building, and indeed the community of St Judes to a greater extent, was now largely invisible to most people, finding itself in the shadow of the huge Cabot Circus retail complex. But Page knew where it was, as did most of his uniformed colleagues.

Connor managed to find a parking space outside the ramped entrance to the building. They took the stairs to the first floor and Page knocked forcefully on the door of Lenny Rhodes' flat. There was no answer so he banged again, this time shouting out: "Lenny. Open the door, it's DI Page."

A clumping sound could be heard coming from the flat and suddenly the door opened enough to reveal Lenny Rhodes, barefoot and dressed in a pair of jeans and a scruffy off-white T-shirt. "What do you want?"

Page stretched out his leg and put his foot in the gap between the bottom of the door and the frame. "That's not very polite. Can we come in Lenny?"

"What do you want? I've not done anything wrong."

"Just a quick chat and then we'll be on our way." Rhodes grudgingly opened the door and stood aside to allow them access. "After you," Page insisted, pointing down the hallway. "And by the way, this is my colleague DC Connor."

Rhodes didn't acknowledge her. "Shut the door," he shouted out and walked along the hallway and into the living area. The room had no furniture in it other than an old, threadbare three-piece suite and balanced on one of the arms of the sofa was an overflowing ashtray. The first thing Rhodes did was sit down and light another cigarette. He stared at the both of them.

"Do you mind if we sit down?" Page asked, not sure he actually wanted to. Rhodes shrugged his shoulders and took a long drag from his cigarette. Interpreting this to mean 'do as you want' Page gestured to Connor and they both sat down. "Thank you," he said, before enquiring: "How have you been keeping Lenny?"

Deliberately blowing smoke across the room towards the two detectives he answered: "I've been keeping my nose clean and staying out of trouble so I don't know what you've been told."

"Who said we've been told anything?" Page asked.

Rhodes laughed. "Because this isn't a bloody social visit out of the kindness of your heart, is it."

"No it's not. You got me there. Look Lenny, I'll be honest with you, a little bird has told us that you've been frequenting certain pubs on an evening…"

Before Page could elaborate Rhodes was straight at him. "Well whoever that was is talking bollocks aren't they. I'm not allowed in pubs on an evening. I've only been out a few weeks and I ain't that stupid. I know I'll end up back inside before long but it won't be for going into a bloody pub, and I can tell you that for free." He flicked the ash from his cigarette towards the ashtray but most of it fell down the side of the settee.

"So why would somebody tell us that you've been seen on a couple of occasions already?"

"I can only guess it's because they want me out of the way again," Rhodes suggested.

"And why might that be?" Page persisted.

"Look, you know how it is," Rhodes said, grinding his cigarette stub into the ashtray. "I'm the enforcer round here for some very powerful people. I don't know who they are but they look after me."

"Not that well," Page ventured, "they don't seem to keep you out of prison."

"That's my fault innit. I probably enjoy my work a bit too much, but they look after me. Trust me, they do. But when I was away this last time a new lot started sniffing around. Started getting to some of the local girls and started trying to supply their own gear around and about. They know that now I'm back it'll be a lot harder for them, and they probably want me gone again. It's them you should be talking to, not me."

"Tell me who they are and I will speak to them," Page replied.

"I don't know who they are but they must have some balls to try this on," Rhodes responded. "I've heard their man on the ground here isn't up to much. A bit of a drinker and a lightweight when push comes to shove. Not in my league anyway. I'm looking forward to meeting him."

"Some competition, a bit of market disruption, always good for the consumer in a capitalist economy," Page joked, but it went over Lenny's head. "Tell me Lenny, you wouldn't happen to know anything about these recent murders in town would you?"

Rhodes sat forward and visibly set himself. "You accusing me of murder now?"

"Not at all. Just wondering what you knew about them. What you'd heard Lenny."

He seemed to relax a little. "They're nothing to do with me. Not my style as you should know." Page did know. Rhodes continued: "And in any case I'm not interested in messing around with them afterwards. Once you've done what's gotta be done, you're done."

"What do you mean by that?" Page asked trying hard not to sound too interested.

"Word is they were undressed, or dressed up, or something after they were dead. Work of a weirdo if you ask me."

Page thought he would have just one more go. "So where did you hear this Lenny?"

"Word on the street. That's all."

Page tried to brush it off. "Don't believe everything you're told on the street Lenny."

"I don't. And I don't believe everything I'm told by coppers either." Rhodes looked at Connor with a leer. "Your girlfriend doesn't say much does she?" He lit up another cigarette.

"Nice talking with you Lenny." Page stood up and Connor followed suit. "Keep out of trouble and keep in touch. We'll see ourselves out."

Rhodes drew a mouthful of smoke deep into his lungs. As he exhaled he shouted behind them: "Shut the door."

Once back in the relative safety and comfort of the car Connor broke her silence. "What a nasty piece of shit he is."

Page laughed. "Not a nice man is he."

"Not at all," she agreed. "Do you believe all that about another gang muscling in on somebody else's territory?"

"I think I do. Lenny Rhodes is a lot of things but he isn't a very good liar, so he doesn't do it very often. And it does make some kind of sense if you think about it." Connor raised an eyebrow as much to say 'really?'. Page continued: "For a start it would explain why a nobody like Stuart Land is inexplicably represented by somebody like Simon Ravell. And remember we commented at the time how quick they were to point the finger at Rhodes."

Connor seemed to be processing his words and perhaps thinking out loud said: "You could be right."

Not really needing the encouragement Page carried on. "Ravell's sudden appearance and unconvincing efforts at sidetracking us could well be about keeping Land in circulation and keeping Rhodes at bay."

"So who is Ravell working for?" Connor asked.

Page shrugged his shoulders. "Not sure we'll ever find that out." He turned to look out of the side window, wondering to himself what their next move should be.

Connor was silent for a while and then asked: "Do you think Rhodes is our killer?"

Page turned back towards her. "No, I don't. Not his style. Do you?"

"I don't know, but if we had his DNA we would know for sure." She sounded a little frustrated.

"But we don't have it," he responded. "Not yet anyway. We will get it though, don't worry. Give him time and he will be arrested for something, but right now there's no point asking him to voluntarily supply a sample, and secretly taking a cigarette stub from his ashtray isn't an option either in case that's what you were thinking of."

"No, it wasn't," she replied earnestly. "Of course it wasn't."

He nodded and smiled. "Our visit wasn't a waste of time. We now know where he lives. We will keep an eye on him, and more importantly he knows that we are watching him."

"I suppose so. And we also know that he's heard the rumours about the bodies. Were you surprised by that?"

Page shook his head. "Not really. Our correspondent from the Post was banging on about the information still being on the fringes but from my experience once something is out there it crosses into the mainstream and spreads very quickly."

"And that doesn't worry you?" Connor asked him.

"Obviously it does. It makes our job a lot more difficult but there's nothing I can do about it." He waited but Connor had nothing to add. He was just about to suggest they go and get a 'proper' coffee when his mobile started ringing. He greeted the unknown caller in his customary manner: "Page."

"Oh hello DI Page. It's Krzysztof Nowak here from Forensic Services. I've just emailed you our report from the dog incident but I got an Out of Office message so thought I would ring you to let you know we'd sent it."

"Thank you, that's very thorough. Hang on a second." He put the call onto the loudspeaker and placed the phone on the dashboard between himself and Connor. "Thanks Krzysztof. You're on speaker-phone and DC Connor is with me too. Can you give us a brief overview of what you found, if anything?"

There was a slight delay and all they could hear was the tap-tapping of a computer keyboard whilst their colleague from forensics was searching for and opening the report. "Got it," he finally confirmed, sounding relieved. "Sorry, it wasn't me that wrote the report. I was just asked to email it to you."

Page rather uncharitably mouthed to Connor: "Work-experience," before adding, "or graduate apprentice." She tried not to laugh.

"Right," Nowak continued, clearly struggling to communicate the information whilst he read ahead. "Dr James drafted the covering email and she says that…" He hesitated. "Shall I just read it to you?"

"Yes, that's a good idea." Page looked at Connor and rolled his eyes.

"She says: 'Jim - report attached. Both the dogs had been poisoned. You can see for yourself the list of other matter from the dogs that we were able to isolate and identify, most of which is common to every pavement outside of every public house in Britain. The two things that will interest you most are: firstly, that we found traces of the same DNA that was present on your two murder victims; and secondly, that both animals had been in very recent contact with an ammonium nitrate substance, most probably fertiliser. Make of that what you will. Speak soon. Charlotte.' Does that make sense?

Page nodded to himself. "Thank you Krzysztof. All the best." He ended the call and retrieved his phone from the dashboard. "So," he said looking straight at Connor, "our serial killer also has a thing against dogs but is partial to a bit of gardening. That should help the profilers narrow down the list of suspects somewhat."

Connor gave him a quick, forced smile. "It's yet another development in the case but with no corresponding progress on our part. It feels like we're going backwards at times." She sounded quite dejected now.

"Come on, chin up," he said. "I know exactly how you feel. We all get days like this, but we'll get our breakthrough. It might not be tomorrow, or even the day after for that matter, but it'll come." She didn't look convinced. Page turned and pulled the seatbelt across himself, clicking it into position. "Come on," he instructed cheerily. "Let's go and get a coffee and a sticky bun."

Working Man

She was always surprised by the big difference a little 'me-time' could make. She'd got home late yesterday afternoon and prepared dinner for later on that evening. She'd then gone to the gym, had a very quick workout, a swim and a relax in the hot tub. After dinner she'd watched television with Aaron and gone to bed with a clear head. She'd slept well and was woken by her alarm. Out of habit she'd checked her mobile before getting out of bed and it was then she'd seen the message from Page telling her he would make his own way in that morning. That was the opportunity for a relaxed breakfast and a chance to see Aaron off to school. When she'd locked the front door behind her she was feeling much more positive and ready to face whatever it was that Monday morning might have in store for her.

Walking across the room to her desk she could see straight away that Page wasn't in his office. She put her bag down and went to go into the kitchen area but noticed PC Sharma sat at a desk in the corner. She went over to him. "Morning." He looked up. She nodded her head towards Page's office. "Is he not in yet?"

Sharma pulled a face. "He's in. Not in a very good mood but he's in."

"What's the problem?" she asked.

"I don't know. He came in about half an hour ago, made himself a coffee and went into his office. It must have been an email or something because all of a sudden he's talking to himself and then he storms out across the room telling anybody and everybody in earshot: 'I'm not having that. Not having it.' And then he's gone."

"Where did he go?"

Sharma clenched his teeth and grimaced. "He's up with DCS Tanner."

"Oh dear," Connor said through a nervous laugh.

Sharma knew precisely what she meant. "I know, and when did that ever end well?" he asked, not expecting an answer.

Connor didn't answer. She smiled back at him and then asked a question of her own. "Did DI Page speak to you this morning about the Seven Stars case?" She could tell from Sharma's blank reaction that he hadn't.

"What about it?" he asked, now looking concerned.

She didn't want to alarm him unnecessarily. "Just a heads up, but the cover sheet to the case file hasn't been completed. We don't think the person that found Clare's body has been interviewed but we don't know who they are."

"Thanks Lou. I'll get on to it now."

"You don't remember who the call was passed to do you? They might have our witness' name."

"I'll have a look. Give me an hour."

"Thanks Jay. One less thing to wind up DI Page at least."

"Yes. Thanks again. Forewarned is forearmed."

Connor made herself a coffee and took it back to her desk. She logged onto her computer and brought up the forensic and Post Mortem reports for Clare Harding and Callum Roberts. Then she opened the forensic analysis from the Full Moon. This morning over breakfast a thought had occurred to her. Dr James' note to DI Page had made explicit reference to the traces of ammonium nitrate found on the dogs but had alluded to the full list of things that had been identified at the scene. Perhaps they were missing something. Perhaps there was something common to all three forensic reports that would help identify the perpetrator, or at least where or how they operated. Yesterday she was lamenting the fact that no breakthrough had presented itself so far, but today with a clearer focus she knew that breakthroughs had to be discovered. She remembered what she had been told when she first became a detective: that successful outcomes were always down to 10% luck and 90% hard work. This morning's job was to cross reference the scientific data and see if there were any surprises or secrets lurking within it.

Connor had been reading through the documents and listing every item that had been found in the appropriate column of her handwritten spreadsheet for around twenty minutes when Page returned. He walked towards his office avoiding eye contact with anyone. She thought she ought to say something but only managed: "Morning."

Page didn't stop but he did respond, albeit cryptically. "The bigger picture Connor. You've got to appreciate the bigger picture." He reached his office and as he went in he was still mumbling something or other to himself that she couldn't quite hear.

It was only two weeks that she had been working with him but already she knew that coffee was the elixir most likely to calm him down. She tapped on his door. "Coffee?"

"Why do we bother Connor?" He was sat back in his chair, arms folded across his stomach, looking totally deflated. She chose not to answer. He gave out a loud sigh that bordered on being a grunt and then in a quiet voice answered her original question. "Yes, thanks. A coffee would be good."

She had found a couple of chocolate digestives in the cupboard and arranged these on a plate. She put the drink and biscuits onto his desk, within easy reach for him. "Do you want to talk about it?"

"Lenny Rhodes was absolutely right. There is something going on." Page then noticed the biscuits next to the drink and smiled. "Thanks. You stole them especially for me."

She laughed. "I'm sure whoever they belonged to won't be involving the police in the matter."

He broke one of the biscuits in half and put the large piece into his mouth all at once. He chewed it a few times and then took a large swig of coffee to help it go down. As if the sugar were having an immediate effect he explained quite calmly: "The case against Stuart Land is being discontinued."

"Why?" Connor asked, surprised by this news.

"The official line is that there is insufficient evidence that the controlled substances belonged to Mr Land. The unofficial story is that our man is only a small cog in a much larger wheel. A wheel that has piqued the interest of law enforcement agencies much more influential and important than us apparently." Page put the other half of the biscuit into his mouth and again swilled it down with a wash of warm coffee. "I told DCS Tanner that this was just a load of bollocks. That we were being played by the Drug Squad, or worse still Simon Ravell, but he suggested that I was failing to appreciate the bigger picture. So I hope you can see the bigger picture Connor, because I evidently can't."

Once again she knew that she should say something but had absolutely no idea what the right thing to say might be. She decided that agreeing with Page would probably be the best idea. "No, I can't see it either, Letting him go just makes us look stupid."

"It's a waste of our time Connor, that's what is. We do all the leg work and then somebody else takes all the glory." He picked up his mug and wrapped both hands around it as though he were hoping the warmth might offer him some comfort. He sat like that for nearly half a minute and did seem a little calmer when he said: "But it's not all bad news. I managed to get Tanner to agree that I can visit Jacob Herring in Lincoln."

"How did you manage that?" she asked with genuine curiosity.

"I told him we had tracked him down and it would help with formal identification of his mother for the coroner."

"And he bought that?"

"Of course not. But he could see that I was pissed off about Land and he doesn't like conflict much our Chief-Super. It was his way of giving me the bad news and not feeling too bad about it himself."

Connor didn't know how he did it, but he always seemed to get what he wanted. Not everything of course, but he often seemed to get the things most important to him at any given time. She knew this was important to him for whatever reason and guessed that he wouldn't delay taking the opportunity he'd been given. "When are you thinking of going?" she asked.

"Tomorrow. I'll contact the prison in a minute and then make my travel arrangements."

It was as she had expected. She thought she knew the answer to her next question too but she asked it anyway. "Do you want me to come with you?"

"No. You've got things to do here. I'll be alright on my own." She was just about to tell him what she was doing with the lab reports when Sharma tapped on the open door. "Come on in and join the party," Page said, sounding much happier again.

Sharma took one step into the doorway but proceeded no further. "DC Connor was asking me about the Seven Stars case file earlier." Page shot a glance at Connor but said nothing. Sharma continued: "I've updated the cover sheet fully now. Apologies for that. Anyway, the person you want to speak to, the person that reported finding the body, is one Jason Trent. Shall I send the details over?"

"Give them to DC Connor," Page said before looking at her and adding: "A job for you to do while I'm away."

"Okey dokey," Sharma acknowledged and set off back to his desk.

Connor felt she should explain her actions to Page before he asked. "Sorry about that. I was in earlier and going back over the case notes when I saw Sharma at his desk and thought I could…"

"That's fine," Page reassured her. "Good to see someone using their initiative. Go and have a chat with Mr Trent. I'm sure it won't be of much use but it is something we have to do."

"Yes. No problem, I'll go later on. Right now I'm going through the forensic reports and comparing them just in case there is something we've missed."

"Such as?" Page queried.

"I don't know. I'm not expecting to find anything in particular but the thought occurred to me that we should not just look at each of the cases in isolation. We should…"

Page interrupted her. "We should look at the bigger picture?" he asked mischievously.

Connor laughed. "Yes. Something like that."

The whole morning had been spent cross checking the scenes of crime reports but with no success. The only incontrovertible fact they still had was that the same man had been present at each of the locations. Connor had got Jason Trent's details from PC Sharma and had managed to arrange a meeting with him that afternoon.

Before setting off for the appointment she had bought herself a pack of sandwiches for a hurried and late lunch. As the weather was good she had decided to eat and walk and was now crossing the new footbridge that curved its way from Castle Park to the recently completed Finzels Reach development. The modern apartments had been built on the site of the city's old sugar refinery, established in the 1600s but rebuilt by the German Conrad Finzel in 1846.

She found her way to the apartment building she was looking for and once outside the flat door she rang the bell. Unsure whether or not it was a camera bell she took no chances and smiled in the direction of the doorway. As she heard the footsteps inside coming towards her she stood up a little straighter.

The door opened and there was a man in his mid-thirties, of average height but quite athletic in build. He seemed to be a little out of breath. "Hi. Jason Trent. You must be Detective Inspector Connor."

"Detective Constable Connor," she corrected him.

"Oh, sorry about that. Not a good start. Do come in," he said, looking embarrassed by his mistake. He started to walk across the very small hall area so she closed the front door behind her and followed him. "This is my living room," he said very proudly.

Her eyes however, were drawn to the full length window and the view it afforded across to Castle Park. "What a fantastic view you've got," she said, contemplating that it was two weeks ago to the day on that very spot on the other side of the river that she had properly met DI Page for the first time.

"Yes. I'm very lucky to live here. Please sit down." He motioned to a small, modern two-seater sofa. Connor sat down and took out her notebook. He looked surprised. "Very formal," he said.

"Nothing to worry about Mr Trent. It's quite routine, but we do need a report for our files."

"Absolutely. No problem," he confirmed.

She thought he was suddenly trying to sound relaxed, but trying just a bit too hard. "Do you live here on your own Mr Trent?" Her first question certainly seemed to unnerve him.

"Yes, but I thought we would be talking about that girl I found."

"We will be. All in good time. So you live alone?"

"Yes, I've already said."

"No pets. Dogs or cats?"

"No. They're not allowed under the lease."

"But you were walking a dog in the early morning when you found Clare Harding's body."

"Yes but that's not my dog. It's my girlfriend's dog."

"Oh I see. Sorry, I thought it was your dog." Connor noticed his relief that the apparent confusion had been resolved, but she remained interested in how quickly he once again became defensive. "And what's your girlfriend's name?"

"What's my girlfriend got to do with this?" he asked.

"We will need to speak to her sometime, that's all. Just to make sure she can corroborate that you were out walking her dog at that time of the morning."

"You don't believe me?" He was now sounding anxious.

"I don't disbelieve you Mr Trent, but it is my job to check what you tell me. Just for the records, you understand." He nodded as if to show he did understand but he didn't answer the question. So Connor asked again. "And your girlfriend's name is?"

"Chloe Andrews," he finally answered.

Connor made a show of slowly writing this down in her notebook before asking: "And where does Chloe live?"

"Off Redcliff Street. Not far from the Seven Stars."

"And she'll be able to confirm what you are telling me?" Connor thought this to be a routine and predictable question and was expecting a straightforward 'yes' in response. Instead she was met with silence and a pained look from the man sitting opposite her.

After some huffing and puffing he answered: "Not really. Chloe was away that weekend and I was dog sitting. She didn't get back until the Monday night." He clearly wasn't keen to elaborate so Connor waited a few seconds, quite a few seconds as it was, remembering what she'd learned on her interview technique training: let silence do the heavy lifting. It worked. Breaking the awkward silence he continued: "I got up early on the Monday morning so that I could walk the dog before setting off for work. I was going to do a quick circular walk but when we saw the body by the pub we had to do something."

"You say 'we'. Do you mean you and the dog?" Connor asked, and once again she seemed to have hit the jackpot.

He let out another heavy sigh. "No. Me and Karen." This time he looked as though he knew what the next question was going to be but he waited for it nonetheless.

"Who's Karen?" Connor duly obliged.

"Karen is Chloe's neighbour, and friend."

"And you just happened to meet her on your early morning walk." Connor delivered this more as a statement than a question but again fell back on her training and waited for further clarification.

"No. I'd arranged to walk with her up to the end of the road where a colleague was picking her up."

Connor said nothing but gave him a look that implied 'you might as well tell me'.

He seemed to be weighing up his options before admitting: "Alright, I'm seeing Karen. Chloe doesn't know about it obviously. That's why I didn't really want you speaking to her."

The reason for his unease was becoming clearer. "That's alright," Connor said offering a smile, "it's not against the law, but it would have been easier if you'd told me at the beginning." He looked away, out of the window and over to Castle Park. "And you spent Sunday night together, you and Karen?"

"No. I was with her most of the day but she was out with friends on the Sunday evening. We arranged to meet up first thing Monday morning as I've told you."

"Tell me how you found Clare's body."

"We were walking to the end of the road to wait for Karen's lift. As we passed the Fleece Karen looked down the lane and said 'What's that?' We thought at first it was one of those shop mannequins but Karen went closer and could see that it was real."

"Did you go into the alleyway with Karen as well?"

"No."

"Why's that?"

"I don't know. Not something I wanted to look at really. I rang 999 straight away and reported what we had found."

"Did you wait for the police to arrive?"

"No. We couldn't wait. Karen had a long journey that morning for a meeting in the Midlands and she had to get her lift."

Once again something didn't seem quite right to Connor. "Karen might have needed to go but why didn't you stay?" No answer was forthcoming. This time it was Connor who broke the silence. "So you just left that poor girl there, all alone, and wandered off as if nothing had happened."

"There was nothing I could do," he responded angrily at first but then in a more measured tone he added: "I didn't know what to do."

"So what did you do?"

"I went back to Chloe's flat, packed my bag, drove to my place and got changed for work."

"And left the dog at Chloe's?"

"No. He came to work with me like he does most days." Connor gave him that 'tell me about it' look again. "I'm out and about all day and Jack, that's the dog's name - he's a Jack Russell, he loves it in the van and most of the time, but not always, he gets to run around outside when I'm working."

"What do you do for a living then Mr Trent?"

"I've got my own business. I'm a landscape gardener."

"Really?" For some reason this revelation had taken Connor by surprise. "Where are you based then?"

Trent was looking more relaxed all of a sudden. "I do most of my work around Bristol. Mainly Clifton, Westbury on Trym, Sneyd Park, there's some big properties around the Downs you know. I've got a storage unit and small yard off Midland Road where I keep all my tools and stuff, so pretty central really."

To Connor's ears this newly acquired confidence made it sound as though he were making a pitch for some work rather than answering her questions. Probably a good place to leave things for now she thought. Putting her notebook away she said: "Many thanks for your time Mr Trent. We will need to see you again, and Karen for that matter. As you were the ones that found the body we will need to take some samples, simply to account for your presence at the scene and to formally eliminate you both from our enquiries." The look of concern seemed to return to his face. "Don't worry, we will be discreet. It's all routine. Somebody will be in touch with you tomorrow to arrange an appointment."

He didn't look overly comforted. He stood up and clearing his throat said: "I'll show you out."

She walked back over the bridge to Castle Park and found a bench where she wouldn't be overheard. She sat down and looked across the water towards the apartments in Finzels Reach wondering whether or not Jason Trent was looking back at her. She phoned Page's mobile but the call went straight to voicemail. "Hi, it's Connor here. Just finished speaking to Mr Trent and thought I'd better update you. He's a very nervous man who is having an affair with his girlfriend's best mate. What might interest you more though is that he was quite evasive about what he did or didn't do upon discovering Clare's body. And then there's the fact that he's a self employed landscape gardener with his own van, and a yard and a lockup in the city centre. Give me a call when you get this if you want to, I'm around most of the evening."

She put her phone away and for a very brief moment allowed herself a ridiculous thought: was this the breakthrough they had been waiting for?

Suspicious Minds

Page was already at home when Connor's message came through. He listened to it and then carried on making the cup of coffee he had promised himself.

That afternoon the prison in Lincoln had finally returned his call and he had been able to make arrangements for a meeting late tomorrow morning with Jacob Herring. The Prison Service should have spoken to Jacob by now and prepared him for the arrival of a detective from Bristol. Hopefully putting his mind at rest that he had done nothing wrong but without telling him the exact purpose of the visit. That had been Page's instructions at least.

With the mug of coffee in his hand he returned to the sitting room and put the drink down on the small table. Picking up his phone he wandered to the window and waited for Connor to answer.

"Hi," was all she said by way of greeting.

"Page here. I got your message."

"Yes. What do you think?"

"I'm not sure I'm thinking anything. You spoke to the man. How did he seem?"

"Nervous and evasive would be a good summary. Socially awkward perhaps. Didn't seem to want to say too much, and what he did say I didn't necessarily believe." She paused before continuing. "I know it's not in the procedural manual anywhere but my gut instinct was one of suspicion the minute I met him."

"Then don't ignore it. Good coppers are born with suspicious minds. There is nothing wrong with gut instinct Connor, providing it is backed up with something more objective."

"And in this case it is," she confirmed somewhat excitedly. "We have a man who puts himself at the scene of our first crime, a crime he had the opportunity to commit by the way, and who has easy access to fertiliser, storage and transportation."

"Not one to prick your bubble Connor, but if he had committed the murder why would he return to the scene of the crime and ring it in to us? That only happens in crap films."

Without hesitation, and without sounding deflated at all, she carried on. "I thought that at first but then there was something not quite right about the way he told me his story of finding the body. Almost as if it was this Karen woman that found the body, not him. I got the sense it was Karen that chose the route that morning and he had to literally go along with her. Left to his own devices he would probably have gone another way or not taken the dog for a walk at all." She stopped talking for a second and asked: "Are you still there?"

Page was staring out of the window watching neighbours coming home from work and vying for the limited number of parking spaces still available but he was listening to what she was saying. "Yes. Go on," he confirmed.

"I also found it strange that he didn't go into the alley with Karen. He let her go in alone. And then once she'd realised it was a real body, he still he didn't go in. Almost as if he didn't need to. As if he already knew what there was to see down there. And having called it in he then didn't wait around. As soon as Karen was out of the picture he disappeared off to work as if nothing had happened. And so I'm thinking none of that seems like normal behaviour."

Page was conscious that Connor had stopped talking. He was watching the man from three doors down who had finally found a parking space big enough for his SUV and who was now struggling to get two young children out of their safety seats and onto the pavement without incident. "Yes. I agree. It doesn't sound like normal behaviour to me either. I guess that once we get a DNA sample we will know for sure."

Connor suddenly sounded a little less positive. "Yes that's all in hand hopefully for tomorrow, but my biggest concern is that we've now spooked him and he will either start getting rid of any evidence still lying around or he will take off and disappear completely."

"Then watch him," Page suggested. "Be at his place first thing tomorrow morning and watch his every move. Follow him everywhere and make a note of where he goes and who he sees. Get one of the others to go with you. Don't let them argue. Tell them I've sanctioned it."

"Are you sure? That's a big call to make."

Page couldn't tell whether Connor was relieved and grateful or surprised and worried. "It's no big deal. As I see it it's simply a precaution we need to take until the formalities of the DNA test are completed." He presumed by her silence that she was happy with this decision. "Right. I need to get off and get ready. Good luck for tomorrow."

"You too," she replied.

His neighbour, now carrying a backpack on one shoulder and with a child holding onto each of his hands, was making slow progress along the street towards home. As they passed the window Page waved and smiled in case he had been spotted watching them. He then turned and walked back to the easy chair and occasional table where his coffee was waiting, now cool enough to drink.

His mind was racing and was fully taken up not with the murder enquiry but with tomorrow's visit. He had no idea how Jacob would take the news. It would be a shock obviously, but would it bring him closure or would it create a bigger sense of loss that he would find hard to cope with? It might be a bit of both. There was no easy answer and certainly no promise of a happy ending.

As he sipped his coffee and reflected on all of this a song came into his head. He got up and went across to his CD shelves on the back wall and picked out the album he wanted. Putting the shiny disc into the machine he pressed play and sat back down again. The room was filled with a short drum roll before a guitar and keyboard driven reggae rhythm took over. He waited and at seventeen seconds the plaintive voice came in. He closed his eyes and let the music temporarily transport him. The mother and child reunion was only a matter of hours away.

Watching The Detectives

Already she felt bored, and it had only been half an hour. She tapped her fingers lightly on the steering wheel and stared at the white van parked a few hundred yards away. It was going to be a long day. Turning to the detective sat next to her she said: "Thanks for agreeing to do this."

"No problem. It gets me out of the office, away from the court hearing preparation I'm stuck with, and in any case, if Big Jim needs help who am I to say 'no'?"

"Big Jim? Is that what you call him?"

DS Brain looked at Connor and smiled. "Didn't you know? Dear old DI Page is known as Big Jim."

"Why's that?" Connor asked. She hadn't heard anybody else refer to him as Big Jim.

"I don't know. He's always been called that as long as I can remember. Probably because he wanders around the office like the big know-it-all sheriff in those old fashioned cowboy movies."

"And does he know?" Connor asked, feeling a little bit guilty at talking about him behind his back.

"I don't think so, and I certainly wouldn't tell him if I were you."

"I'm not going to, don't worry."

The two women sat in silence for a while, both alternating their attention between the parked van and the entrance to the apartment block. DS Brain broke the silence. "How are you getting on with Big Jim?"

The question surprised Connor but she was more concerned about the answer she now had to give. She didn't know Anna Brain at all. She'd seen her around the office obviously, but had never had anything to do with her. She might have spilled the beans about Page's nickname but she was still a senior officer, as of course was DI Page. "I like him," she started to say, knowing that she couldn't just leave it there. "He can be hard work at times, doesn't always communicate that well but he cares, and that's important." Consciously trying to shift the focus away from herself she turned to look at Brain and enquired: "How about you? You know him better than me."

Brain smiled. "I like him too. He does care, you're right, but that's not always enough. He's been around for a long time now and perhaps it's time for him to hang up his spurs. Time to let some younger talent rise and challenge the established patriarchy."

Connor hadn't expected such candour and certainly hadn't expected her own immediate reaction to be one of disagreement and loyalty to Page. She valued his experience and accepted that they didn't always agree. She had never felt that he was holding her back, in fact if anything she felt he was letting her do too much at times. But perhaps that was DS Brain's point: that it was still the women in the rank and file who were doing the work and bidding of the men. Nevertheless Connor didn't feel inclined to agree with her colleague, but neither was she prepared to voice her dissent. She wanted to avoid any bad feeling so a difficult silence threatened to ensue until Jason Trent suddenly appeared in the doorway. "There he is," Connor pointed out, relieved that they could now move on, both figuratively and actually.

"Got him," Brain confirmed, checking the time and entering it into her notebook.

Trent crossed the road to his van and got in. Connor started the car engine. "If he's told us the truth then he'll be going to Chloe's to pick up the dog."

As expected he made the short journey to his girlfriend's flat. He disappeared for only a matter of minutes before returning to the van with the dog trotting along by his side.

"Where will he be going now?" Brain asked.

"Probably to his lockup in Midland Road," Connor suggested.

As the van pulled away Connor prepared to follow at a safe distance, but instead of retracing his journey and making for Old Market he turned left and crossed Bristol Bridge. Connor had to speed up to keep him in sight and as she was halfway over the bridge she saw him turn onto Baldwin Street and head towards the Centre. Another left turn took them onto Anchor Road and Connor could drop back a little as they progressed past the Aquarium and on along the waterside until they could see Brunel's SS Great Britain on the other side of the harbour. At the roundabout Trent almost did a full u-turn back the way he'd come but instead he took the last exit and drove very slowly up St George's Road. Connor pulled in as soon as she had left the roundabout, worried that Trent had realised he was being followed. She watched him drive another hundred yards before he indicated and pulled into a Resident Only parking bay. She waited, a little concerned that he was going to get out and continue on foot. "What do we do if he leaves the van here?" she asked. "I hadn't thought of that."

"I'll follow him," Brain said. "He's not seen me before and won't know who I am."

But nothing happened. Trent didn't leave the vehicle. He didn't even open a window. They sat there, eyes fixed on the white van. A couple of students walked past them, crossed the road and continued on their way to College Green. Connor followed them with her eyes and then she saw the sign. "Hang on a minute," she said sounding surprised, "I recognise this place. That's the Three Tuns pub up there on the right, and on the left are the steps up to Brandon Hill."

"Yup," Brain agreed, clearly knowing her way around this part of the city better than Connor did. "And the significance of this might be?"

"It's the location of our second murder." Connor hesitated before continuing: "And our prime suspect has just brought us here."

The two detectives looked at each other. "It might just be coincidence," Brain cautioned, but the look on her face suggested she didn't believe in coincidence any more than any other detective.

"So what are you up to?" Connor was thinking out loud. "It's too early to be waiting for the pub to open."

"Perhaps he's waiting for someone," Brain suggested.

"Possibly. He might have arranged to meet Karen, his girlfriend, I suppose."

Brain looked confused. "I thought his girlfriend was called Chloe."

"She is," Connor confirmed, "but his other girlfriend is called Karen. Don't ask."

She didn't, but after a further couple of minutes of sitting and waiting she said: "Shall I take a walk up to College Green to get a coffee or something and have a look at what he's doing as I go past?"

"I'm not sure. Don't you think that's too risky?"

"There are other people walking around, why would he notice me?"

"He might see you getting out of the car. He could be watching us watching him." Connor smiled to herself. She was starting to think and sound like DI Page.

Brain seemed to be mulling things over when she suddenly leant forward. "There's somebody walking down the hill, I could go now."

"Wait," Connor instructed, her eyes fixed on the male figure approaching Trent's van. As he reached the vehicle the passenger door swung open. He walked around the open door before turning and getting in, slamming the door behind him.

Connor was staring out of the windscreen. She looked shocked. "Are you alright?" Brain asked.

"I'm fine. I just can't believe my eyes that's all. The man who's just got into the van with Trent is Sean Wilson, the manager at the Seven Stars, the location of our first murder." Connor paused to gather her thoughts and turned towards her colleague. "Now this certainly cannot be coincidence."

Brain didn't contradict her this time. "I agree. They're meeting here for a very specific reason. By that I don't mean that they are meeting for a specific reason, which they obviously are, it's more that they have deliberately chosen this specific location for the meeting." Connor looked at her with a slight frown. She continued: "These two could meet anywhere in Bristol. For starters Wilson runs a pub very close to where Trent's girlfriend lives, and not far at all from Trent's own place in Finzels Reach. If they are worried about being seen together then why choose a place for a meeting that is even less private than any of the options they have available closer to home?"

Connor looked out of the window at the van parked up the hill. "Unless of course, the whole point of the meeting was to be seen." She was definitely turning into Page. "Perhaps they are just playing us."

"Perhaps," Brain agreed, "but still the question remains: why choose this specific location? Why bring us here?"

Connor didn't know. She couldn't really begin to think why. If Trent was their killer, why would he bring them here? "Audacity or stupidity," she said aloud.

Brain looked at her. "What do you mean?"

"I'm just answering the question. If Trent is our man why would he lead us here? Audacity or stupidity?"

Before they could consider this any further the van's passenger door swung open again. "Here we go," Brain said, instinctively sitting back in her seat. Wilson climbed out of the van and then leaned back in as if to finish off a conversation. Then he stood up straight, stepped back and slammed the door shut. Instead of returning back up the hill he turned and started walking down towards them. Connor got her phone out and thrust it between her and Brain. "Look at this," she instructed. "Make it look like we are checking something." The two women were hunched together over the screen as Wilson stepped closer. As he came alongside the passenger window Connor shot him a furtive glance. She wasn't absolutely sure but she thought he bent down slightly to try and catch her eye and then acknowledged her presence by making a waving gesture with the fingers on his left hand. And then he was gone, on down the hill towards the Bag of Nails pub.

"Shall I follow him?" Brain asked quickly.

"No. Let him go. We know he's not our man. Let's follow Trent." With that the white van pulled out of the parking bay and drove slowly up the hill, turning left opposite the Central Library heading for Park Street. Connor followed at a distance although by now she was convinced that Trent wouldn't let her lose him. "Do me a favour," she said to DS Brain. "Contact the office and make sure they phone Mr Trent to make an appointment for him to have his DNA test later today."

"To keep the pressure on?" Brain asked knowingly.

"Yes," Connor answered, "and to let him know that we are watching him watching us."

From the Three Tuns Trent drove to the yard in Midland Road, but he didn't take the most direct route. It was clear from the route he did take that he was deliberately wasting their time. When they had finally arrived at his workshop and parked up a few hundred yards from the entrance way Connor couldn't have been any angrier. "What the hell is he doing?" she'd asked through gritted teeth. "Who the hell does he think he is?"

DS Brain was updating her notebook with a summary of the morning's key events whilst Connor, a little calmer now, was watching the entrance way to the industrial units where Trent had disappeared nearly half an hour ago. The silence was broken by the ringing of Brain's mobile. "It's the office," she confirmed before answering the call. The two colleagues were sat close enough to each other that Connor could hear both sides of the conversation. Despite this, once the call was over, Brain turned to her and checked: "You got that?"

"Yes I think so. Mr Trent has been very cooperative and has agreed to attend the station this afternoon to provide a DNA sample." There was more than a hint of frustration in Connor's voice. "And in the meantime we are sat here while he's in there doing whatever it is he's doing."

A look of slight concern came over Brain's face. "We are sure he is in there aren't we?" she asked.

"Yes," Connor responded without hesitation. "I checked the maps yesterday. There is only one way in and out of the estate for vehicles." As soon as she had said it she felt her stomach tighten. "Shit." She started the car and drove slowly into the service road. The first few units were occupied by motor-part dealers, electrical wholesalers and a self-storage facility. Parked directly ahead was a burger and coffee van doing a steady mid-morning trade. She manoeuvred around the mobile cafe and the units now coming into view were smaller than the ones nearest the road. There on the right hand side were three grey metal-shuttered frontages and parked outside the middle one was Jason Trent's van. Connor pulled up behind it, blocking it in to prevent any quick getaways.

Brain was first out of the car and she made her way quietly along the passenger side of the van, staring intently at the door mirror for any signs of movement within. She got to the side window and knocked on it loudly with her left hand, using her right hand to pull on the door handle. She was met with a dull thud and a pain in her wrist. The door was locked shut and the van was empty.

Connor was at the front of the building banging the metal shutter with her fist and kicking it with her foot, but this too was locked and secured. "Shit," she said again and turned to Brain. Together they walked around the building and right up to the six foot wire boundary fence at the rear. It only took a few seconds for both detectives to spot it. "He was no Houdini was he. Didn't need to be," Connor lamented nodding at the gaping hole in the fence. This short cut was evidently well used. The gap in the fence allowed access and egress with just a bend and a bob of the head, and on the other side the grass was so well trodden that a pathway could be seen running first alongside the fence line and then veering off downhill towards The Dings Park. Connor stared into the distance. "Shit. What's DI Page going to say when I tell him we lost him?" she asked shaking her head and feeling thoroughly defeated.

"When we tell him that he lost us," Brain corrected her. "Don't be so hard on yourself. You've already ascertained that he's been stringing us along all morning. This was all part of his elaborate plan."

"And that's supposed to make me feel better is it?" Connor challenged her colleague.

"I'm just saying that it isn't all your fault."

"I know what you're saying, and it's appreciated, but I'm more concerned about what DI Page will say."

Brain put her hand on Connor's shoulder and gave it a quick squeeze. "I don't know what he will say, but I do know what he'd say if he were here right now."

Connor gave her a smile. "He'd say, let's get a coffee. That's what he would say."

"Correct. Come on then," Brain said walking away. "The queue at that coffee van back there might have gone down by now."

Counting Out Time

Half an hour Page had been sat in the interview room. A windowless room that smelled of lies and lost hope. He tapped his fingers lightly on the table in front of him and looked around the room once again but nothing had changed. There was still nothing to see other than the table and the empty chair opposite him awaiting the arrival of Jacob Herring. He had nothing to use as a distraction: his phone and everything else in his pockets had been taken from him at the airport style scanner in the reception area. Everything had been itemised and put into a locked deposit box ready for him to collect when he passed through the scanner again on his way back to the outside world. Everything that was apart from the plain brown envelope containing the two photographs that was now positioned on the table under his fingertips. He stopped his tapping, leant back in the chair and looked up at the ceiling. He hated prisons. He had only ever visited them in a professional capacity but he was always so keen to escape. He couldn't imagine spending years at a time in such places. They were all the same: hermetically sealed establishments not where time stood still but where every heartbeat you felt was the steady tick of your existence ebbing inexorably away. That was the real punishment he had always thought, worse even than being sentenced to death. You were sentenced to a life where you counted every second and not one of them counted at all.

He was roused from his thoughts by the sound of footsteps approaching along the corridor. He sat himself up and waited for the door to open. Almost immediately it did and a prison guard took a large step into the doorway and announced the prisoner's arrival like a butler announcing a highly decorated dignitary at some swanky garden party. "Prisoner 341 - Jacob Herring." He stood aside and on cue Herring entered the room, looking nervous and tired. Before Page could stand up the guard had disappeared, shutting the door behind him, so he remained seated and stretched out his arm towards the empty chair. "Please, sit down." He watched as Jacob awkwardly pulled the chair away from the table and slowly lowered himself into it. He looked like he did in the prison service photograph, although he seemed to have had a haircut. More of a trim really but he looked a little tidier. Page wondered whether or not this might have been on his account. Once Jacob looked as comfortable as he was going to be Page introduced himself. "Good morning Jacob. I'm Detective Inspector Jim Page and I work in Bristol." Jacob nodded but otherwise didn't respond. Page continued: "Thanks for seeing me today," and then he paused very briefly. "I am very sorry but I think I have some bad news for you."

Jacob shrugged his shoulders slightly as if to say 'don't worry' and then he spoke for the first time. "It's mum, isn't it."

Page reached out for the envelope and withdrew the top photograph: the prepared mortuary shot showing Shirley with her hair coiffured and face made-up resting on a pillow with her shrouded shoulders exposed above a silk coverlet. He turned it the right way around and passed it across the table. "Is this your mum Jacob?" Jacob moved only his eyes, gave the picture the most cursory of glances and looking back at Page nodded. "I am so sorry Jacob. This must be such a shock for you."

Instead of the silence that Page was expecting the response was instantaneous: "Not really. I've been waiting for this every day. Not hoping for it, but knowing that if I ever saw her again she would be dead."

Page reached into the brown envelope once more and offered the old school photograph to Jacob. "This is you, isn't it?"

This time Jacob took the picture from him and gazed at it. "Yes, that's me and my brother Josh. Where did you get this from?"

"It was among your mother's belongings."

Jacob smiled. "Good," and as if he could predict Page's next question he volunteered: "I gave it to her."

"When was that then, because your mum had left home before this picture was taken hadn't she?"

Jacob put the picture back onto the table. "Yes. This photo was taken just before Josh died and it was the last picture I had of him. I carried it everywhere with me. About six months later I started at the big school and on my very first day there she was, standing to the side of the entrance gates under the shade of the big apple tree. She told me she couldn't stay and that she couldn't see me again but that she wanted to say goodbye properly this time. I told her Josh was gone and she said she knew. And then she said that I had always been her favourite. Can you imagine how that made me feel? How it still makes me feel?"

Page could only say: "No."

"So I gave her my photograph and told her that she had to remember and love us both equally. She took it. She made no promises mind, but she took it. And now I know she took it with her to the grave." He stopped and stared red-eyed at Page. "Do you have any idea what it feels like to be abandoned as a child. For your mother to get up and go and leave you behind without any explanation, just leave you behind, disappear and never come back?"

Page bit hard into his lower lip and took in a deep, audible breath. "Actually I do, and that's the reason I worked so hard to put a name to your mum, to find you, and why I had to personally come here today to tell you what I'd found."

Jacob looked away but Page could see the tears welling up in his eyes. "How did she die?"

"She wasn't in the best of health and was sleeping rough. Her drinking didn't help." He thought he'd leave it at that and luckily Jacob was happy to leave it there too. "If you'd like me to, I could have a word with the Governor and see whether it might be possible for you to attend the funeral."

Jacob wiped his nose on the back of his hand and gave a short sniff. "No thanks, you're alright. I don't think I need to be there. I think I buried her that day she left me at the school gates."

"I get it," Page tried to console him, "but if you change your mind then let me know, because I will be there. I'll definitely be there."

"And why will you be there?" Jacob asked. "For her, for me or for yourself?"

There didn't seem to be any malice in the question but it hit Page hard. "For all of us," he answered but deep down he knew it was for himself really. His chance to finally lay his own ghosts to rest.

"Was that it then?" Jacob asked, obviously keen to get back to the surroundings and routine he was more comfortable with.

"Yes, unless there is anything else you want to ask me." Jacob shook his head. Page pointed to the two photographs on the table. "Would you like to keep these?"

Jacob reached for the picture of him and his brother. "Just this one."

Page nodded and smiled. "OK. Let's get you back to where you need to be." He scraped the chair backwards as he tried to stand up and before he had even taken a step the door opened and the guard appeared.

"Finished here?" he asked gruffly, and without waiting for an answer he barked: "Come on Herring, back to reality."

Page watched as Jacob stood up and left the room, his eyes staring at the floor as he went and both hands holding tightly onto the old school photograph as if making sure it could never again slip from his grasp. Once they were gone Page picked up the picture of Shirley left on its own in the middle of the table and returned it to the brown envelope. He smiled to himself ironically. How wrong he had been. It hadn't been about reuniting a mother and her son after all. That might have been the most important thing for him, but for Jacob it was clearly all about being reunited with his little brother.

He had been back out in the free world for about half an hour and almost at the train station when his phone pinged to indicate he had a message. When he checked it seemed that the message had been left earlier that morning. The phone of course had been turned off and then kept for a few hours in a thick-walled vault so he presumed that it had taken a while for all the various connections to be reestablished. Squinting at the screen he could see that the message was from Connor and that it simply said: 'Give me a call when you can.' In his experience short text messages were never good news. People were always keen to leave long rambling voicemail messages when they had good news to impart otherwise they always seemed to resort to brief monosyllabic missives that offered no useful information whatsoever.

With a coffee now in his hand he walked to the very end of the platform and sat himself down on the bench. One more big sip and he was ready for whatever it was that Connor had to tell him. As soon as she answered he started speaking, cutting short her introductory pleasantries. "Page here. Sorry I missed your message earlier."

"No problem. I knew you would be tied up and without your phone. That's why I left a text message. How did it go?"

Page clenched his teeth together and pulled a face, a 'tell' that he knew full well Connor couldn't see, and then he replied: "It went well. Yes, very well. As well as could have been expected." There was no need for Connor to know that despite all his hard work Jacob had been pretty ambivalent about the news of his mother's death, so changing the subject as quickly as he could he enquired: "And how has your day been?"

"Pretty shit really."

"I thought so," Page interjected without allowing her the chance to expand further. "Hence the cagey text message. Go on then, spill the beans."

"We lost Trent," she said matter of factly. "Or rather Trent lost us. He led us on a wild goose chase and then disappeared."

"Disappeared?" Page asked, trying to understand what had been going on.

"Yes, disappeared, but not before taking us close to both our murder scenes and then meeting up with Sean Wilson from the Seven Stars just for good measure."

"Oh dear," Page said, trying to sound sympathetic but failing.

"It's not funny," Connor countered before adding: "He knows we are on to him and now he's gone."

"How do you know he's gone?" Page asked trying to establish whether or not there might really be a problem or whether it was just Connor overreacting to her disappointment.

"He drove his van to his depot, dumped it there and then disappeared somewhere on foot with his girlfriend's dog in tow. He is due to come into the station later this afternoon to provide a DNA sample but I can't see that happening, can you?"

Page got off the bench and started pacing up and down. "Probably not, but we shouldn't forget that this morning Jason Trent was simply a witness. We might have had our suspicions but we had nothing else that would have allowed us to arrest him." He walked towards a waste bin and tossed his empty cardboard cup into one of the three coloured sections without checking whether or not he had chosen the appropriate recycling option. He walked back towards the bench. "And despite today's pantomime we still have no evidence to justify an arrest. However, given what you have seen today, should he fail to appear this afternoon for his appointment then I would say he starts to become a person of interest."

"And what difference does that make if we don't know where he is?" Connor asked, still sounding annoyed with herself.

"It means we can start to look for him, and more importantly, let him know that we are looking for him. The longer it is that he stays AWOL then the stronger our case becomes." Connor didn't respond. Page continued: "And another thing of course is that if he fails to attend his pre-arranged, voluntary interview then we might start worrying about his wellbeing mightn't we. And it would be negligent of us not to check his home and workplace wouldn't it, just to make sure that nothing untoward hadn't befallen him of course."

Page could almost hear Connor smiling and already her mood seemed to have lightened as she finally answered him: "And that's what years of experience bring: the ability to spot an opportunity even when faced with an overwhelming set of lost causes."

"Are you being sarcastic?" he quickly checked.

"No, not at all. I mean it."

Page laughed as he sat back down on the bench. "Don't let anyone tell you I'm past it. There's life in this old dog yet."

Connor laughed too and Page was pleased that it seemed he had been able to get her back on side. "So you cheer up," he told her. "Don't worry about today, have a nice evening and pick me up in the morning raring to go again."

"Will do, and thanks."

Before she could say anything else Page ended the call and sighed. He wasn't really feeling as positive about things as he had implied. He had to let Shirley go now. Tomorrow he really needed to start focusing on the murder enquiry and somehow they had to start looking for Jason Trent. He would have to pull himself together. It seemed that DC Connor at least was counting on him.

On The Run

"There. Over there," Page shouted extending his right arm so quickly that he nearly hit Connor in the face.

She glanced across the road. "What is it?"

"Pull over," he barked. "There's a space outside that coffee shop."

The Gloucester Road was always busy at this time of the day and even as a non-driver Page recognised an opportunity that had to be taken when it presented itself. As an actual driver however, Connor looked less keen to accept such opportunities but on this occasion she made an exception. She stopped the car abruptly, indicated and then slowly nudged her way towards the oncoming flow of traffic until somebody flashed her across and she could claim the parking space. A successful manoeuvre but one that nonetheless drew the ire of the driver behind, who as he passed demonstrated his displeasure with both a hand signal and beep of his horn.

"The things I do for you," she said as she turned the engine off.

"And I am grateful," Page conceded. "Would you like a drink?"

"No thanks. I had one before I left home."

Connor had arrived to pick him up that morning but he hadn't been ready. He hadn't slept well. He hadn't been able to shake off the one lingering impression from his prison visit: the image of Jacob shuffling back to his cell clutching the photograph of his brother like a child on his way to bed cuddling his favourite teddy-bear. He had over slept and when Connor had arrived he still had no shirt on, and he certainly had no time to stop and make coffee.

Coming out of the shop and walking towards the car he gave Connor a big grin and lifted the coffee cup towards her as if it were a glass of champagne and he was toasting her good health. As he got in she smiled back at him. "Better now?" she asked.

"Absolutely. Everything in the world is good again."

"But for how long?" she teased him.

"Probably until the next idiot comes along and ruins my day completely."

"Not long then!" she laughed.

"Probably not, so let's make the most of it."

As predicted Trent hadn't keep his appointment and so the search had begun. Page had suggested that they start at the lock-up and when they pulled onto the forecourt Trent's van was there.

"It doesn't seem to have moved since yesterday," Connor advised.

"Let's have a look around while we're here," Page suggested. Out of the car he walked around the van trying both of the front doors and the back doors in turn. "Locked," he confirmed. He walked up to the metal shuttering and gave it a push and a pull.

"Locked," a voice said.

Page turned to see where the voice had come from. It had come from the adjoining unit where a blue-overalled man stood wiping his hands in a rag. He was short, in his mid-forties and looked like he could never be anything other than a car mechanic. "Is it always locked at this time of the day?" Page asked.

"It's locked when nobody's here."

"I guessed that, but has anybody been here this morning?" The man started to look concerned at all the questions so Page walked over to him, showed him his warrant card and out of habit introduced himself: "DI Page."

"Oh," the man said without really looking at the ID. "I'm Andy Brown," and looking down at the oily rag he added: "I won't shake hands."

"No offence taken," Page replied as DC Connor joined the two men outside the car repair unit.

"That is Jason Trent's van over there?" she asked.

Page acknowledged her arrival with a nod of his head. "This is my colleague DC Connor."

"Hello," Brown said. "Pleased to meet you."

Page was starting to get impatient with Mr Brown's overly polite manner. "That's the introductions out of the way. Perhaps you could now answer our questions." Brown looked at the two detectives as if he needed help remembering what the questions were, so Page obliged. "I asked you whether Jason Trent had been here today, and DC Connor asked you to confirm that the van over there belongs to Mr Trent."

"Yes," Brown answered. "I mean, yes that is Jason's van, and no, he's not been here this morning. In fact I didn't see him yesterday either." Page glanced at Connor. Brown continued: "I was later getting in yesterday morning. I had to pick up a car from a regular customer, a nice old boy, and he always insists that I have a cup of tea with him before I leave with the car. Anyway, when I got here to open up, Jason's van was here but there was no sign of him."

"And you didn't see him later in the day?" Connor asked.

"No. I was here until quite late for me but I didn't see Jason at all."

"Is it unusual for Jason to leave his van here?" Page enquired.

"He never leaves it here. He comes on a morning to put whatever he needs into the van and you don't see him then until the next day."

"So other than first thing on a morning this unit is normally locked up all day?" Page asked pointing at the property next door.

"It's only locked up when nobody's here," Brown explained again before adding: "But when Sean's here it's not locked, obviously."

This time Connor gave Page a look. "And who is Sean?" she asked.

"I don't know his full name. Just know him as Sean. He shares the lock up here with Jason."

"Does he now," Connor mused. "And is Sean a landscape gardener too?"

"No. He owns a bar I think."

"Why do you say that?" It was Page's turn to lead their witness.

"He uses the lock-up to store bottles of spirits and boxes of crisps. He calls in probably twice a week. Always speaks. 'Stocking up' he says."

"And when did you last see Sean?" Page followed up.

"A few days ago now. But he'll be here soon. He'll need to stock up won't he."

"I'm not sure he will," Page confided, "but if he does turn up then perhaps you would give us a call."

"Of course." Brown looked so pleased that he had been able to help them with their enquiries. As Connor handed him her business card he studied it, then looked up at them both. "It's the very least I can do."

Back in the car Connor asked: "What did he mean - 'it's the very least I can do'?"

Page shook his head. "I don't know. He's just an obsequious little man. Desperate to please. Too desperate if you ask me."

Connor laughed. "Your good mood didn't last long. Not even an hour."

"An hour? That's good going for me!"

She stared ahead at Trent's van, seemingly abandoned in front of the locked unit. "What's going on here then?"

"Do you mean with Trent or Wilson?" Page turned to look at her. "If you ask me the two aren't necessarily linked. Wilson is using the lock-up to store his contraband and is probably selling it surreptitiously in the pub as a side-line with all the profits going to him and not the pub owner. Trent met him yesterday to warn him not to go near the lock-up because he was being followed. Wilson didn't need to know why Trent was being followed, he just needed to stay away from Midland Road, for his own good."

"So what's going on with Jason Trent then?" Connor asked, starting to sound frustrated.

"He's on the run. We need to find out what it is he's running from, and we need to find him, but he's on the run. No doubt."

The office was busy and noisy. Page's mood had gradually deteriorated as the morning had gone on. After leaving the lock-up they had gone to Trent's apartment, and then made calls on both of his girlfriends, but all to no avail. They had even called in at the Seven Stars and although it wasn't yet open they had been advised by a staff member that Sean Wilson wasn't expected in for the next few days. He had taken leave apparently.

Page pushed the empty sandwich wrapper away. "That was bloody awful. It's given me indigestion already." Without a word Connor picked it up along with her own rubbish and put it into the bin beside Page's desk. "Thanks," he managed before sitting back in his chair and running his tongue across his teeth in an attempt to remove any remaining evidence of his unsatisfactory lunch.

"What do we do now?" Connor asked.

Page clapped his hands together. "If we can't find Mr Trent then we get somebody else to find him."

"Like who?"

"Like our friends in the fourth estate."

Connor looked uncertainly at him. "Do you think Tanner will agree to holding a press conference?"

Page chuckled. "There's no way Tanner would sanction a press conference. No, we need to use the back door for this."

"Meaning?"

"Meaning our friendly journalist on the Evening Post."

"The Bristol Post," she corrected him, looking uncomfortable with what was about to happen.

Page picked up his mobile phone from the desk and scrolled through the Recents tab until he found Matt Hall's name. He looked up at Connor. "Are you staying or going?"

She got up, walked to the door and closed it before returning to her seat. "One or both of us might regret this," she cautioned.

Page hit Matt Hall's name, selected the speaker option and put the phone down on the desk so that he could speak into it and Connor could also hear the conversation. A loud ringing at first and then Matt Hall's voice: "Good afternoon DI Page. How are you?"

"I'm well. Can you talk?"

"Yes. No problem at all. Do you have something for me?"

"No. Not yet anyway, but I was hoping that you might be able to help me." Page looked at Connor, smiled and continued. "Out of interest, you didn't run with the full-moon canine-sacrifice story after all."

The journalist laughed. "No, you were right DI Page. It was a bit too Sunday Sport, and I guessed if I kept my powder dry there might be a bigger story somewhere down the line."

"And you guessed right too. That's the reason for my call Matt. There is nothing I can tell you just yet, but I was hoping you could do some groundwork for me and in return I would do my best to make sure you got the big story before the 'nationals'. No promises you understand, but best endeavours."

"OK. What was it you wanted?"

Page couldn't help himself. "Great song Matt. Do you know it?"

"Know what?"

"The song by Bob Dylan. 'What Was It You Wanted', from the Oh Mercy album."

The young man sounded confused. "No, I don't think I've ever heard it."

Connor stared at Page shaking her head. He gave her a broad grin in return and then bent towards the phone on the desk again. "Give it a listen Matt. It's a great album, one of his best." He waited a second for some acknowledgement of his recommendation at least but nothing was forthcoming so he returned to the main purpose of his call. "Look Matt, I was hoping you could run a little piece about a missing person, but not on behalf of the police. This would be from the perspective of a concerned, but anonymous friend."

There was a brief silence. "And this person, are they real, and are they really missing?"

Page smiled at Connor. The reporter seemed to have taken the bait. "Oh yes, they are real. And they really are missing."

"And you are the concerned friend who would really like to speak to them," Hall extrapolated. "So would this person by any chance be wanted in connection with the murders you are investigating?"

"They might be," Page answered tentatively. "Who knows? But right now they are wanted on suspicion of handling counterfeit spirits, but that is between you and me you understand."

There was another brief silence before Hall responded. "This story: what will it say?"

"Don't worry about that, I'll send something over to you, but essentially you have been contacted to help find the whereabouts of this person. The disappearance is completely out of character says a concerned friend and any sightings or information about them can be reported anonymously on a phone number that you will have set up. As a responsible newspaper journalist any information you do receive relating to a possible crime must of course be reported to the police. And luckily, you have my number."

"You make it sound so easy," Hall reflected.

"Nothing that a man of your ability and ambition can't cope with I'm sure."

They could hear the journalist moving around: obviously thinking through the pitfalls and upsides of the proposition and trying to weigh each of them up in his own mind. "This isn't something I can get into the newspaper," he concluded, "but it is the sort of thing we might be able to run with on the Bristol Live socials, and importantly pull it pretty quickly if we have to."

"Socials?" Page asked.

"Showing your age now DI Page," Matt Hall joked, clearly feeling a little more relaxed about things. "Socials is just a way of saying we can post the story on our Facebook page or Instagram and Twitter accounts. People tend to interact with these sort of items but they also forget about them pretty quickly, which might be a good thing for all of us."

"The ideal communication channels for the generations born with short attention spans," Page noted with a large hint of sarcasm.

"Don't knock it, it's the future," Hall opined.

"Then God help us." Page despaired of the way things were going. How everybody now seemed to only live for the moment. How people were so easily persuaded by the dishonest soundbites dished up by those in positions of power; and how nobody seemed to pay heed anymore to the valuable, empirical lessons of the past. Social media had a lot to answer for in his book. "Anyway," he sighed, "thanks for your assistance with this Matt, I won't forget it. I'll send you over some words in a minute and perhaps you could conjure together your dark arts and get the story out onto the internet later tonight if possible." He didn't wait for any confirmation of whether or not this would be possible. "Speak soon," he said and reached forward with his extended middle finger to end the call.

Connor looked no less worried than she had at the start of the call. "That's a high risk game you're playing there. Are you sure you can trust this Hall guy?"

"I reckon so. He thinks he's better than what he's doing every day for the Post. He's fed up with reporting on car crime in Staple Hill. He's waiting for the big one."

"I hope you are right, but it's not a risk I would have thought you would take."

"Not sure it is a risk in one sense. I suspect that by tomorrow morning thanks to Mr Hall we will have a number of sightings and some additional information that will be extremely useful. But I know what you mean Connor, and right now I'm not sure I care. I'm fed up with being given the run around. I just want to find Trent and get it all over with."

"But that is presuming he's our man."

"Not at all. He seems to fit the bill but a simple DNA test will tell us. If he is our man, then job done. A big pat on the back and doubles all round. If he isn't, then it's game over. Tanner will have me off the case, send me on gardening leave for a week and yet again ask me to use the time to consider whether or not retirement might really be in my best interest. Either way, chasing dead-ends to find a deranged dog-hating killer won't be my problem any more."

Connor looked concerned, both for herself and for her boss too. "Is it that bad working with me?" she asked with a large smile clearly designed to lighten the mood a little.

Page knew what she was trying to do but he could also sense her anxiety. "It's not about working with you at all. It honestly isn't. It's just me," he confirmed. "You'll be alright, you can't lose. We'll either get Trent or you will be part of the new team that will inevitably be given an increased budget, big enough in fact to DNA everyman and his dog in Bristol."

She smiled. "You are joking, aren't you."

"Only a bit," he conceded and smiled back at her. He was actually enjoying working with her. Despite her inexperience and some of her strange beliefs she made him laugh more often than she made him angry. And she was quietly effective at times. They were shaping up to be a good team. He should have told her. He'd had the chance a few seconds ago, but that just wasn't how he was wired. People had to guess what he was thinking, he rarely told them.

"What do we do now?" she asked.

Connor's default query brought Page back from his thoughts. "Not a lot we can do really. I'll get this story over to old Piers Morgan and you can make yourself look busy. Check the case files are all up to date and then I suggest we call it a day. Start again tomorrow. Maybe in a better frame of mind."

"And maybe with some credible leads," she proffered.

"Maybe," Page acknowledged. "You never know."

Father And Son

As it was most Wednesday evenings the Annexe was almost empty. Page had used the second entrance door that opens directly onto the bar area. Looking back towards the cage he could see that Frank was already at the table, waiting for him as he always was. And Page knew that he would already have bought himself a pint. Looking at the row of pumps on the back wall he tried to decide what he fancied. Usually he stuck to the same beer all evening, so the choice of the first pint was important. He plumped for the Wye Valley HPA. His reasoning was that for a pale ale it still delivered a good bitter taste and at 4% three or four pints wouldn't be giving him a thick head in the morning.

It wasn't until he approached the table that he noticed Frank wasn't alone. "Who's this then?" he asked, although he was pretty certain of the answer.

"This is Edward. My little boy. Although you're not so little now are you?"

Edward gave no response. Page smiled and nodded to him. "Hi Edward. I've not seen you for a very long time. In fact, you were still a little boy when I last saw you. Do you remember me?"

Again there was no response so Frank stepped in. "This is Jim, my friend. The friend I meet every Wednesday evening."

And then turning to look at Page he apologised. "Sorry Jim. He's a bit shy when he first meets people."

"So am I. Nothing wrong with that," Page offered trying to take the attention away from Edward.

Frank's boy had certainly grown since he'd last seen him. He had the frame of the adult he now was. He was in his late twenties, not overly tall but well built. Not somebody that could physically be pushed around that easily, but of course he was vulnerable in other ways. His learning disabilities had never been that severe but they had always been very evident. As a young child the round-lensed, wire-framed glasses that Frank had chosen for him had done nothing to help his cause; and then as he got older he gradually got left behind: in the classroom, on the sports field and by those he thought were his friends. His mother had died days after he was born and Frank had devoted his whole life to bringing him up as best he could. It hadn't been easy. The help that he really needed had never materialised, either due to a lack of funding or limited resources, so Frank had done it alone. Page had always marvelled at this dedication, at such unconditional love, knowing full well that it was something he himself was wholly incapable of. And yet despite all of this it was something they rarely spoke about. Perhaps because they were two men of a certain age who preferred to avoid talking about their feelings, or perhaps because Wednesday nights were crib-night where they could both forget their day-to-day worries and talk about something else instead.

Page held his beer up to the light. It looked as good as it tasted. He took another sip and put the glass down on the small circular table that they were all sat around. "You had a busy week then Frank?"

"Not really. Can't even remember what I have been doing." The two friends laughed. "Oh yes, I had to go to the doctors for a blood test on Monday. Routine, nothing to worry about, but that took most of the morning. You get there for a 10:30 appointment and the nurse doesn't call you in until 11:00. By the time you're done and got back home it's lunchtime."

"That's why I don't bother going," Page agreed. "You wait around for hours surrounded by people that are coughing or sneezing and you come out more infectious than when you went in."

"And here ends the informed critique of the National Health Service's General Practitioner provision," Frank smirked, raising his glass in a mock salute.

"My God Frank, don't we sound like a couple of grumpy old men."

"No Jim, we are a couple of grumpy old men." They smiled at each other and clinked their glasses together.

"And long may it continue," Page toasted.

Frank placed his glass carefully onto the beermat. "How about you Jim, you had a busy week?"

"It's certainly been interesting. I was in prison yesterday morning in Lincoln, but they let me out for good behaviour."

"Work related though," Frank checked.

"Yes," Page confirmed, and then glancing towards Edward, and with a little nod of the head, he said: "I'll explain another time." Frank nodded back to indicate he understood. "And how about you Edward. You had a busy week?" The young man shook his head.

"You've been out for your walks haven't you," his father reminded him, seemingly encouraging him to engage with the conversation. "Tell Jim about your walks."

He scowled at his father. "I'm not a child and I'm not stupid. I can talk you know. I listen first, then I speak if I want to."

"Alright Edward, calm down. I was only trying to involve you in things."

Frank was starting to raise his voice and Page was feeling uncomfortable so he stepped in. "It seems very wise to me. Always better to listen first rather than go jumping in and make yourself look like a fool. That's apparently why God gave us two ears and only one mouth."

Edward was now looking directly at Page. "Do you believe in God Jim?"

It was a question he hadn't been expecting, but one that he could easily answer. "No I don't. I don't believe in God. Do you?"

"No, not in a God that looks after us but there are people like him, people with powers that hurt us."

"Do you mean people in power or people with special powers?" Page asked. It seemed an important distinction although he wasn't sure Edward would understand the nuance.

"People with special powers who make people do things, bad things."

Frank was looking awkwardly at his son but Page was intrigued. "What sort of people?"

"Wizards, witches, devils and angels."

"That's enough now," Frank intervened. "Jim doesn't need to hear this nonsense."

"It's not nonsense," Edward hissed at his father.

"It's alright," Page reassured them both. "I'm interested to listen and learn. How do these people influence us then?"

But Edward had already been dissuaded. He was now looking down at the floor and snarled: "It's not important. You can laugh like all the others but I'm not an idiot."

"Nobody said you were, and nobody's laughing at you," his father tried to reassure him, "but these games you play upstairs, they aren't real Edward, these devils and angels don't exist."

"That's what you think, but you are wrong."

"Edward," Frank implored stretching out his hand but his son slapped it away so hard that it knocked the empty beer glass over on the table with a loud clunk.

Page leant forward and stopped the glass rolling onto the floor. "OK, let's all calm down. No harm's done. Frank why don't you go and get another round in."

Edward was on his feet. "I'm going. I'm going for a walk, and then I'm going home."

Page, his arm under the table, gave Frank's knee a supportive squeeze. His friend looked back at him and then up at his son. "Have you got your keys?" Edward held them aloft almost sarcastically and jingled them together. "Go steady then," his father said in a quiet voice. "I won't be too late home."

With a pint in each hand and the peace offering of two packets of crisps hanging from his clenched teeth Frank reappeared at the table. He let the crisps drop. "I'm sorry about that," he said before he had even sat down again. "Sorry that you had to hear all of that."

"Not a problem mate. Are you alright?"

Frank took a large gulp of his drink, put the glass down and stared into the beer as if he were trying to see what the future might hold. Without looking up he confided: "Things haven't been good these last few years if I'm honest. I'm getting older and Edward is getting more difficult. We've stopped communicating properly. Hardly see each other. He's either up in his room with his dungeon and dragons games or whatever they are, or out walking the streets on his own."

"Hey," Page called out, and Frank lifted his head to look at him. "That all sounds quite normal. Edward isn't a kid anymore. I know you worry about him, he needs extra support sometimes, but he can look after himself. He's a big boy and he's nobody's fool." Frank nodded as if he knew all of this. Page went on: "A lot of kids his age have left home, only see their parents every now and then and still manage to fall out. You two are living in each other's pockets and are bound to have words from time to time. When did fathers and sons ever see eye to eye?"

Frank sighed. "You're right, but I'm tired. Tired of the constant confrontation. It didn't use to be like that."

Page gave him a reassuring smile. "No, I'm sure it didn't, but as we just discussed, it is nothing more complicated than the fact that you are getting older and Edward is growing up.

He doesn't need you in the same way as when he was a child. You have to try and accept that, but it's hard I know."

Frank looked back down at his beer. "I know, but it's not just that Jim. I'm worried about what will happen to him once I'm gone. I'm 76 now, nearly 77, and who knows how long I've got left, but there is no way he could live and cope on his own. No way."

Page didn't respond at first. He stared at his friend who was undoubtedly looking older and less well than he'd witnessed before. And then he noticed that Frank was looking at him. Looking at him for an answer. An answer that wasn't the one he already knew and didn't much like. Honesty seemed the best policy. "Frank, I do think you are right to be thinking about this but you have to face up to some practicalities. You and Edward both need to know that things will be alright if anything happens to you. But that's not something you can sort out on your own. You need help with thinking these things through and with making some plans, even if it is too early to be making firm decisions just yet."

"And where does this help come from?"

"Ultimately from Adult Social Services." These words brought Page up sharp and he realised he risked going into 'work mode': dispensing dispassionate advice in a caring voice that managed to hide the likelihood that the third party organisation being discussed would be of no practical help whatsoever. Frank deserved more. "Do you have a social worker contact already?"

Frank pulled a face that clearly said 'what do you think?'

"Would it help if I spoke to a colleague in the Family Liaison team and got a name for someone in the council that you could contact. Somebody that our team rates and who will actually give you a call back and talk things through?"

"And what would we talk about?"

"You could just talk about how you are feeling if you want to; or you could talk about options for finding Edward somewhere appropriate to live, which he might actually want to think about sooner rather than later. There are lots of different options for supported living these days you know. Or you could just talk about the chances of Roger Waters and David Gilmour patching up their differences and making a new Pink Floyd concept album based on one of the plays from a Morecambe and Wise Christmas Special."

Frank looked at him and burst out laughing. "You don't change Jim, do you!" The two friends sat in silence for a few seconds, but it was a comfortable silence. "Thanks. It might be helpful to talk to somebody. Would you do that for me?"

"Of course I will. That's what friends are for."

"Thanks, and sorry again if I ruined your evening."

"Don't be stupid, of course you didn't ruin my evening. It was honestly really good to see Edward again. If you think it might help I would be more than pleased to come round one evening and spend some time with the both of you. Maybe we could even play dungarees and drag queens. Is that what it's called?"

Frank laughed again. "That would be good." He picked up his glass and downed what was left of the pint.

"Do you want another one?" Page asked.

"No thanks. I'm going to make a move now. Get in before Edward comes back. Is that alright?"

"Absolutely. I think I'll stay and have another one but I'll see you in here next Wednesday all being well."

Frank got to his feet. "Great. Look forward to it. Perhaps we can discuss that new Pink Floyd album?"

"Definitely. Take care." Page watched Frank walk slowly to the door and disappear into the night. He didn't turn and look back at all. Had he done so he would have seen his friend smiling to himself, already starting to think of suitable album titles for this most unlikely of rock reunions. Frank was right: Page never changed.

Night Comes On

It was hardly home sweet home. It was lacking all creature comforts. There were no windows, no form of heating and he was starting to feel the cold, but that was the way it was going to be. There was nowhere else for him to go. He would wait for the last light of the day to dim to darkness before he grabbed a few hours sleep. And then tomorrow morning he would make the final preparations and steel himself for his next show of strength that he would execute later that evening. He still wasn't sure in his own mind whether what he was doing was meting out justice or passing judgement. He wasn't even sure whether or not there was a difference. And if there were, did it really matter?

But for now, as the night came on, he tried to make himself as comfortable as he possibly could. He put another hessian sack behind his back, wriggled it into position, let his weight rest against the leg of the workbench and pulled the old dust sheet up under his chin. The smell of oil and rotten grass from the garden machinery weren't the bed fellows he would have chosen, but this was the company he would now be keeping. For the foreseeable future at least.

Turn Of The Cards

She was in the kitchen area making coffee for herself and DI Page. She was deliberately not rushing, running everything through in her mind one last time.

She had spent most of the previous evening trying to work out what she was going to say. How she was going to explain it to him. At first of course she had wondered whether she needed to tell him at all. She knew what he would say: that it was just another one of her 'bonkers ideas'. But it wasn't. She was sure of that now. She had been through it over and over, and each time she had been more persuaded. But convincing Page might be something else altogether.

The drive into the office had been completed in near silence. The usual greetings when he had first got into the car but then not much else after that. Luckily he seemed to have been preoccupied too and hadn't employed his standard practice of filling long silences with questions. Questions about her activities the night before, or worse still, questions about songs or albums she had never heard by bands she had often never even heard of. She might be used to these questions by now but she still couldn't answer them. This morning's long silence had seemed to suit them both.

She gently pushed his office door open with her foot. In her hands she was carrying a tray with two mugs of coffee and some chocolate biscuits that she had brought with her from home. He looked up and cleared a space at the front of his desk so that she could put the tray down. His eyes lit up when he saw the biscuits. He seemed to be a bit more like his normal self. "Good news," he announced, before she could even move his mug from the tray to the coaster waiting in front of him. "Forgot to tell you earlier, I heard from our friend Mr Hall. The article went up late last night and we've had five sightings of Jason Trent already. Three around the Bristol area, one from South Wales and another from Berwick-upon-Tweed. If we wait an hour or so we should have some more. We can then do a sweep of the local ones ourselves and review what to do with the others once we've sorted out the wheat from the chaff." He certainly had perked up.

She put the plate of biscuits onto his desk. "Thought these might help."

"Well done Connor. There's not much in life that can't be sorted by a milk chocolate Digestive." He reached over and took a couple of the biscuits before adding: "But today feels like a two-Digestive day already." He bit into the first biscuit and a shower of crumbs found their way onto the desk and into his lap.

"To be honest, the biscuits come with an ulterior motive," she admitted.

"Oh yes. What's that then?"

"There's something I need to tell you and I don't want you interrupting me."

Page caught his breath. "Is everything OK?"

"Yes. It's nothing like that. Nothing personal, but it's important."

"About the case?" he queried.

"Yes. About the case."

"OK. I'll eat my biscuit then and keep quiet."

Connor pulled the thin strap of her handbag over her head and put the small leather satchel onto the floor beside her chair. 'Start at the beginning' she reminded herself, clasping her hands together. She looked at Page, took a deep breath and started. "Last night I went to my relaxation class and after we'd finished I stayed behind and had a drink with the course leader. She's called Sky." Connor saw Page move in his chair and she shot him a glance that said: 'I know, stupid name, but don't say anything.' He took a bite from what was left of his first biscuit. She carried on. "Sky knows what I do for a living and I must have told her that I was working this case, anyway, she said to me that some of her even more alternative friends, my words not hers, had been reading about the murders online and had told her a bit about how the bodies had been left. She also knew about the dogs."

Page's mobile phone started to ring on the desk. He picked it up, checked the caller-ID and rejected it. "Sorry," he said. "It was Matt Hall. I'll call him back in a minute."

Connor nodded to accept the apology. It wasn't Page's fault after all. "So, obviously, I just played dumb and then she asked me whether or not we'd made a link between the murders and the Tarot."

"The Tarot?" Page clearly couldn't help himself.

"You know about the Tarot?" she asked him.

"I know of Tarot cards but I know nothing about them."

"OK. I've been doing some research. Basically it's a pack of cards. The precursor to the packs we use today. But in a Tarot deck there are 78 cards, each featuring a unique picture. The classic deck is the 1909 Rider Waite version with illustrations by Pamela Colman Smith. The main pack is divided into four suits and there are fourteen cards in each suit: Ace through to ten and then Page, Knight, Queen and King. The four suits are Pentacles, Cups, Wands and Swords."

Page couldn't help himself. "The King and the Queen of Swords, that's where it comes from then." He was suddenly looking interested.

"Where what comes from?"

"The lyric from Bob Dylan's Changing of the Guards."

Another of his music-based connections she mused, but this one certainly had some relevance to the matter they were discussing. "Indeed," she conceded, knowing now at least that he was still listening. "But in addition to these four suits there are another twenty-two cards known as the Major Arcana. Think of them as trump cards. They are numbered 1 to 21 with a final single card known as The Fool. We know it nowadays as the Joker in the pack." She reached down, opened her handbag and withdrew a white envelope. Making space on the desktop she then took out the twenty-two cards from a Rider Waite deck that Sky had let her borrow the night before and started to carefully place them down in order starting with number one and naming each in turn: "The Magician, The High Priestess, The Empress, The Emperor, The Hierophant…"

"Bloody hell Connor, what are you going to do - read my fortune?"

She was surprised it had taken him this long to mock her, but she was nearly there. "Let me finish," she asked of him, placing the remaining cards down without comment so that there were now two rows, each of eleven cards, facing her. "Please, indulge me. Come round to this side of the desk."

Page stood up and a host of golden crumbs fell to the floor from the front of his trousers. He wiped the rest away as he walked around the desk to join her. "So what do we have here?"

She pointed to the first card in the second row and tapped it with her index finger. "The Hanged Man," she clarified and stood back a little as Page leaned forward to take a closer look at the card. Hanging upside down by one leg from the branch of a tree was a man, with what appeared to be a halo around the back of his head. "Excuse me," she said as she reached across him, tapping on the card in the middle of the same row. "The Star," she confirmed. This card showed a naked woman, kneeling by a pool. In each hand she held a water jug. Above her head was a large yellow star that could be construed as a halo. Surrounding it were a number of smaller, white stars. Seven stars in fact.

Page turned back to face her. "This can't be for real," he said, looking quite shaken.

"And the next one," she instructed him.

He looked back at the desk and moved his eyes onto the card immediately to the right of The Star. "Shit," was all he managed to say. The next card was The Moon, depicting at the top in the centre a large circular yellow moon with a caricature crescent face and below it, with their heads raised together as one, were two dogs.

"Now tell me I'm imaging it," she challenged him, not quite sure what it was she really wanted to hear him say.

But he said nothing. He stood there motionless looking at the cards. He shook his head, then perhaps conscious of the silence he confessed: "I don't know what to say. For once, I just don't know what to say."

"So you don't think I am seeing things then. Reading too much into it all?" she asked him.

"Sadly not. I fear you are right. Every picture tells a story Connor, and this story is one of the strangest I've ever come across." He walked back around the desk and plonked himself into his chair. "Perhaps there is black magic afoot after all, although I don't see Jason Trent as some occult magician do you?"

"No. There were no signs of anything like that I could see when I was at his place the other day, but perhaps we need to take another closer look."

"Perhaps we do," Page pondered aloud. He leaned forward, picked up the last biscuit from the plate and took a big bite. Almost immediately his mobile rang.

"That'll be Matt Hall chasing you again," she surmised.

He picked it up, glanced at the name on the screen and shook his head. "It's not," he corrected her with a mouth full of biscuit, before swiping to accept the call, swallowing hard to empty his mouth and offering his usual greeting: "Page." She watched as he frowned. He was either listening intently or unable to get a word in. "Alright, calm down. Tell me again." He stood up and went to the window, his back to her. "There could be lots of reasons," he flustered into the phone and started pacing up and down. "Look, don't panic. Stay where you are and I'll come over now." He ended the call, turned around and tossed his phone onto a pile of paperwork on the desk.

"Everything aright?" she asked, knowing full well it was a stupid question.

"Right now I could do with this like a hole in the head," he complained, taking his jacket off the back of the chair. "Can you give me a lift?"

"Of course. Where are we going?"

"Anywhere around here will do," Page suggested.

They had turned off the Gloucester Road and were now approaching a small crossroads of sorts. Page didn't live too far away but even to him the narrow streets and bay-windowed Victorian houses of Bishopston all looked the same.

As they'd left the office he had explained to Connor that the call was from his friend Frank and that he was worried because his son hadn't come home last night. He'd explained to her that although Edward was nearly thirty years old he had some learning difficulties and that was why Frank was so concerned. He hadn't told her that he had been with the both of them the previous evening.

Connor found a space to park the car and before she turned the engine off she asked: "Do you want me to wait here or come back and pick you up later?"

"Don't be silly, you can come in with me. It might even be a help."

Frank's house was on a corner. Not actually the corner plot but the first house after it. It had a very small front garden and the rear garden wasn't much bigger, but the property backed onto Horfield Common with its grassed open expanse, children's play area, tennis courts and small cafe. As they stepped from the pavement up onto the garden pathway the front door opened. "Thanks for coming Jim. I didn't know what to do."

Page waited until they were inside and the door was shut behind them before he introduced Connor. "Frank, this is my colleague DC Connor. She's also my chauffeuse."

Connor smiled. "Hello Frank. Please call me Louise."

The old man led them into the small living room. It was clean enough but a bit cluttered: a brown leather three piece suite, a large coffee table with empty mugs on it, a tall wooden plant stand bearing a plant that had seen better days and on the floor were various piles of newspapers and magazines. "Please sit down." Frank had already lowered himself into one of the armchairs.

Page sat down on the end of the settee closest to his friend and Connor took the remaining chair. Page sat forward. "When did you notice that Edward wasn't here?" he asked, trying hard to sound like a friend and not a detective.

"After I left you I came straight home."

Page noticed Connor react. "Crib night," he reminded her, "Wednesday nights are crib night." She nodded and he turned back to his friend. "Carry on Frank."

"When I got home he wasn't here, but there's nothing unusual about that these days. I waited up an hour or so and then went to bed and read for a while. I normally hear him come in, the early hours sometimes, but last night I must have fallen asleep. And then this morning when I called him for breakfast there was no reply. And that is unusual. So I went up and knocked on his door, and nothing. No answer, so I knocked again. Still no answer, and then I opened the door and he wasn't there."

"And had the bed been slept in?" Page asked.

"No, It didn't look like it to me."

"So you are thinking that he wasn't here at all last night."

"Yes."

"And you don't think it's the case that he just got up early this morning, made his bed and went out?"

"No. He's never done that."

Page looked at his friend, waiting for him to make eye contact so that he could offer a reassuring nod or smile but Frank had his eyes screwed tightly shut. "Frank, I'm sorry about all the questions but they are important." Frank dropped his head onto his chest. "Is there anything missing from his room?" Page asked.

Frank looked up and opened his eyes. "I don't know. I haven't checked," and then with a worried look on his face he queried: "Should I have done?"

"Frank, don't worry, you've done the right thing," Page tried to reassure him, before giving Connor a subtle nod, a heads up that he was going to bring her into the conversation. "Louise has got a teenage son. She knows what sort of things they get up to far better than you and I. How about she pops up and has a look at his room and I'll make us a cup of tea."

"That sounds like a good idea. Can I stay here? I'm a bit wobbly on my legs this morning."

"Of course you can," Page confirmed, standing up and patting his friend on the shoulder.

Connor stood up too. "Which is Edward's room?" she enquired.

"Top of the stairs, first on the left," Frank advised.

At the bottom of the stairs Page gave Connor a grateful smile. "Thanks for doing this. He's a good friend."

"No problem."

"Tea or coffee?" he checked as he walked along the hall towards the kitchen.

"Tea for me," she confirmed, halfway up the stairs.

He had put the kettle on, taken three mugs from the wooden mug-tree next to the microwave and was still looking through the cupboards to find where Frank kept the tea and coffee when Connor appeared in the kitchen doorway.

"You need to come and see this," was all she said.

They walked back to the foot of the stairs and Page furtively peered into the living room. Maybe not asleep but Frank was resting: eyes shut, head back, mouth open.

Once on the landing Connor stood outside the open door to Edward's bedroom. "After you," she insisted.

Page went in. His eyes were immediately drawn to the large window on the right. Beneath the window was Edward's bed, exactly as Frank had described it, properly made and evidently unslept in. Next to the headboard on the small wall behind the door was a shelf unit. The top shelf was full of miniature fantasy models, dragons, wizards and monsters, all painted and carefully arranged among groups of gnarled trees and the ruined facades of buildings. The next couple of shelves housed his books and on the bottom shelf various board games were precariously stacked: Game of Thrones and Lord of the Rings role play games, some darker looking board games with strange names that he didn't recognise like Scythe and Skyrim, as well as the old familiar favourites of Monopoly and Risk. The long wall at the other end of the bed was taken up with fitted wardrobes. He slid open one of the doors. "Have you checked in here?"

"Not yet." Connor was still on the landing watching him through the doorway.

"We'll need to have a quick look in a minute," he said turning to his left. Here there was a desk and a chair and above them on the wall a large pinboard had been affixed. Page stood stock still. Instead of the random collection of letters, newspaper clippings and photographs that usually adorn such boards, this one had been carefully curated. There was nothing else on the board apart from the shape of a large capital letter T that had been formed using five colourful cards. Five colourful cards that Page had never seen in his life before until earlier that morning, and here they were again. "This is a joke isn't it. A sick joke," he stammered. "We've been set up."

Connor came into the room and stood by his side. "I didn't put them there if that's what you're suggesting."

"That's not what I meant, but this is unbelievable. Last night I was out with Frank, and I briefly met Edward for the first time in years. You were out as well and somebody puts the idea of Tarot cards into your head. And then today Edward goes missing and low and behold we find Tarot cards on his wall."

"So it's my fault, all of this, is it?" She was starting to sound angry.

"Of course it isn't, but you have to admit it's a bloody strange coincidence."

Neither of them spoke for a few moments but then Connor broke the silence. "I'm sorry for getting mad. I don't like this anymore than you do." Page acknowledged the apology and hesitantly she continued. "You are right, we are faced with deciding between two scenarios both of which on face value are difficult to countenance. Either we are being manipulated, somebody has fed us the Tarot spiel and then kidnapped and framed Edward, or…"

Page interrupted her. "Or it is just that: a bloody big coincidence that we end up here like this and Edward is our killer."

She looked at him, her face reddening. "Sir, neither scenario is straight forward but from an objective standpoint, if I may say so, we really need to consider the more plausible explanation first, however unpalatable that might be."

Page stepped nearer the pinboard and had a closer look at the arrangement. The top of the letter T, the horizontal arm, was made up from the three cards that seemed to depict their crime scenes: the Star, the Hanged Man and the Moon. The vertical stem extended down from the Hanged Man and was completed with two more cards: The Fool and Death. The longer he stared at the cards the clearer it became that Connor had a point. As much as he personally didn't want to believe that Edward was capable of such things, that was the starting point. It had to be. After all, that was what the evidence was suggesting, even though at this stage it was purely circumstantial.

"What are you thinking?" she asked, still sounding nervous.

"I'm thinking you are right that we have to start with the assumption that things here are actually as they seem, but I'm hoping you are wrong and that this is all an elaborate hoax to distract us from the truth."

"So I'm forgiven?"

"For now." Page forced a smile for her but he didn't feel much like smiling. "Probably best that we don't mention any of this this to Frank. Do you agree?"

"Agreed."

"Right then, let's get back downstairs."

Page was first into the sitting room, a hot drink in both hands. He put them onto the coffee table and swapped the empty mug in front of Frank for one of the freshly made teas. Connor brought her own drink with her and returned to the chair she had previously sat in. She looked over at Frank. "I've had a look at Edward's room and it all looks very tidy. It doesn't look like anybody went through his clothes snatching things in a hurry, and that's a good sign."

"When we see this," Page picked up the narrative, "it normally means that the person who has gone missing hasn't planned to stay away long. They either intended to be away for only one night, or often they didn't intend to stay out at all but became distracted, ended up at a friends or somewhere else where there was no public transport home at that time of the night."

Connor waited a second and then followed up with the inevitable question. "Frank, is there anywhere you can think of that Edward might have gone? Any friends he meets or any places he likes to go?"

He shook his head. "No. I'm not aware of any friends that he sees. He's quite a loner. He goes out every day for walks, for hours sometimes, but I've always had the impression he's walking around, not going to any specific location."

Page knew they needed somewhere to start but didn't want to press his friend too hard. "So there's nowhere you've taken him that he might remember? Nowhere you can think of that he used to like going as a child?"

"No," Frank repeated, staring absently out into the hallway. "We never really went away anywhere. We were stay at home kind of people, if you know what I mean." He turned to look at Page and explained. "We didn't really need to go away. I had the allotment along the road, used to grow some veg and flowers up there and Edward could run around until his heart was content. The old potting shed was his den and when he wasn't racing about outside he would sit in there and read and whatnot. Door closed, happy in his own little world."

"The good times," Page reflected out loud, as much for Connor's benefit as Frank's. "Have you still got the allotment?" he asked.

"Good God no. Gave that up a long time ago. I've not been up there for years."

"And how about Edward, has he ever mentioned that he's been back there?"

"No. Never."

Page's mug made a brittle scraping sound as he put it down onto the tile-topped coffee table. "I think we've got enough to be going on with Frank. If you let us know where your allotment was we'll have a look on our way back to the station. If there's no sign of him there then when we get back I will raise a formal Missing Person alert. The sooner we do that the more chance we have of finding him safe and well. And try not to worry. I know it's easy for me to say, but trust me, most missing people are found very quickly."

Frank didn't look convinced but Page hadn't expected him to. "Thanks Jim. Hope I'm not making a fuss about nothing."

"Not at all. You've done the right thing. I'll call you later. If Edward gets in touch or anything happens then let me know straight away." Page got to his feet and Connor followed his lead. "Louise will take these dirty mugs through to the kitchen for you and you can tell me where we might find this old allotment of yours."

The allotments themselves were only a couple of hundred yards from Frank's house but the entrance was located a few streets away. After a longer walk than they had expected they reached the gap in the row of houses. At the end of the short lane was a new-looking five bar gate that afforded vehicular access to the site. It was padlocked shut. Next to it however, the similarly constructed but smaller pedestrian gate was only secured by a metal throw over loop on the top. Once on the site they were met with rows of neatly tended garden plots, some covered in green netting, some peppered with plastic tunnel cloches and some sporting full sized glass greenhouses.

They made their way to the far end of the gardens where Frank had directed them. Here there was a single strip of four allotments that no longer seemed to be used. They were tight up to the hedge and at one end two of the allotment plots also found themselves beneath the overhanging canopy of a large tree. Not much would grow in these dark and damp conditions. At the other end was an old shed. It was in poor condition, the roof needed re-felting and the side panels a lick of wood preserver, but it wasn't in danger of falling down. The door was shut but it wasn't locked. The hasp was resting outwards at 90° and hanging from the loop on the door frame was a shiny new combination padlock.

Page noticed it immediately. "Look at the lock," he whispered to Connor. Slowly he walked towards the shed and beckoned for her to follow him. "Stay on my outside," he mouthed, reckoning that two abreast they had a better chance of foiling any escape attempt. When they were both in position they stood still, listening for any activity within, but nothing could be heard. "Edward, are you in there? It's Jim." Nothing. "I was with you and your dad last night. He's very worried about you. Is everything OK?" Still nothing. "I'm going to open the door, is that alright?" He waited and then looked at Connor. He gave her a nod and together they walked the last few feet to the shed door. "I'm coming in," he advised, his tone now slightly more authoritative. He reached for the metal hasp and pulled it forcefully towards himself. The door stuck at first but then swung open. There was nobody there. He was relieved.

"Somebody's been here," Connor noted.

"It certainly looks like it." Page stepped into the shed. On the back wall was an old work bench and hanging on the wall above it was an early model Flymo rotary lawn mower, its once bright shiny orange plastic cover now faded to a mottled dirty cream colour. Around it on the wall were various gardening tools, all of their wooden handles cracked by weather and time and the metal components themselves dirty or rusty due to neglect. The floor under the workbench was stained with oil, and in the very corner were two silver dog bowls. The floor in front of the bench had been covered with fertiliser bags and a large dust sheet was screwed up by the door. It was however, the half full bottle of Coke, the chocolate wrappers and discarded crisp packets that both detectives had first spotted. Coming out of the shed Page gave Connor a look that barely hid his disappointment. They were too late. So close and yet so far. "Whoever it was here is long gone and they're not coming back here anytime soon," he bemoaned.

"Otherwise they would have locked the door," Connor concluded.

"Exactly," Page agreed. "They are done here and we will have to start looking somewhere else."

"Do you think it was Edward that was here?" she asked.

"Almost certainly, but there's nothing here to help us discover where he might have gone and that's why we need to make this official now." Connor nodded in agreement but the look she gave him left some room for doubt. "Is something wrong?" he probed. "We are agreed aren't we?"

"Yes. Yes, of course. It's just that… Well, just to be absolutely clear, what is it we will be making official? A MISPER case?"

Page let out a long breath. He knew what the question was that she was really asking and why she was asking it. "In my heart I wish it was just a MISPER enquiry, I really do, but I don't think it is. My head tells me we've got a manhunt on our hands Connor." Page thought she looked relieved, in the sense that she now knew where she stood and what they had to do. "Agreed?," he asked again for the avoidance of all doubt.

"Yes," she confirmed. "I'll call it in now and get SOCO down here. And then we'd better secure the scene ready for their arrival."

Page gave her a nod. He didn't think she needed his permission or approval but he needed to say something. "Well done," he said, and then he got to what he really wanted to say. "Thank you."

Angels

He was conscious of the growing restlessness in the room outside. The full team was assembled and waiting for his briefing. He listened as one or two familiar voices could be heard above the others, talking nonsense but eliciting loud guffaws and mock disagreement. He smiled. It was this camaraderie that made the job worthwhile.

"Are you ready?" Connor was in the doorway.

"On my way." He slipped his jacket on and went out into the large office. He walked to the wall where the incident board had been positioned. The noise level dropped but still a few people were talking and laughing. He waited for a couple more seconds and then raised his voice: "OK you horrible lot - listen up." The room fell silent. "After weeks of endless enquiries and multiple false starts there have been some significant developments over the last two days." He turned and knocked on the large whiteboard where the two photographs had been placed, pointing to the one closest to him. "This gentleman here is one Jason Trent. Some of you will recognise him as the witness that called in the first murder. He has also been seen visiting the scene of our second murder. He had agreed to provide a DNA sample to eliminate himself from our enquiries but he failed to attend the pre-arranged appointment. It seems he is friendly with the manager of the Seven Stars and at the very least they are both involved in some dodgy scam involving knock-off booze. Mr Trent has gone missing and the possibility still exists that he is our man."

"But you don't believe that, do you," a voice from the back of the room called out.

Page couldn't see who it was but answered anyway. "No, I don't believe it but I don't want to completely ignore the possibility either. DC Connor has a list of sightings of Jason Trent to hand out at the end of this meeting and it is still a priority that we find him as quickly as we can." Page paused. He watched the reactions and waited for the inevitable dissent. "Look, I fully understand that it seems counter intuitive for a murder enquiry to spend time looking for somebody that probably didn't commit the murder, but we simply cannot be seen to not follow this up."

"Eggs in one basket," Anna Brain announced. Everyone in the room turned to look at her. "We can't afford to put all our eggs into one basket. If our prime suspect turns out to be a dud and this guy gets away then we will all look like a bunch of clowns."

For once Page was pleased with the interruption. "Thank you DS Brain. And as the ringmaster it will be me that gets fired from the cannon not you lot." From the corner of the room someone started chanting the Entry of the Gladiators, the tune synonymous with clowns and the circus. Others joined in amid general laughter. Page let the levity go for a while and then restored order. "OK," he called out. He pointed to the second picture on the board. "This is Edward Slater. He might not look it but he is a vulnerable adult and whatever happens I want you to remember that." Again he paused to make sure that this message had been understood by all. "Edward is also missing as of last night, and as of this morning he is now our prime suspect."

"Is there any evidence on which to base this assertion?"

Once more it was DS Brain. It was a fair question. Page looked across at Connor and then back at the sea of faces waiting for an answer. "Yes, there is compelling circumstantial evidence that infers Edward Slater is linked to our murders but at this stage we do not have any direct evidence." He knew that he would need to elaborate further. And he knew that there wasn't anybody in the room who would, even for the slightest moment, believe that he was convinced by the suggestion of any connection to the occult. And normally of course, he wouldn't be. He looked at Connor for help.

She stood up and cleared her throat. "When we searched Edward's room this morning we found a display of Tarot cards that accurately revealed details of each of our murder scenes."

"But those details have been doing the rounds for nearly a week now. That doesn't prove much." This time it wasn't DS Brain.

"OK, that's enough," Page was back on his feet. "Don't shoot the messenger, let DC Connor finish. Trust me, we haven't jumped to this conclusion based solely on some cards from a fortune telling pack. And while we're at it, any connection with these Tarot cards goes no further. It stays in this room. Understood?" The silence suggested that it was understood.

Connor waited for Page to sit down and then continued. "In addition to the cards we managed to gain access to an old allotment shed not far from Edward's home. This shed once belonged to his father. Inside was evidence of somebody having slept there within the last few days. Two dog bowls were also in the shed, and they had recently been used. We suspect tests will reveal that they were used to poison the two dogs found at the Full Moon."

"Thank you DC Connor." Page walked back to the white board. "From speaking to his father, Edward has no alibis for the nights our murders took place. He is often out and about until the early hours. We are not aware he has any specific contacts in town but our three crime scenes are all relatively close together and so it would make sense to focus our initial searches around the Old City area. Any questions?" He didn't expect any and there was none. "OK. Get to it."

The murmur of voices grew louder as team members commented to each other on what they had just heard. Colleagues gathered around DC Connor to pick up copies of the intelligence on Jason Trent and the pictures of both wanted men. After a short while the room emptied leaving just its usual occupants and soon the normal background sounds of people being quietly busy were reestablished. Back in his office Page could hear himself think again, and he had a lot to think about.

"A penny for them." Connor startled him. "Sorry. You seemed miles away."

"Yes I was. I'm worried about Frank. Worried whether or not I should tell him what's really going on."

Connor came in and sat down. "I'm not sure we do know what's going on, do we?" Page didn't respond. "You said yourself in the briefing just now that we need to keep an open mind. Suspicions are much more dangerous than facts. I think I'd wait before I said anything else to him."

"But I don't like the thought of lying."

"You're not. You are doing as you promised: mobilising a search for Edward. If you want to be pedantic then you are omitting to tell him everything, but you are not telling him anything untruthful."

"Sounds more like sophistry than pedantry if you ask me."

"I don't know about that, but I do know that not telling him right now would be the kindest thing. The kind of thing that a good friend would do."

Page nodded. "I suppose so, but it still doesn't feel right."

"It's for the best, it really is." She gave him a smile.

He smiled back at her. "For the greater good, as our colleagues in Sandford would say," but the allusion clearly wasn't understood.

On arrival they were told to park on the pavement. A space seemed to have been kept for them. Outside the car, all around them, was pandemonium. A line of uniformed officers was standing in front of a billowing blue and white Police Incident tape as a large crowd jostled to get as close to the front as possible. Already at the front of course were a couple of press photographers taking pictures of everything and anything in the hope that something would be of relevance and of use to them later on. Immediately behind the cordon he could see what looked like an Armed Response Unit, the tailgates of their vehicles open in the air as they retrieved their guns and ammunition from the onboard safe and made the final fitting adjustments to their body armour. Page was anxious about the situation but still a little surprised to see armed back-up in place already.

He had been at his desk when PC Sharma rushed into his office without knocking. That was the first sign that something was wrong. "There's an ongoing incident at Castle Park," he reported breathlessly. "Witnesses say there's a man walking around the church building with a bladed weapon, and that he seems agitated." The look Page had given him must have said 'So what?' because Sharma didn't wait for a spoken response and qualified his initial statement with: "The first uniform on the scene recognised him from the briefing photo as Edward Slater." Page had grabbed his jacket and shouted over at Connor. Together they had left Bridewell not knowing what awaited them at Castle Park.

Stepping out of the car they were ushered through the protective line. As he stooped under the tape a voice shouted out: "DI Page - can you tell us what is happening here?" Page turned and spotted a young man holding a digital voice recorder over the heads of the people in front of him. "Matt Hall, Bristol Post," he helpfully clarified.

Page made brief eye contact, enough of an acknowledgment for the journalist to know that he had been seen, but other than that he offered no response at all. He strode to the uniformed officer that had been put in charge of the site. "DI Page and DC Connor," he announced. He waited for their names to be added to the log and then in a loud voice he demanded: "Who's in charge of firearms then?"

"That'll be me." Page turned around and stood directly in front of him was a tall figure clad in dark blue combat overalls with his Heckler and Koch sub machine gun slung across his chest. His features were hidden by a balaclava and under his arm was the kevlar helmet waiting to be put on. "DI Page I presume. I won't shake your hand, no offence."

"None taken."

"Inspector Law. Harry Law. How do you want to play this?"

Page took a few steps away from the people milling around. "To be honest, I would rather you weren't here. In fact I don't really know why you are here."

"Reports of an armed male in a busy public place, quickly followed up by the intel that the individual might be wanted for a series of murders. Other than that, probably a pure over reaction."

"I'm not going to argue with you. For a start you've got a machine gun and all I've got is a mobile phone, but I know this individual and your deployment here is over the top. He could well be a killer but as daft as it sounds he is not dangerous in an immediate sense. He is perhaps a strangler or a poisoner, but he's got no history of using weapons."

"Maybe so, but that's not a risk I'm prepared to take, even if you are."

Page could only see Law's eyes through the slits in the balaclava but he knew he didn't like the supercilious look on the rest of his face without even seeing it. It wasn't worth arguing with him though. "Stay well behind me, and try not to make your presence too bloody obvious." Law nodded and without a further word returned to his unit. "Prick," Page muttered under his breath and looked around for Connor.

The sky was growing darker. Darker than normal for this time of day. A group of black clouds were ominously moving towards the park from the city centre, bringing with them the threat of rain. Having checked that the firearms officers were ready and in position Page walked slowly towards the ruined church. At first there was no obvious sign of anybody else. He walked to the right of the building and from this vantage point he could see the police presence below blocking the two obvious escape routes down by the river. He retraced the path back to the front of the tower and this time went to the left. He was sure he saw a shadowy figure dart back against the dark grey stonework. "Edward, it's me Jim," he called out. "We met the other night." He continued walking slowly along the length of the wall. "It's OK Edward. There's nothing to be frightened of. I just want to talk to you." He stopped. He heard a rustling sound ahead. And then from the shadows a figure emerged. It was Edward. He looked dishevelled. Both arms were hanging by his side but in the dimming light it looked as if his right hand had been replaced by a hook. As Page stepped slowly closer he could ascertain that Edward was holding tightly onto an old garden sickle. The blade was a dull red colour and in that moment it was hard to be sure whether it was covered in rust or dried blood.

"Don't come any closer," he instructed Page.

"Alright, no problem. I'm just glad I've found you. Your dad is really worried you know."

Edward took a few steps towards Page and stopped. "I hope my father forgives me. He didn't know what I was doing."

"And what were you doing Edward?"

"Helping them to be noticed."

"Helping who to be noticed?"

"People like me. People that are taken for granted. Taken for granted until they're not there. People that aren't seen, or if they are seen then they are ignored."

"And why did you need to help them?" Page asked, aiming to keep him talking.

"Do you know what it feels like never to be noticed? To be out shopping and people say to your father: 'My he's grown, how old is he now?' Or they ask 'Is Edward working these days?' or similar stupid questions that they could easily have asked me. And if they do speak to me, then they treat me as a child, they presume I don't have all my faculties and they either patronise me or they offer me pity. It's not pity I want, it's respect."

"I understand that Edward. That's what we all want, and what we all deserve. So how did you help them get noticed?"

"I turned them into angels."

"You turned them into angels."

"Yes. Not everybody can see angels but they are all around us. If you believe in them hard enough then you will see them. You can recognise them by their halos. They can live anywhere, not just in old churches like this one, and they live forever and they help people. To be chosen as an angel is an honour, a recognition of your full worth."

Page wasn't sure what to say. He knew he had to carry on as if this were the most normal of conversations. He had to keep Edward calm but he wasn't sure where to start. A question maybe? So he asked: "Are you an angel Edward?"

Edward laughed. "No, of course not. I haven't got a halo have I, and you have to die to become an angel." His tone of voice seemed to imply that this was something everybody knew. "You have to die to become an angel," he repeated and took a step closer towards Page. Raising the sickle above his head he asked: "Are you afraid of dying Jim?"

From nowhere two loud thudding drumbeat sounds suddenly rent the air. The sickle fell from Edward's hand as he crumpled backwards to the floor. Page went to dash forward but was halted by the shout from behind. "Stand still. Armed police. Stand still." He wasn't sure why he stopped. The warning wasn't aimed at him surely? But then again, if it had been intended for Edward then it was far too late. Three firearms officers, weapons drawn, approached where Edward lay. One knelt down beside him, stretched out a gloved hand and touched the young man's neck, testing for a pulse. Within seconds he was back on his feet, shaking his head.

Page's legs felt unsteady. Everything around him seemed to be happening in slow motion and in total silence. He was frantically looking for Harry Law but the firearms' uniform was deliberately designed to afford its wearers full anonymity. He grabbed the nearest armed officer he could. "Why the hell did you do that? Why did you do that?" he screamed. The blue suited figure gently moved him aside as he walked over to the Armed Response Vehicles where the firearms team was assembling.

"Are you alright?" Connor was holding onto his arm.

"What the hell has just happened here?"

"I don't know, but are you alright?"

"I'm not injured if that's what you mean, but I'm not alright by any stretch of the imagination."

"You're in shock."

"I'm not in shock but I am shocked that some asshole can do this and just walk away." Page was starting to get angry with Connor and that wasn't his intention. It wasn't her fault. He gave her an apologetic smile. "I need to see him," he said, and so they both walked slowly towards the body. Edward was on his back with his two arms outstretched as if he had been crucified. A dark stain had spread across his chest where Page presumed the two bullets had entered his body. The hood of his jacket was up behind him and the draw stringed front edge had formed a halo like circle around his head. There seemed to be a smile on his face. "Cover him up," Page said to the uniformed officer that had appeared by their side. He turned to Connor. "What a shitshow. What an absolute shitshow."

It was nearly an hour now that Page and Connor had been waiting in the car. They had been allowed to move it and park behind the cordon from where they could see everything that was going on. Page had watched the firearms team disarm themselves, disrobe and then disappear like a circus troupe leaving town. The uniformed reinforcements had dispersed the crowd and extended the exclusion zone by closing the roads that bounded the park. Twice Page's phone had rung and both times it was Matt Hall. He had ignored them. The Bristol Post could wait.

Page saw the estate car pull up and watched as Charlotte James got out, walked around the vehicle and opened the tailgate door, balancing herself on the edge of the boot and pulling the white forensic suit up over her trousers and jumper. As she picked up her bag and slammed the door shut Page got out of the car and called across to her. "Good evening Dr James."

"Evening Jim."

He walked towards her and gave her a wry smile. "For once I'm here before you and I won't be asking those annoying questions you hate so much, because I already know the answers. I could have saved you a journey."

"So it's my turn to ask 'what have we got here?' is it?"

"Yes, and I say 'Male: late twenties. Cause of death: shot by a trigger happy storm trooper. Time of death: almost certainly one hour and twenty minutes ago.' And how do I know? Because I was there. Does that help?"

She could clearly sense his anger. "It can't have been nice. I do feel for you. I have been briefed on the circumstances surrounding the death and my report will be going to the coroner and to the Independent Office for Police Conduct. I'll be as thorough as I can be."

"I know you will. Look after him won't you." Page's anger had been replaced by an apparent vulnerability.

"Of course I will." Dr James went to go towards the incident tent that had been erected alongside the external nave wall of the church but she sensed that Page still had something to say. "Was there anything else?"

He hesitated and then very quietly said: "He was a friend of mine."

"Oh Jim, I'm so terribly sorry." She put her bag down and gave him a big hug.

It was well intentioned but it made Page feel uncomfortable. "You'd better be getting on," he said, taking a step backwards. "I hope you don't mind but I waited here so that I could personally entrust him into your care."

She gave him a warm smile. "Leave him with me Jim. I'll look after him."

"Thanks Charlotte." And then without even thinking about what he was saying he added: "You're an angel."

Motherless Children

The sun was streaming into the living room lending everything an artificial brightness. He was sat in his armchair balancing a mug of coffee on the arm and listening to the stereo. The music was loud, but he always thought that Neil Young sounded better loud. And living alone meant you could play your music loud without fear of either comment or contradiction. But the music wasn't so loud that he didn't hear the knock on the door. Taking his coffee with him he walked into the bay window and peered out. He recognised the car parked outside immediately and went to open the front door.

"Good morning, and what brings you here?" he asked playfully.

"Thought I'd call by and see how you were doing."

"Come on in. I'll make you a coffee." He led the way into the living room, picked up the remote control and stopped Cortez the Killer in his tracks. "Have a seat." He gestured to the settee. "I'll put the kettle on."

When he came back in with the coffee Connor was stood at the back wall, her head cocked to one side, reading the spines of his CDs. "Looking for anything in particular?" he asked.

She straightened up and seemed embarrassed that she had been caught. "You've got so many. How do you ever find what you want?"

He laughed. "A thing called alphabetical cataloguing by artiste that is then sub-divided chronologically." He put her drink onto the coffee table and sat himself down in his chair. She walked across the room to the settee. "But you didn't come here just to talk about my CD collection did you?"

Connor took her seat and leant back into the large cushion behind her. "No I didn't, but I'm still not sure I should even be here."

"Why ever not?" Page challenged her. "I'm not suspended - I've just taken a few weeks as compassionate leave, with the full support of the Chief Super I'll have you know."

"I know. I wanted to see how you were getting on and update you on things if you wanted, but I don't want to upset the boss."

"Ah now we have it," he teased. "Yesterday's man already am I?"

"I didn't mean that."

"I know, only joking. So who is the new boss?"

"They've made DS Brain acting DI until you return."

"And how are you getting on with acting DI Brain then?"

Connor hesitated. "It's funny you should ask that. When I first properly met her that day when we were following Jason Trent she asked me exactly the same thing: How are you getting on with DI Page?"

"Except, I bet she called me Big Jim, not DI Page." Connor blushed a little. "It's alright. It's a joke her and a few of her contemporaries like to share. She doesn't have much time for me. Professionally I mean. As far as she is concerned time is running out for her and her ambitions and old dinosaurs like me are in her way. She thinks it's time I handed my badge in and hung up my spurs, as do a few others, but she's a good copper."

"And you're a good copper too," Connor insisted.

Page remained silent for a few seconds. "I'm not so sure I am these days. DCS Tanner has agreed to this leave of absence hoping I come to the conclusion not to return, and when I look back at the last few weeks I tend to think he might have a point."

"You can't blame yourself for what happened."

"Ask yourself this: would it have happened if Anna Brain had been in charge?"

Connor looked at him, almost angrily. "You can't say that. You can't possibly know."

"Perhaps if I'd spent less time on Shirley's case and more time helping you we might have resolved things more quickly."

"You did help me, more than you will ever know, but you also resolved things for Shirley's son, and DS Brain would never have done that. She doesn't care about things the same way as you do and that really sets you apart from her in a good way."

Uneasy with even the faintest of praise Page knew this was the opportunity he needed to take to finally put the record straight. "Look, I've not been entirely honest with you about Shirley's case." He was expecting some reaction from her but there was nothing. She simply leaned forward and picked up her coffee as much as to say: 'Go on then.' He took a sip of his own drink before starting. "I didn't know Shirley at all but it was still very personal for me. My mother walked out and disappeared when I was ten years old and I've never seen her since. I saw Shirley's death as the chance to bring an end to somebody else's uncertainty, and maybe even mine if I'm totally honest."

Connor looked at him. "I'm sorry to hear that, but it doesn't change anything. I always knew there was more to it than you said but figured it was your business. And it was. In any case you still brought some closure to Jacob Herring, and not many other people would have bothered with somebody like him."

Page smiled ironically, remembering how Jacob had reacted to seeing the photograph of himself and his brother Joshua. "Yes, I did bring him some closure," he reflected ruefully, "but perhaps not in the way I had intended."

"But that's not important. The point is that you cared enough to try and you actually made a positive difference one way or another."

Page shrugged his shoulders dismissively. "I think it was too late to make a difference, if indeed any difference could ever have been made. The real damage was done years ago." He took a gulp of coffee and clumsily put the mug down onto the table. "I've been thinking about this sat here at home these last few weeks. We're not much different the three of us: me, Jacob Herring and Edward Slater. Three men who from a very early age have spent most of their lives trying, and failing, to come to terms with the sudden and inexplicable loss of their mother. Three men who have consequently retreated into themselves and avoided any relationships that required even the slightest bit of commitment for fear of once again being let down and abandoned." He looked at Connor sat opposite him. "This inability to trust anyone stays with you your whole life you know, your whole bloody life, regardless of how short, how hard or how successful that life might be. You hear a lot from these right-wing sociologists blaming juvenile delinquency on the absence of a father figure, but you never hear anything about the long term effects of not having a mother do you. Which is staggering. A child needs its mother like nobody else. Your mother is the only person who you can guarantee will be there with you when you come into this world. Anybody else is a nice-to-have, but you need your mother to be there at that moment, and then you need her to stay around." Connor looked as if she were trying to think of something to say. He saved her the effort. "You've still got your mother haven't you," he checked with her.

She nodded. "Yes. She lives locally, can be demanding at times, but we generally get along fine. She's a real help to me."

"Good. Then make sure you keep it that way." He gave her a smile. "Anyway, that's enough from me. I've had too much time on my hands recently, spent too long feeling sorry for myself, and you've already heard too much about it I'm sure. So tell me, how are things back at the ranch? Have you managed to tie up all those loose ends yet?"

Connor moved herself to the front of the settee as though she were about to share a big secret. "For starters, Jason Trent handed himself in on the Friday of the very same week he went missing. I think we've got your friend Matt Hall and Bristol Live to thank for that mind you. Trent got fed up with friends contacting him saying they had seen his name in the news. It seems that him and Sean Wilson were running some pub scam which was big enough to get HM Revenue & Customs all excited. It's not clear whether they were the masterminds behind it all, I doubt that very much, but they will certainly be taking the rap."

Page nodded. Nothing there he hadn't expected to hear. "And our murder case?" he asked.

"Case solved. The DNA samples from our three crime scenes and the allotment shed were all a perfect match for Edward. Nobody else appears to have been involved. I guess we are now just waiting to hear from the Crown Prosecution Service on what happens next."

"Nothing happens next. Edward is dead and from what you say he acted alone, so the CPS is unable to make a charging decision. Prosecution and public trial is the sole preserve of the living. The dead are excused such rituals." Page paused, and then asked the question he was most interested in. "And what is happening about Edward's summary execution at the hands of the state?" He was starting to sound angry already.

Connor looked at him apprehensively. "You know how it is. We don't really get to hear too much about what is going on, but apparently there is an independent enquiry underway. Word is that they are trying to make a case for confusion around when precisely the 'armed police' warning was given and when it was that Edward threatened you."

"That's bullshit and they know it." Page really was angry now. "For a start Edward never threatened me and they never gave a warning until after they had shot him. Shot him not once but twice, just for good measure. He wasn't a threat to anyone."

Connor put her hands out, almost it seemed in self defence from his anger, and then she said in a calm voice: "Look I had to give a statement about it all the other day. I'm not allowed to discuss what was in my statement, but I did tell the truth. I honestly did. The full truth, with no omissions."

"I'm sure you did. Thank you." Page managed a smile. He didn't want to be angry with her. Deep down he knew that she was on his side. He waited for her to acknowledge the smile and then continued. "I haven't spoken to Frank yet. Didn't really know what to say, and didn't even know whether he would want to speak to me. And then last week a letter arrived from him, apologising for what he had put me through. Apologising to me, can you believe that? Apologising to the man that killed his son." The room fell silent but after a few seconds Page could tell that Connor wanted to say something. A simple nod was enough to give her the permission and the space she needed.

"You are not to blame for Edward's death," she started, "and Frank knows that. Of course he is not to blame either. In your own ways you will each feel some guilt I'm sure, but your friendship will prevail. You must speak to him. He's written to you, reached out to you. Give him a call and arrange to meet."

Page knew the ball was in his court, knew he had to contact his friend, but actually doing it was a different matter. "I will," he said, "I'll give him a call," but he still wasn't sure when that might be.

Connor could clearly recognise the reticence on his part. "Well make sure you do, it's really important."

"I know. Message understood."

He was about to change the subject when Connor looked at him. She had her serious face on. He remained silent and let her speak. "There's something else I need to tell you," she said, her voice not so confident now. "You might not want to know, but you would find out when you came back to work, and I wouldn't want you not to know."

He could tell that she was grappling with this. Not sure what she should do for the best. He wasn't sure he wanted to hear what she had to say either, but he wouldn't know for sure until she'd said it. "It's alright, you can tell me," he encouraged.

"It's about Frank," she confirmed. "When all the forensic reports were back, and all the DNA samples had been catalogued and cross-referenced, then it became clear that…" She hesitated. "You might already know this, but the DNA samples showed conclusively that Frank was not Edward's biological father."

Page was dumbfounded. He wanted to say that there must be some kind of mistake, but Connor had chosen her words very carefully. Nevertheless, he asked the question: "Are you sure?"

"Yes. Positive."

"And who knows this?"

"Me, DS Brain and Dr James."

"So Frank hasn't been told?"

"No."

Page looked relieved. "Good. Then he mustn't find out. It's not for us to tell him in any case."

"But do you think he already knows, or at least suspects?" Connor asked.

"Good God no, and if he found out now then that would finish him off. It would be like losing Edward and his wife all over again, but this time it would be ten times worse."

Page went to pick up his mug but noticed it was empty. He pushed it across the table. Connor put her mug down, perhaps in solidarity. "I'm sorry to be the bearer of this news," she said. "Are you OK?"

"Yes, I'm fine. It's just a shock, that's all."

"So what are you going to do, now you know?" she asked.

"Nothing. I'm going to take your advice and say nothing. It's what a good friend would do, isn't that right?"

She smiled at him. "Yes it is."

He returned her smile. "Thanks for telling me. I know it wasn't easy for you. It wasn't something I really wanted to hear, but you were right, I needed to know."

He watched her pull away and gave an awkward hand gesture resembling a wave just in case she was watching him in the rear view mirror. He shut the front door and walked back into the lounge. He now had even more to think about than before: what he was and wasn't going to say to Frank; and what exactly it was he was going to say to DCS Tanner about his future intentions. He picked up the remote control, turned the volume up and restarted the album he had been listening to when Connor had arrived. He tossed the remote onto the sofa, picked up the dirty mugs from the table and headed for the kitchen to make himself another coffee.

AFTERGLOW

The sun was still setting when he left the house but the streetlights above his head were already illuminated, their sodium glow growing brighter as the daylight dimmed.

Connor's impromptu visit had been a godsend. It had shaken him out of his malaise and for the first time in weeks he now knew where he was heading.

Right now he was off to meet Frank in the Annexe. It seemed strange, it was Friday, it wasn't crib-night, but Connor was right, they needed to get their first meeting over and done with. Frank had been pleased to hear from him, and although Page wasn't necessarily looking forward to the meeting itself he was relieved that they were meeting at long last.

As he turned into Nevil Road he quickened his pace. There was a discernible spring in his step. A renewed purpose. He was smiling to himself. Around four o'clock that afternoon he had made contact with DCS Tanner's office. Knowing full well that the boss would already have finished for the weekend, he'd left a message with Julie to confirm that he would be back at work first thing on Monday morning.

Big Jim wasn't going to hand in his badge or hang up his spurs: he was getting back into the saddle.

About The Author

Stephen Cook was born in Bristol in 1962. He was educated at Sir Bernard Lovell Comprehensive School in Oldland Common and studied German at Warwick University. In 2016 he published *Words for Lost* - a short collection of poetry and prose. *Angels in the Architecture* is his first novel. Stephen now lives in Bristol again but has lived in Sussex, Germany and Wales.